DESERT
Jewel

NATALINA REIS

For information, contact the publisher, Hot Tree Publishing.
www.hottreepublishing.com
Editing: Hot Tree Editing
Cover Designer: Claire Smith
Formatting: RMGrapx
ISBN-10: 1-925448-44-4
ISBN-13: 978-1-925448-44-3

10 9 8 7 6 5 4 3 2 1

Dedication

To Africa with love.

Desert Jewel

"No, I won't do it!"

Not a very princess-like attitude—she was well aware of that. With her face buried in the pillow, Milenda kicked the bed until the bedclothes fell to the floor. "Asha, go tell the Elders I won't do it."

The young girl stopped midchore and stared at the princess, a mixture of confusion and fear on her face. "Most Exalted, I can't—"

Milenda interrupted her, flipping herself over on the bed. "I know you can't tell them that, Asha. I can't either." She sighed loudly. "What's the point of being the Jewel of the Crown if I have no say in anything I do?" It was a rhetorical question, and the young servant knew that. "I hate being the royal heiress. Just hate it…"

Being the Crown Jewel of Natale was not all it was cracked up to be. Milenda was almost eighteen and expected to follow traditions that had been created and shaped long before her people ruled the kingdom—obsolete and often cruel traditions that made absolutely no sense to her or to those of her generation. On the occasion of her eighteenth birthday, she was expected to follow and obey one of those ridiculous rites of passage—she was to choose a husband from Natale's ever-dwindling population of eligible males.

On one hand, she was allowed to choose pretty much anyone, any age, from any walk of life, as long as the chosen male was not already married and had passed the fertility tests. After all, the kingdom needed an heir. In theory, Milenda could let her heart choose who was to be her consort for the rest of their natural lives—and beyond, if traditional beliefs were to be trusted. However, nothing was that simple in Natale. She often wondered if her nation's founders had been pranksters who took pleasure in providing as many obstacles as humanly possible to finding a chance at an easy, happy life.

As part of the consort-choosing process, Milenda was to first allow a few select candidates to try and win her good graces and possibly her heart. Those chosen by the Elders—a group of men older than sin who were, if truth be told, the true rulers of Natale—had to pass a series of strict and often dangerous tests, from medical exams to bravery and strength trials. The Elders seemed to become more creative with each passing royal wedding, and the history books were full of examples of tryouts going terribly wrong. It was not uncommon for one, or even all of the candidates, to lose a limb or their lives in the process. Should those unfortunate souls not be successful at winning her love, no matter how much the Trials had cost them, they would be pushed aside and sent home, whole or whatever was left of them, in disgrace. Milenda cringed at the very idea of having the lives of those men in her hands even more than the idea of picking a husband so early in life.

The first candidates were about to be brought to her this evening, and there was much preparation to be done. Tradition demanded that the bride be thoroughly primped; she would spend most of the day in the hands of hairdressers, stylists, and makeup artists. The best jewelers in the kingdom had been called to decorate her like a hanging chandelier, and even as she rose from her bed that morning, a meticulous and complicated bath routine was being prepped next door.

With a sigh, Milenda accepted her fate for the day and followed her attendants to the scrubbing of a lifetime.

After hours of preparation and lots of fussing from the part of servants, Milenda was ready to do the one thing her whole being rebelled against: the introduction to the poor contenders for her hand.

The rumble of thunder in the distance, foreshadowing some terrible storm, seemed to carry the undulating movement of hundreds of bodies crammed across the lawn, anxious to witness their princess bless what was, by any standards, a cruel and ancient ritual.

The Crown Jewel twitched, and in spite of all the mental preparation for this moment, she could feel beads of perspiration collecting along the edges of her ceremonial *gele*, a traditional and elaborate scarf arrangement that towered above her head. The crown room was brightly illuminated with candles that sparkled and reflected off the diamond-encrusted chandeliers hanging from the high ceilings. Spread in front of her throne, a long, royal blue carpet set the stage for the procession of consort hopefuls about to begin.

The men entered quietly, dressed in traditional white tunics and pants embroidered in rich silk thread and decorated with tiny, iridescent diamonds. Their heads, bowed in respectful observance of their devotion, were covered in the ceremonial white veils that kept their identities a mystery even to the Jewel. She sat silently, trying to control her shaking hands, mentally preparing herself for what was about to start.

It all seemed so wasteful and useless. Milenda whispered a little prayer, "Please, God, let all the hopefuls be strangers." It would be hard enough to send innocent men on this arduous journey; it would be heartbreaking to send someone she knew, or worse, someone she cared about. In her heart, she had already chosen her consort, and nothing under the sun would sway her otherwise. The boy she loved was a commoner, a young academic in the local university whom she had met in one of the many classes she attended to fight the boredom of palace life. He was single, just a few years older than herself, and fertile—she had checked his medical records. He was also beautiful. When he smiled, she felt as if all the planets in the universe aligned, and every star in the never-ending skies shimmered just for her.

Jaali was unusual amongst her people; alabaster skin, blue topaz eyes, and hair the color of pearls. When he walked outside, the light reflected off him in glistening rays, mesmerizing everyone who saw it. To her, he seemed to glide rather than walk, and the sound of his soft voice was all it took to melt her heart. Nothing on this earth would steer her from her decision to pick him as her royal husband.

That night, before the candidates came to be presented to her, the Elders had sat down with her to explain this year's elimination process. With horror and disbelief in her heart, she listened attentively as they described in great detail what had to be, in her young opinion, one of the worst and most dangerous processes yet created.

The five candidates would be dropped in the *Jangwa Pori*, a mostly arid expanse of land that stretched for hundreds of miles in every direction and was inhabited by some of the wildest, most dangerous creatures in the kingdom. The consort-hopefuls would be provided with a bottle of drinking water, a small blanket, and a few other meager supplies; whoever survived the journey back to the capital would then have a chance at winning favor with the princess. Only then would she be allowed to make her final decision—accept their hand in marriage or choose someone else. One way or another, she would be the reason for a lot of misery in the next few weeks.

The first man approached the throne, fell to one knee, and said, "Your Majesty, I beg for your infinite love and mercy to allow me to prove myself to you, so I may deserve the joining of our bodies and souls in holy union. I am Zakia, son of Malik and Zahra."

Taking a corner of his veil, the man uncovered himself to reveal his identity to Milenda. Her heart skipped a beat; she knew this man. She had seen him in the market many times, selling his wares and entertaining the crowd with his beautiful singing voice. This well-liked man was about to embark on a journey from which he may never return.

Swallowing bile, Milenda rose to her feet, not sure her weak legs would hold her. "I accept your proposal and look forward to attesting to your courage and strength in the trials ahead." The ritual words were said almost unconsciously as her hand reached to Zakia to take symbolic possession of his soul. The veil he handed her was of the purest of silk and felt as if it would evaporate at her touch. Slowly, as she had been taught all her life, she brought it to her mouth and kissed it, thus sealing both their promises. The dark-skinned man rose and moved to take his place in the contenders' row.

Three more men came to stand in front of her, fell to their knees, uttered the ceremonial words, and handed her their metaphorical souls before taking their seats.

Only one man remained. As he walked down the blue carpet, Milenda felt the first pangs of recognition. Like the others, he fell to his knee and uttered the meaningless words. Except, this time, they were not meaningless to her. Even before he removed his veil, her heart began bleeding.

"No, not you. Anyone but you…," she whispered in a pained voice, tears stinging the back of her eyes. Fate was a cruel lover, it seemed. For when the veil was removed, Jaali's beautiful pale eyes were staring back at her. Her world shook and crumbled one piece at a time, like a deck of cards in an earth tremor. Her vision blurred, her pulse slowed, and her limbs went numb. The room darkened as she sagged, unconscious, back onto her throne and slid all the way to the carpeted floor in front of it. Oblivion welcomed her in its cold arms.

The Boy and The Lizard

———————————————

Class finished, and Jaali packed his books into his bag. It was a calculated, slow ritual that he followed every day after the students left. The more he delayed his departure from the class hall, the better his chances of walking across the building without being noticed. Eyes lowered, chin down, body covered from head to toe, he hurried through the marble corridors of the building, hoping no one else was around and that for once he would go unnoticed. A trifle of a hope, for invariably eyes would follow him—the man with the silver hair and the ghostly skin, the man with the eyes that glowed in the sun like ice-blue topaz. Jaali should be used to it by now, but he still felt the pinch of anger at being ogled like a freak. Being free did not change his status as an exotic creature who stuck out no matter where he went or what he did. He couldn't hide his past, for his coloring yelled out, loud and clear, his history as a slave, an *indent*.

Today was no different. By the time he reached the main doors, small pods of people had stopped, heads bent together. They whispered as they stole furtive—or often bold—glances at him, the Fjorden who had escaped captivity to become a scholar in the university.

There weren't that many ex-*indents*. Those who had won their freedom found living among those who had enslaved them unbearable, and they often moved across the continent to other lands. Jaali had no place to go. He could barely remember his homeland, and he had no way of knowing whether his family was still alive. For him, there was no good choice; he had elected to stay in Natale, the only home he knew.

A peek out the glass door told him a storm was imminent. The wind furiously blew leaves into small funnels of air and debris. The skies had darkened as a screen of thick, pregnant clouds blocked the suddenly shy sun.

He knew he'd better hurry. His *hema*, the humble building he called his home, was still some distance from the university, and he was in clear danger of getting drenched before arriving home. Pulling the collar of his shirt a little higher to hide the whiteness of his skin and holding his bag tight against his body, Jaali crossed the threshold and sped across the lawn. The ominous skies and wind prevented people from paying too much attention to his pale figure zigzagging between them, crossing paths and avoiding obstacles in a frantic race to beat the storm. A quick look up told him he was not going to make it. As a fat drop fell on his forehead, Jaali decided to take refuge in the library just around the corner.

The clouds, tired of carrying their weight, opened up and released their contents all at once. No sooner had the rain started falling than Jaali was soaked to the bone. Tightening his hold of the bag with his precious books and class materials, the young Fjorden turned the corner—and crashed head-on with someone. Her books dropped to the flooded ground and a flow of curses escaped her lips.

Aware that she wasn't too happy with him, he immediately began collecting her books and apologizing.

"I'm sorry, *msichana*," he said, as he bent and tried to save the books from a thorough drenching. When he raised his eyes to her, an electric shock went through his body and mind.

He had never seen such a lovely creature. She was staring at him as if in a trance, and for a moment, he forgot who he was.

"Well, you really should be more careful," she said. The golden brown of her skin, now covered in rivulets of rain, seemed to glow in the gloomy light. Her eyes were vibrant emeralds sheltered by arched, raven-black eyebrows.

Her wet sleeves had slid slightly down her arms to reveal the most amazing markings on her skin. Were those tattoos? Their color, just a shade darker than her amber skin, denied it. He had heard of it, but had never seen it; *matangazos*, the telltale markings of a Nyota. Who was this girl?

***

The heavens had just unburdened themselves of a massive amount of water. The world blurred, melting around the edges as Milenda navigated through the throng of hurrying students making their way to or from classes. No matter how many times she walked the campus, she still stared in wonder at its wild beauty. The university campus had been carved off the jungle, a human intrusion the wilderness was fighting back at by surreptitiously invading the large building areas with greenery and trees. Throughout the years, those trees had grown into true giants with sprawling and far-reaching arms that sometimes poked through roofs and even windows.

Milenda had spent most of her first semester in a lecture hall seemingly built around two massive trees. In reality, the trees had stubbornly sprouted from underneath the marble floors, pushing and shoving the offensive obstacle aside and growing to their full height within the confines of the hall. The tree branches now touched the high, vaulted ceilings, threatening to push through the decorative frescoes and the glass of the skylights.

As she headed toward the library, Milenda bowed her head, trying to keep the rain from hitting her face. With an armful of books and a satchel hanging from her right shoulder, she sprinted through puddles and bumps on the path, anxious to find a dry place. Her comfortable cloth slippers were drenched, and she was tempted to remove them altogether and run barefoot instead. As she turned around the corner of the library, a mere few steps away from the dry haven of the kingdom's largest repository of books, she bumped into someone. The impact surprised her so much, she lost her balance. Trying to steady herself, all of her books fell to the sodden ground at her feet.

"Son of a wicked shaman," she exclaimed, forgetting her royal station for a moment. "Will you look where you're going?"

When she lifted her eyes to the culprit, she was met with the strangest, purest azure eyes she had ever seen. "I'm sorry, *msichana*," the ethereal creature said in a warm, melodic voice that covered her in goose bumps. "I wasn't watching where I was going." Scrambling around her, the young man bent to retrieve her books from the watery surface.

Princess Milenda, used to being recognized, was shocked to realize this man did not know who she was. Even though she knew the incident had been as much her fault as his, she was not about to admit that to him. "Well, you really should be more careful."

The mystifying blue eyes returned to hers and she felt oozy inside, as if her innards had just turned to jelly. *"Nasikitika, msichana,"* he apologized.

In spite of her irritation at the fact that he was so apologetic and so exotic, she felt her anger deflate completely as he stood before her, dripping rain from every inch of his tall, slender body. Books in hand, he reached out to her, seemingly oblivious to the pouring rain.

"Asante," she thanked him, regaining possession of her texts. "What's your name?"

"Jaali, *msichana*." His head bowed in the traditional gesture of respect. He raised his pale eyes back to hers, water dripping from his eyelashes. "I would like to ask for yours, but maybe we should seek shelter before I do."

Giggling a little, she agreed and, side by side with this strange creature, she headed to the library door and ducked inside.

The cozy hallway was warm and, thankfully, dry. She could almost feel steam escaping her soaked clothes. Jaali gallantly guided her to a bench not far from the door, where they could dry out a bit. Milenda set her wet books by a vent in hopes they would dry faster and with minimal damage, but she was not holding her breath. The young man sat down beside her, satchel set aside, water forming a small puddle by his feet as he twisted his platinum hair in his hands.

"I'm Milenda," she told him, fascinated by his coloring. "You're not from around here, are you?"

Jaali laughed softly. "What gave me away? My lack of coordination?" They both laughed. She felt oddly comfortable with this stranger. "I'm not, even though I have lived in the kingdom since I was twelve. I was brought from the Outerlands by Mabaya warriors."

Milenda's eyes opened wide, startled by the information. How quickly she had forgotten that her beautiful and sophisticated kingdom still tolerated slavery in various forms. Mabaya warriors were not well regarded by the public in general, but were a necessary evil. They often kidnapped people in foreign lands and sold them to the highest bidder. It was shameful that such things were still happening among a people who prided themselves on their culture and high moral standards.

"*Nasikitika.* I'm sorry." What else could she say? As a princess, her political and legal powers were virtually nonexistent. No matter how repugnant she found the legislation that allowed human beings to be bought, sold, and used like merchandise, there was not much she could do, other than voice her displeasure, which she did often.

"Don't trouble yourself with it, *msichana*," he said, waving a hand as if dismissing any reason for sorrow. "I paid my way into emancipation some years ago. I have a good life now."

"You go to school here?" Milenda asked, shivering now that her wet clothes stuck to her body.

Jaali stood and produced a blanket from his satchel. "I teach languages," he explained while covering the princess's shoulders with the colorful wrap.

Milenda brushed a hand across the soft, woven, red and black fabric. "One of the few things I was allowed to bring from the Outerlands. It belonged to my mother," he said.

"It's beautiful, Jaali," she told him, grateful for the gesture and the warmth.

Milenda felt guilt nibbling at her toes. As the heiress to the crown, the Jewel, as she was often called, she was kept away from politics. Her royal father and the body of Elders wove a protective shield around her, keeping all the uncomfortable realities at bay. When Milenda had insisted on taking classes at the centuries-old university campus, she had almost caused a national crisis amongst the governing bodies. She would be exposed to facts and rumors they'd rather have hidden from her. She had been relentless in her desire, and at last they had given in.

All along, they'd had her followed. It was hard to ignore a giant hulk of a man, wearing the flamboyant uniform of the Protectors, always a few steps behind her. It was not hard to dissuade them from keeping a close guard on her; a few not-so-veiled threats of improper conduct and she soon lost her bodyguard. Everyone knew who she was and for the most part, much to her dismay, they kept their distance, too scared of committing some faux pas and of the government's retaliation. Even the professors were guarded around her.

So, it was refreshing to really talk to someone who did not recognize her at all. To be treated like an ordinary young woman, even for just a few moments, was exciting and new.

"What do you study?" Jaali asked her, his pale blue eyes trained on her face. She felt a rush of heat crawling up her neck. The unusual young man tilted his head as if fascinated by what he was seeing. "Is it normal for your spots to shine?" he asked.

Damn it! My traitorous spots.

Her people's typical skin spots were known to glow and shimmer when they got excited, embarrassed, or happy. Spots were distinct. Not one person from Nyota stock had the same pattern of *matangazos*. The location of the markings also changed from one person to another, but they were all in at least partially visible places of the body. Hers began on her right cheek by her ear and spilled in a flowing pattern like a cornucopia down her neck into her shoulder, dissolving at her shoulder blade. Her *matangazos* resembled the spots of a leopard, but on others, they were shaped like round dots or elongated ovals or even hearts. She remembered trying to hide her markings, which were naturally a slightly deeper color of amber, with makeup as a young teenager, trying to look more like the Wazi, whose skins were unmarked and smooth like sanded ebony. Her markings didn't bother her anymore, though. She had grown to love and accept them as a part of what made her an individual, and nothing made her prouder than being regarded as her own person.

"Yes, the *matangazos* of my people have a mind of their own," she joked, trying to hide her embarrassment. She realized he didn't know the significance of her glowing. More relaxed, she said, "I'm studying the arts."

"Any art in particular?" His sincere interest made her glow even more. It was not every day she had someone really interested in her as a person, not as the Jewel.

"Not really, even though I'm quite partial to dance," she confessed. "Do you like art?"

"I paint a little," he said, a shy smile on his pink lips, "and I dabble in sculpture. I like bringing raw materials, like sandstone or wood, to life in my hands. I'm not sure I'm any good at it, though."

The words were out of her mouth before she even knew she was going to say them. "I would love to see them sometime."

Jaali's exotic face lit up in a big smile. Obviously pleased by her interest, he lowered his eyes to his satchel and rummaged through it. His platinum hair spilled over the sides of his face, and he had to brush it back with his hand when he looked up at her again.

He held out a card to her. "This is my address," he said. "I'm home every evening and when school is out. Come anytime, and I'll show you my sculptures."

He seemed so eager to share his art, Milenda found herself smiling from ear to ear and ignoring the nagging voice on the edge of her consciousness telling her this was a bad idea; princesses did not fraternize with the population at large.

She surprised herself the next day by standing in front of his small home, timidly knocking at the door. He lived on the outskirts of town, closer to the jungle than most city dwellers, in a quaint *hema*. Milenda knew they still existed, but she had never been in one. They belonged in another time, a time when modern comforts were still unavailable to most, and the general populace couldn't afford living anywhere else. Houses were now made of solid, sturdy materials that provided straight walls and smooth floors. Most had central air-conditioning and glass windows. Jaali's place seemed primitive by comparison, made of what looked like artisan stone bricks glued together with clay or some other dirt-like material. The few windows were small and covered by colorful curtains that billowed in the breeze. The door was a plain, big piece of wood fashioned to fit the frame with a simple iron handle. Copper sheets comprised the roof, half-rusted by the elements.

"*Msichana*, you came."

Her eyes left the puzzling building to rest on Jaali's happy face. The door was now opened wide, but the sun outside was so bright, she could only see shadows inside. "You sound surprised," she said, knowing all too well that he was not the only one. "I told you I would come."

The pale young man smiled, amused. "Many are polite enough to say it, but not interested enough to actually go through with it." He invited her in with a sweeping gesture. "Welcome to my humble home."

As soon as she stepped inside, she knew she had been very wrong in assuming the house was primitive. The air was cool and, in spite of the antique-looking architecture, the home was cozy and beautiful. Shock must have shown on her face because he chuckled as they stepped in further.

"Wow!" she exclaimed. "This is amazing."

"I built it myself for the most part," he said, pride coloring his voice. "This was an abandoned *hema*. I bought it for a song and brought it back from the dead. I told you I like doing that." He had a silly smile on his face, like a little boy showing his mom a drawing he made in school.

Not many people must visit. Being a foreigner, and an ex-*indent* for that matter, must not inspire many people to associate with him. His exotic looks probably also scared a lot of people off. People were often afraid of the unfamiliar.

Jaali signaled her to a chair that, by its looks, had been handcrafted and lovingly carved out of soft brown wood. Milenda gingerly sat, afraid of damaging the artistic item. Jaali's gentle laughter reached her ears.

"It's pretty sturdy, *msichana*," he said.

"Did you make these chairs?" She was in awe of the mixture of carved wood furnishings in his *hema*, each piece an individual expression of beauty and functionality.

The exotic young man, liquid eyes examining her with some amusement and obvious pleasure, waved his hand in an expansive gesture that encompassed everything in the small *hema*. "It took me years, but yes, with a few exceptions, this is all my work. Do you approve?"

Her mouth slightly open, the Jewel looked at him

incredulously. "Approve? I love it!" she exclaimed, her voice exploding in the small space. "How can anyone be so talented?"

Jaali sauntered to the small section of the room that served as a kitchen and poured a hot beverage into two old, but pretty, ceramic cups. "My people are expert carpenters and carvers," he explained, bringing her the beverage. "There's a rumor that Fjordian people were genetically enhanced for that end. I personally think it amounts to pure traditional genetics, not fabricated DNA, but who am I to disagree with beliefs that have been around longer than I have?"

Holding the warm cup in the palm of her hand, Milenda watched him with growing interest. "Does that belief have anything to do with your kidnapping?" she asked, hoping she wasn't being too personal.

"Yes, it does," he admitted, sitting down across from her. "They sold me to a furniture builder at first, but when the workshop burned down, I was appropriated by the insurance company and sold to a private home." His voice trailed off, as if unpleasant memories had crept up on him.

Without thinking, Milenda jumped to her feet and crossed the short space between them to crouch in front of him. "I shouldn't have brought that up," she said. *"Nasikitika*, Jaali, *nasikitika."*

The Fjorden's pale eyes trailed to her hand resting on his knee and he smiled. He covered her hand with his, and she wondered at the sharp contrast of their coloring; his pearly complexion somehow complemented her skin. He caressed her hand with his thumb and stared into her eyes. From the corner of her eye she could see her spots sparkling like jewels in the shadowy space. His smile got wider. "You are beautiful, *msichana*," he whispered. "Truly beautiful."

Her smile spread from ear to ear at the compliment. Yes, she heard flattery all the time, but it was never sincere. Or, at least, she didn't think it was. People flattered her because she was the princess, the heir to the throne, the Jewel. It was in their own interest to "butter her up" in case they needed a favor later. Jaali didn't know who she was. His flattery sounded genuine and heartfelt.

She thought he was beautiful too and wanted badly to tell him so. But her upbringing got in the way. A proper young lady would never tell a boy such things. A proper young lady would not allow her hand to be held and caressed like that. But it felt so right, she couldn't pull away. In fact, she wished he would linger there, his warm, calloused hand over her tiny, almost insubstantial fingers sending shivers of pleasure throughout her body, making her heart quiver in delight.

Their meetings became more frequent. Milenda often visited him at his *hema*, but sometimes they would meet in the thick jungle that surrounded the college campus. Small study stations had been built within the trees. Seats and tables were carved directly off the green giants that claimed the space as their kingdom—a kingdom over which even her father, King Melchior, had no power or authority. Her favorite spot was an old wicker arbor seat, built to look like an elongated egg and hidden among a copse of trees and heavy greenery deep in the forest grounds. Someone had laid a comfortable, weatherized, overstuffed cushion inside of it, and Milenda had brought her own collection of big pillows to turn the niche into an inviting reading and studying spot. She suspected her bodyguards had made sure the spot was left alone by everybody else, for she had never found anyone occupying it, even when the rest of the forest seemed to crawl with humanity in search of quietude.

"Does it bother you that you were indentured?" They were reclined in the arbor seat, surrounded by the pillows and a pile of books Jaali always seemed to carry around with him. "Stupid question," she chided herself, "of course it does. What I mean is, does it affect your life as it is now? The knowing that at one time you were not free."

The fire in his eyes belied their color, and not for the first time, she felt tempted to get lost in them. "Sometimes it does," he replied, fluffing another pillow with his hands. "Memories are hard to eradicate. Impossible even. At times, they come flooding back, and I feel like I'm enslaved all over again." He pulled on the pillow edges and shifted in the seat. "Not a good place to be." He glanced at her and quickly looked away.

"*Nasikitika*, I made you uncomfortable," Milenda said, her hands gently squeezing his knee. Scooting closer to Jaali, she lowered her voice. "I won't bring it up again, I promise. My father often tells me I have a big mouth and no brains to control it."

Jaali raised his eyebrows and chuckled. "Your father does not sound like a very nice man," he said, tilting his head to one side like a bird. "You've never told me about your parents. I assume they are still alive." There was a question in his tone as he blinked and scooted closer.

Her heart flip-flopped. The dreaded moment was here.

Lying was not an option, not to Jaali with whom she felt at home for the first time in her whole young life. Truth had to prevail, no matter how reluctant she was to tell him who her parents were. Her hands went to the small pendant around her neck and she twisted it around in her fingers, gathering courage.

The young Fjorden bit his lip as he waited for her response, but it never came. A sudden clatter behind them startled them onto their feet. With a squeal, Milenda threw herself into Jaali's arms and buried her face in his linen shirt. His long arms went around her protectively as he surveyed the grounds for the source of the noise. Looking up at the tree directly behind him, Jaali gasped at the sight of a huge green eye peeking through the knot of a lower branch.

"*For søren!*" he exclaimed, jerking his head back as the big eye blinked. "What is that?"

Milenda lifted her head tentatively and stole a glance toward the mysterious apparition. Her hand flew to her throat and a peal of laughter escaped her lips.

"Mjusi *msitu!*" she yelled, as if that explained everything. Her body relaxed in his arms as her fear dissolved into nothing. She knew this creature. "You're bad, Mjusi," she yelled out, laughter in her voice. "You scared us to death."

The eye that fully filled the big oval knot on the branch blinked again and crinkled at the edges as if the creature were smiling.

"What creature is this, *msichana*?" he asked, in awe of such a sighting even as two massive green wings unfolded from behind the tree trunk and flapped in the air.

"That's mjusi *msitu*, the forest lizard," Milenda explained, dropping her arms from around his neck. She smoothed her soft blue *kanga* with one hand. "He's my friend."

"You have a giant lizard as a friend?" Mjusi's wings were now totally unfurled and causing bursts of wind with their flapping. "Correction. You have a giant flying lizard for a friend?"

Milenda laughed softly at his obvious shock. "Until you came, Jaali, I didn't have many friends at all." The creature detached itself from the tree and came to perch on a fallen branch nearby. Soft, gentle sounds came from it as it stretched its neck to offer the enormous green head for petting. Milenda obliged. "Mjusi is very gentle. He often comes and keeps me safe when I'm in the jungle."

Jaali stared at her, his mouth still half open and a look of astonishment on his face. Her hair beads had slid a little over her forehead, and her colorful *isigolwani* neck hoop was hanging all the way back. Distractedly, he reached out to straighten the hoop around her neck.

"Why wouldn't you have many friends, *msichana*? You are beautiful and smart." The giant creature growled, not liking the fact Jaali was touching her. "Protective creature," he whispered in awe.

Milenda smiled and her heart melted a little more at the sound of his flattering words. "The Jewel does not inspire friendships," she said, casting her eyes down. "The Jewel inspires fear and respect."

His hand, still on her neck loop, fell alongside his body and his ghostly eyes shot up to her face. "Jewel? Like in the

Jewel of the Crown?" he exclaimed. "Like in heiress to the throne?"

She pulled back from him, taking a step closer to the flying lizard. "Yes, I am the Jewel." There was no going back now. The truth was out, and she feared she had just lost the only human friend she had ever had.

Secrets Untold

———————————————

The solitude of her room was a comfort for once. Normally, the lack of character and personal touches in the chamber officially assigned as her bedroom would have been oppressive and lonely. She welcomed the emptiness that her overwhelmingly white room provided.

She had not waited around to see Jaali's reaction to her revelation the day before. Too scared of what his face might reveal or of what his words might bring, she had run away as fast as her legs could carry her. Mjusi had followed her at first, flapping his awesome wings behind her and uttering that peculiar guttural sound he always made when sensing her distress. Milenda had sent him home, promising she was all right, but she wasn't sure he believed her. His big green eyes were doleful when they parted ways just outside the palace's gates.

This morning, the silk sheets underneath her body felt cool against her bare skin. As was her habit, Milenda had unwound herself from her blue *kanga* and slipped into a pair of loose satin pants and a cropped top. Her shoes had been unceremoniously thrown into the corner of the room. Had she not dismissed her maids—quite forcibly—they would have fussed over the neglected pieces of royal clothing strewn around.

Not for the first time, her heart swelled with hate for her social status. Why did she have to be of royal stock? Why couldn't she be just another girl taking classes at the university? She despised people walking on eggshells around her, avoiding eye contact.

Jaali was different though, not just another of her future subjects. Her heart had come to feel so much more for him than what she had expected at first. She needed him the same way she needed sustenance or water. He was the drop of normalcy that made her life worth living, a kindred spirit of sorts—totally different, but equal at the same time. Jaali gave her balance in a world where she felt off half the time. Now, with one tiny revelation, he had joined the ranks of those who looked at her as a freak, an idol to be admired and adored but not to be touched or truly loved.

Tears soaked the pillow, and she angrily wiped them with the expensive and hard-to-replace sheet. Let them send emissaries to the far Outerlands in search of replacement linens for the ones she was staining with her makeup. Let them spend an obscene amount of money on a totally unnecessary object to validate her social importance, her shallow, meaningless notability that afforded her only loneliness.

Hours may have passed; she couldn't be sure. She nodded off after her furious crying.

A faint knock came from the outside door. She sat up, sniffling a little, distantly curious as to who dared interrupt her slumber. The door cracked open, and the head of one of the chamber maids popped in shyly.

At first, Milenda couldn't make out what she was saying. The girl, wrapped in the traditional red *kanga* that marked royal servants, cleared her throat and repeated a little louder, "Royal Jewel, I have a message for you." She held a white piece of paper in her outstretched hand. "May I enter?"

"Of course, you silly girl," Milenda said, immediately regretting her snappiness. If she weren't careful, she would indeed turn into a real royal, full of self-importance and no respect or consideration for others. "Sorry, Asha. I'm indisposed. Come right in."

The young Asha, a tiny, willowy girl, stepped timidly into the room, closing the door behind her. Her *kanga* was wound so tightly around her, Milenda wondered how she was still able to walk. Over her head, she wore another wad of red fabric, the edges falling over and wrapped around her shoulders. Only her childish dark face was visible.

"Holy Jewel," she said, coming to kneel in front of Milenda. "Most exalted one." Milenda chuckled, being quite certain she looked a fright for someone so exalted. The young girl looked up at her, confusion in her eyes.

"Never mind, Asha," Milenda said, reaching out for the note. "Who is this from?"

"The guards told me it came from the university, from a professor there," the girl said, her eyes still blinking at her princess's reaction.

Milenda opened the note and read it. Her face relaxed as the words, written in beautiful, artistic handwriting, quickly brought the sun back into her heart. The note was from Jaali, who had obviously used his teaching position at the university to get a message to her. Clever.

"You can go back to the common room," she told Asha, wanting no witnesses to the pleasure the message brought her. It was personal, intimate even, and she wanted to enjoy it on her own.

Dear Milenda,

I am not sure why you ran away. I tried to call you back, but you can run faster than anybody I know. Are you all right?

I was very surprised by your revelation. I can't believe I never made the connection. I think I was way too happy thinking of you as just a girl I met. I never stopped to wonder why people talked to you in such a reverent way, or why the professors never looked you in the eye. I told myself it was because you are so beautiful. Beauty often intimidates people. And you are indeed beautiful, Milenda. You are like a walking work of art, and I am in awe of you. When you told me who you are, I did not know how to react, but I do now.

At the risk of having my head chopped off by your overzealous guards, I will tell you I'm not ready to give up on our friendship. I don't have many friends. I'm different in more ways than one, and people look at me with suspicion. There aren't that many Fjordens running around free, and I remind Natalians that slavery is still very much alive. I make people uncomfortable, so I carry on alone. It didn't bother me until I met you. Now, I don't want to lose you.

If you feel the same way, come and see me. We can talk. I would love to talk to you. Please, come…

P.S. - Trying to make friends with Mjusi, but he is being difficult.

A sigh of pleasure escaped from her lips. The young princess jumped out of bed with the letter tightly squeezed against her chest, *matangazos* sparkling like fireworks along her neck and shoulder. This time she thoroughly enjoyed the tickling feeling of warmth they created, since they were singing for joy. Jaali did not hate her; he didn't even seem too intimidated by the fact he had been hanging out with royalty. Milenda spun, letter still held against her body as a precious treasure.

He thinks I'm beautiful.

Heart full of a happiness she had never felt before, the Jewel raided her closet, never once letting go of the note. She picked out a brightly-hued *kanga* in shades of blues and browns to cover her slim body and an *iqhiya* hat to cover her unruly thick hair. She didn't want to spend a lot of time with it, so she skipped the *santulo*. He thought she was beautiful; she didn't need any further ornamentation. If she could, she would fly to his place in her undergarments, as inappropriate as it may be. Her heart and soul craved his company, her restless eyes longed to behold his tranquil blues, and her body ached for his touch, however restrained.

The palace servants glanced curiously at her as she propelled herself barefoot through the long, marble-paved hallways, her scarf flowing behind her like wings.

Jaali's *hema* was not far from the palace, which had been built strategically on a hilltop on the outskirts of town, a vantage point in case of attack. Not that Natale had been attacked in the last two hundred years, but the palace had been built before peace had graced their nation, at a time when the ethnic groups in the region fought against each other for reasons that time forgot. Wazis, Nyotas, and even Outlanders all seemed to have forgotten the gripes of the past and lived side by side in peace.

The sight of her friend's small *hema* brought tears of happiness to her eyes. She couldn't remember the last time she had a real friend; in fact, the only friend she could ever remember having was the daughter of a kitchen maid, who at the age of three had been too innocent to realize who Milenda really was. That friendship had ended as soon as her royal tutors had a private conversation with the little girl's parents. Needless to say, her first and only friend never set foot in the palace again.

She might be the Jewel of the kingdom, but Jaali was the jewel of her life.

Knocking was unnecessary since the front door stood ajar, but she still rapped her knuckles on it as a polite warning that she had arrived. From inside, she heard that gentle, modulated voice that made her skin go all bumpy and triggered chaos with her *matangazos*.

"Come inside. The door is open."

Hand on her *iqhiya* to make sure it was in place and not showing her unkempt hair, Milenda stepped inside, feeling her legs shaking beneath her. Why was she so nervous? It was not like they had never met before. They had been together just yesterday in the jungle. So, why all the jitters inside of her now?

Jaali didn't give her too long to ponder. He took two giant steps, and before she could react, he was standing right in front of her, holding her small hands in his and drowning her eyes in the crystal lakes of his own. "*Msichana.*" His gentle voice dropped an octave, and for a second, she wasn't even sure he had spoken.

Afraid that she would lose herself in his eyes, Milenda dropped her gaze to his full lips to confirm he had indeed spoken. They were moving again, but this time not in speech. He was going to kiss her.

A princess cannot allow a boy, of lowly or high birth, to kiss her. The old, traditional directive came to her as a scream inside her head, making her wince and involuntarily step away from him, their hands yanking apart.

Jaali looked disconcerted, confused. There was a question in his eyes that she couldn't answer. That kiss was so desired by her heart and by her lips, but a lifetime of etiquette brainwashing had taken its toll. It was too soon for her, no matter how much her body yearned for it. She dropped her eyes to her feet, which she belatedly noticed to be bare. What would her tutors say? Barefoot and alone in a boy's house. Fodder for scandal, she was certain.

His hand, which had been raised slightly, fell like a

deflated balloon along with his whole demeanor. "*Nasikitika*," he whispered, "I shouldn't have—"

Her hand shot up to grab his wrist and pull him closer to her. "No, I am sorry, Jaali," she said, her eyes pleading. "I have these voices in my head telling me what I should and should not do." His eyes danced with amusement. "Well, not voices literally. That would be crazy." She giggled and his face opened up in a smile.

With a gentle tug, he twisted his wrist in her hand and held it, palm against palm, fingers interlaced. Their bodies were mere inches from touching, and his eyes glittered with excitement. "And what are those voices telling you not to do?" he asked, his voice low and meaningful. He tugged her closer to him, their linked hands now resting between them.

The strange hot-cold feeling she always felt when her *matangazos* were glowing spread from her face to her shoulder as the heat from Jaali's body seeped into her skin underneath her *kanga*. With a shiver, she lifted her head to meet his eyes. He was taller than her by at least a foot, and as they drew closer, he had to bend down in order to look at her face and mouth.

Jaali's head dipped lower and his lips touched hers. They lingered there, as if asking for permission to go any further. Milenda reveled in the feeling, but was too afraid to move.

"Is it all right?"

She felt his lips move over hers, and losing all control, she wrapped her arms around him and pulled him even closer. She had never kissed a boy before, but she found she knew how— or rather her body did. Instinct seemed to have taken over, and her lips latched on to his with a passion she didn't know she had. Under her touch, Jaali's lips opened, welcoming her exploration. Her legs weakened and liquefied under her and she braced herself against him.

As Jaali held her up, Milenda felt her *matangazos* burn like they never had before as she tasted the sweetness of his mouth. It was not an altogether unpleasant feeling, but it gave her pause.

What if those voices are right? What if it is wrong for a young woman to be this close to a man? She pushed him gently away. "I should go," she mumbled, her face still so close to his, all she could see was the whiteness of his skin.

He sighed deeply and, after a moment's hesitation, took a step backward, creating a narrow space between them. Milenda felt oddly bereft, as if a part of her had gone missing. That small space might as well be a chasm, for at the moment, the chaperone voices in her head would not allow her to cross it again.

"Will I see you again?" His voice shook, and his eyes searched her face for a clue.

She needed to do some soul searching. The significance of everything she had done and felt was not all that clear to her. The need for guidance overwhelmed and daunted her, but she had no one she could talk to about this. Her mother had passed away many years before, and her father was as distant to her as he was to all his subjects. In his world, she existed only as his heir, someone to take over his royal seat once he was gone. She had long lost her cravings for his attention, for his love. Her youth did not preclude her from the wisdom of understanding the futility of yearning for something you could never have.

If a moment ago, while in Jaali arms, she had felt grown-up and sure of herself, she now felt like a child, small and helpless, unsure of what to do or how to feel. She had this overwhelming need to run into her mother's arms, knowing all too well she couldn't. Mortified, she noticed her lower lip quivering and her eyes hot with tears.

I am not going to cry.

Jaali looked concerned as he held her by the shoulders at arm's length. "What's wrong?" he asked. "Something is wrong."

Milenda's head moved side to side in denial. "No, it's fine. I just need to go home." As she moved toward the door, she turned slightly to assure him, "See you tomorrow? In the study spot?"

Quietly he nodded, the look of concern still twisting his mouth a bit. She couldn't stand it anymore. Her *matangazos* were burning so hot, she was sure they would scorch her skin. She left, half walking, half running, already hating herself for it. Putting space—lots of it—between the two of them seemed to be the only good choice at that moment.

Instead of going back to the palace, she ran all the way to their corner of the university jungle, hoping it would bring her some clarity and solace. However, as she sat in the usually comforting arbor seat, she felt more and more restless, her confusion multiplying tenfold as she sat against the fluffy cushions, surrounded by nothing but silence and earthly greens.

"Why can't I make sense of what I feel?" she asked out loud.

A low purr answered her question. Two great big green eyes appeared around the side of the seat, quickly followed by the magnificent, scaled body of Mjusi. The great beast stepped slowly toward her, his head down, soft growls coming out of his mouth. Milenda welcomed her friend with open arms and the creature came to settle in a large, curled mass by her feet, head propped on her lap. Mjusi's adoring eyes made the princess smile.

"My good friend," she whispered, caressing the rough, warm head. "You always know what to do when I'm blue." The beast growled again, his long forked tongue licking her hand lovingly. Her heart was now beating at a normal pace, her *matangazos* didn't burn anymore, and her mind cleared just enough to afford her a sense of momentary peace. "Sweet Mjusi, being a grown-up is more complicated than I thought."

***

Confusion didn't even start to explain what he felt. Milenda had stormed out of his *hema* after having shared with him the first moment of real intimacy he had experienced in his adult life. One minute, she had seemed to be fully invested in their mutual feelings, the next she was acting as if she had been stung by a dozen bees. Jaali knew she had felt it, just like he did, since her *matangazos*, barely hidden by the *isigolwani* she was wearing, had glowed brighter than flames. Was she embarrassed to share such an intimate moment with a former *indent*? Had she realized suddenly how unwise their relationship was, considering her royal status?

With a hand swipe over his snow-white hair, he made himself move in spite of his protesting muscles that were still basking in the afterglow of their bodily contact.

He was expected for a lecture on Outlandish languages at the university. The term always made him smile; there was nothing outlandish about the tongues of the northern lands. It had been an unfortunate choice of words for whoever had first coined the term that included the languages of every nation not in Natale or its neighboring lands. Anything outside the massive continent of Afrika was commonly known as Outerlands—largely thought of as barbaric lands filled with odd people and even stranger languages. But trade had to go on. Afrika needed the skills and the talents of the northern people, fabled for their mastery of carpentry, engineering, agriculture, and manufacturing. A nation could not live off their riches or intellectual prowess alone. People needed to eat, to live under a roof, to protect themselves from the elements. For all that, the proud people of Natale and other Afrikan nations traded and collaborated with the land of the savages they so abhorred. Jaali built bridges between them by teaching them the languages that would make their differences less insurmountable, opening the lines of communication and, he hoped, mutual understanding.

By the time his lecture was over, he couldn't remember a word he had said. His mind constantly fled to Milenda, incapable of staying away for too long. He knew he was being foolish, allowing himself to fall for a creature of such beauty and status. Milenda was an adult by Natale's definition, but he couldn't help noticing she was purer and more innocent than most of the other girls her age. Her station in life must have somehow sheltered her from the world at large, a world that could be cruel and ugly at times.

Jaali knew all about it, his innocence lost many years before he was of age. Being an *indent*—just a less ugly term for slave—had left its mark. His first few years working at the furniture factory had been lonely, but all in all, only mildly traumatic. He had missed his family bitterly and had gone to bed every night more exhausted than he had ever thought possible. But he had gone to bed whole, unharmed, fed, and warm.

Life took a sudden and unwelcome turn to a dark place after the fire. Sold as a piece of furniture to the highest bidder by the insurance company trying to recover the funds they had lost, Jaali came face-to-face with a world of evil he, in his young naïveté, hadn't known existed. Or hadn't wanted to know existed.

Banish your thoughts. With a shake of his head, symbolically clearing his mind of such disturbing memories, Jaali collected all his materials and headed home.

Immersed in his own mind, he failed to notice that the path he took did not lead him home. Instead, he found himself standing before the arbor seat he had shared with Milenda for the past couple weeks.

What exactly did he expect was to happen between them? She was the heir to Natale's throne—the only heir, for she had no siblings or cousins. His knowledge of local history told him she would soon be expected to choose a consort, someone who would provide her and the nation with heirs to the crown. He also knew she would be allowed to pick a husband of her own choosing as long as the male in question proved to be in good health and fertile. But only after the ceremonial trial.

Legend had it that many princesses in Natale's past had chosen one of the competitors, not for love, but because of their sense of duty, possibly strongly encouraged by the Elders. It was a smart political move to soothe the populace, a thank you of sorts for having risked their people's lives trying out for the crown. Even if she wanted to choose him for her consort, Milenda would be bound by honor to pick one of the poor bastards who survived the dangers of the selection. She may even think she wouldn't, but he knew her by now—her true self, the young woman with a heart of gold and an honorable soul. She would do the right thing, even if that meant being unhappy for the rest of her life. There was no future for them. Even their friendship would come to an inevitable end once Milenda assumed her right and duty as a married royal.

Legs stretched across the seat, Jaali reclined on the cushions, hands cradling his head, eyes closed. He couldn't explain what he felt for the princess, not even to himself. They had known each other for such a short time, and yet he felt this inexplicable, intense attraction to her. It was not a mere physical attraction; it was an attraction of body, mind, heart, and soul. When they were together, he felt fulfilled, whole, worthy. When apart, he felt incomplete, small, and insignificant. Never had he felt this way for anyone before, nor had he needed someone this desperately. It was exhilarating.

It scared him half to death. What was he going to do? What could he do?

***

That special spot in the jungle had always been a favorite of Milenda's, but now it held such a deeper meaning for her. She couldn't think of it without being assailed by images of Jaali's beautiful pale face, his near-white hair flying in the breeze, and his soul-penetrating azure eyes locked on hers. Her heart quivered, and her stomach became the home for a thousand butterflies. Was this what it felt like to be in love? In her young heart, Milenda had hoped she would one day feel love, but deep inside she thought she wouldn't. As the princess, she was expected to follow the path of so many royals before her: responsibility and duty. Certainly not love. After all, she couldn't remember a single instance of feeling loved. Her mother had died when she was too young to remember her, and her father... well, her father had never shown her anything but a passing, distracted interest.

Reclined on the arbor seat, supported by several soft pillows, Milenda put the open book down on her lap and closed her eyes. She wanted to dream of the warm, exciting feeling Jaali's lips had brought upon her body. Even her ever-present invisible chaperones couldn't find any fault with a dream, could they?

His long, artistic fingers traced the contours of her face—chin, cheeks, eyebrows.... The calloused skin on his fingertips just deepened the thrill they caused as they brushed gently and slowly over her lips. Instinctively she opened her mouth and allowed his finger between her moist lips. A low growl of pleasure and frustration grew in her throat and left her before she realized this was no dream.

Milenda's eyes popped open to meet the sky of Jaali's unusual eyes. A wave of hot, red lava climbed and spread on her face. "Jaali, you're here," she gasped, embarrassment choking her. "I didn't hear you."

The Fjorden was flushed, his cheeks ablaze, and his eyes feverish. His breath came out ragged as if he had been running. His fingers lingered by her lips and, without thinking, Milenda laid her hand over his, trapping his fingers against her skin. His breath quickened to match hers.

"Will you sit with me?" she asked, finally letting go of his hand.

Jaali seemed to have lost his power of speech as he sat down by her in silence. His eyes asked her a million questions she couldn't answer. How could she? This was all so new to her. Amazing, exciting, but also frightening. She felt so much and so strongly, it seemed sometimes as if her heart would explode. Milenda had no answers. Only more questions.

"You ran from me again yesterday," Jaali said, regaining his voice. "Why? Did I do something wrong?"

Milenda shook her head fiercely. "No, you did nothing wrong," she said, reaching out to him. Jaali swathed her hand with his. She smiled shyly. Her *matangazos* prickled like tiny electric shocks. "It scared me a little."

Jaali's eyebrows shot upwards. "Scared? Of me?" he said, sitting straighter. "I would never want to hurt you. You know that, don't you? I—" Seemingly lost for words, the young scholar licked his lips. "I just wanted—needed to kiss you."

With the heat rising within her and along her markings, Milenda took a deep breath. "And now?" she asked, so quietly she couldn't be sure he had heard her.

A generous and brilliant smile spread across his lips. "I need to kiss you again," he whispered, inching closer to her.

A side of her wanted to flee, but the other wanted to feel his lips on her again. So badly, tears rose to her eyes. "So, what are you waiting for?"

Jaali bent down slightly, slipped one hand behind her neck and pulled her face toward his. "My jewel," he uttered before molding his lips around hers.

All her doubts, all her fears dissolved as her breath mingled with his, and his hand cradled the back of her head. This was what home felt like. It turned out she could indeed love and be loved.

The Dream

Milenda stretched across her bed. She wondered if there was anything she could do to dissuade the Elders from carrying on with the traditional trials, but deep inside, she knew it was a lost cause. Tradition was deeply inlaid in their culture, and to break it was almost sacrilegious. It would take a divine act for them to be swayed into change. Even though she had been prepared—and brainwashed—to accept this day without question, she couldn't.

There was a war raging inside of her that she couldn't control. She had picked her consort already. In her heart, she knew exactly what name she would utter the day of the Choosing, following the Trials. Jaali was her choice; he had stolen her heart, and she couldn't imagine choosing someone else. But the Trials would still be held, and men would be hurt or even killed in the process of trying to prove themselves worthy of her hand. By not picking any of them in favor of one who had not stood trial, the Jewel knew her conscience would be heavy with guilt. It wasn't an easy decision, but it was one she was determined to make. Jaali would be her consort one way or another. Unless he decided against it.

Oh gods! What if he doesn't want to be my husband? The thought had not occurred to her until then. He was obviously attracted to her, and their friendship had grown exponentially as weeks went by. They had kissed and hungered for one another to the point of near panic in her case, but they had never really talked about where to go from there. How to go from feeling to doing, from the abstract to the concrete. So far, all they had was the present, the moment; the future had not entered their minds as of yet. Until now. She wanted him to stay by her side for the rest of her life, to be there when she opened her eyes, and to be the last thing she saw before falling asleep. Forever. She wanted him forever. Her insides quivered at the thought he may not feel the same way.

Asha came in, eyes subserviently lowered, hands locked together making her look much older than she was. Milenda realized with horror that she did not know how old her faithful maid really was.

"Asha, how old are you?" she asked on impulse.

The girl was startled into looking up at her mistress, but quickly regained her composure. "Thirteen, Holy Jewel," she replied, her eyes back on the floor. "Do you require help with the dress?"

Milenda smiled. That was the young girl's way of

reminding her she had an appointment with the Elders and she was still in her night clothes. "Yes, I do need your assistance," she said, reluctantly rolling herself off the bed. "What shall I wear for this most exciting and important meeting?"

Her sarcasm was lost on the young servant, who immediately sprinted to the closet in search of appropriate garb. "Maybe the purple *kanga*. Purple is a very serious color," the girl replied, ruffling through the closet and fishing out a wad of purple-colored cloth. "This one would do nicely, I think. Does it meet your expectations?"

With a sigh, Milenda accepted the cloth from the girl. It was indeed a beautiful, formal kanga and totally appropriate for a meeting with the Elders, but she was in no mood for serious; she longed for something fun and relaxing. Pink would be a good color. Or blue. Blue was always a nice, calming hue for her. "Yes, it is beautiful," she said, accepting the fact she had no choice. "Will you help me put it on?"

In no time, Asha had the fabric artistically wrapped around her mistress's body, another wad of cloth draped around her shoulders, and a somber-looking *iqhiya* on top of her well-coiffed hair. Finishing it all with the ceremonial beads around her neck and a collection of wide bracelets that covered at least half of Milenda's forearms, the young servant finally gave herself a moment to rest. "You look beautiful, my sweet Jewel," she said. "The gods will be pleased."

Feeling itchy and hot, she made her way down to the council room where the Elders held their court. She hadn't seen her father in over a week, but his presence at the meeting with the Elders was most likely not needed. She had to wonder how much of his input was even taken into consideration in matters of the state.

The two large doors opened as if by magic, and she entered the room. The inside of the council room was surprisingly small, with a row of chairs along the front wall, a small desk with a computer to the left, and a long sideboard along the right wall. A young man sat at the desk typing away, and when she entered the room, he looked up for a moment before returning to his industrious work. The Elders in all their dignity and advanced age graced her with a nod.

Curtsying slightly—a princess is always gentle and courteous to her elders—Milenda stared at the familiar and, yet, ever-distant faces.

"You summoned me, honored ones?" It was a rhetorical question. She had indeed been summoned—why else would she be there?—and she had a good idea why.

"Yes, young Jewel," one of them said. "It is time to start the selection for the Trials, and we need your blessing to do so."

Her heart skipped a beat. "Yes, I understand," she said. "Not meaning any offense, honored ones, but may I ask whether it would be acceptable to skip the Trials and go straight to the Choosing?"

From the corner of her eyes, she noticed the Elders cringe a little, as if bothered by an annoying fly or mosquito. "We understand and acknowledge your question, dear one, but tradition must be upheld," the same one replied, his voice showing no shadow of doubt or trepidation.

"If mankind never attempted anything new, reverent one,

nothing would ever be invented or made better," she protested, emboldened by the lack of reaction from the ancient ones. "Maybe it would be wise to try a different way. It may save lives."

The Elders' spokesperson closed his eyes briefly as the others around him stole silent glances at each other. When he reopened them, he took a deep breath and allowed the air to come out from his lungs in a long, quiet whoosh, as if releasing unwanted particles of oxygen from his body. His sharp, deep-set onyx eyes cut straight into her soul, or so it felt.

"Your most exalted Jewel, you are very young and understandably naïve about the way of the world," he said. His voice was quiet and gentle, and yet she felt as she had just been slapped. "This tradition was given to us by our gods. Both our divinities and the common folk of this land expect this law to be upheld."

"How can that be?" she asked, forgetting the formalities. "Chances are that common folk, like you call them, are the ones who would be hurt or even killed by these trials. So, how can that be?"

"Common people are superstitious," the Elder explained, his voice slightly higher now. "They are afraid of what may happen if tradition is not followed."

Let it go. There's no point. "I understand, wise one," she said. "Please forgive my impertinence. I was just trying to look out for my future subjects."

"We understand and appreciate it," he said.

She could tell he did not. Like most of those in power, he wasn't willing to change things for fear of loss of control.

She knew he was right about the people of Natale being superstitious, but she also knew they were smart enough to realize things could be better for them.

The rest of the meeting was spent on a mostly one-sided conversation about the rules and the details of how the Trials would be run. By the end of the meeting, Milenda had broken out in hives along her *matangazos*. As she had recently learned, her spots would glow and heat up—something she hadn't known until she met Jaali—when she was sexually aroused. Now, it seemed they turned into an itching nightmare when she was scared or anxious. The itchy burn was agonizing, and she longed to be out of that room and alone, so she could indulge in an old-fashioned scratch.

The details about what her consort-wannabes would have to face in order to be considered as her future husband horrified her. How could she face her own people after being the reason for such cruel games?

That evening, she ate her meal in her room. She couldn't forget what she had heard, and she couldn't face anyone while that knowledge lurked in the corners of her mind.

With the half-eaten dinner in the discarded tray, Milenda opened the massive windows of her room and whistled a little tune. It wasn't long until the sound of flapping wings reached her ears.

"Mjusi, I need you tonight, my friend," she said as the winged beast alit on the wide windowsill and stretched his head to her. "Have you seen Jaali today?"

The creature had taken upon himself to check on the Fjorden like a protective mother hen. The low growl he offered in response told her he had indeed been to see him already.

"Is he well?" she asked, closing the window. She offered Mjusi a bowl of water. The creature waved his head and Milenda relaxed. Jaali was all right.

With the scaly creature curled up by her side, she fell asleep on top of her soft bed linens and dreamed.

Milenda stood at the end of the equally bright red carpet stretched endlessly in front of her, the red ceremonial kanga tight against her hot skin. She was conscious of only one emotion—the desire to disappear. In the distance, she could recognize human forms slowly approaching. They looked more like ghosts than humans, with their wispy shapes and foggy contours. Somehow, she knew they were coming toward her, even though she couldn't really discern who they were. She waited for hours, and yet they didn't make any progress. Drops of sweat fell from her forehead into her eyes, and her sight became blurry. Her eyes stung from the salt of her own perspiration, and her kanga clung uncomfortably to her moist body. She couldn't move, though. The ceremonial rules were very clear; she must wait as still as the air in the desert until such time as whoever was coming had reached her. So she waited, feet itching for movement, legs cramping, lips dried from the lack of water.

As she blinked the sweat beads out of her eyes, she saw them; they were indeed humans. Men to be exact, three or four of them making their way along the carpet. Their clothes were in rags, as if they had just gone through a shredder, and as they got closer, she could tell they were also covered in blood. For the first time, she noticed they all walked in an awkward way—one dragging a leg behind him, another hauling what looked like a long bag of sorts. It was not long before she realized the bag was actually his arm, half-hanging from the shoulder, bloodied and purple, his muscle and bone sticking out. She swallowed bile and tried to turn and run, but her feet wouldn't move. Frozen in place, she watched with horror as the four disfigured and bloodied male figures closed in. They were so close now she could smell them, the nauseating sweet smell of rotten blood hitting her nostrils and making her heave. The closest one reached his hand to her; instead of fingers, he had only bloody stubs. She cringed as he tried to touch her.

"Pick me," the man said, his voice hoarse and blood dripping from his mouth. "I fought bravely for you, my jewel."

With a start, she knew. This was the day of the Choosing, and those poor human remains were her choices.

Milenda sat upright in her bed, gasping for air. It was only a dream. Only a dream. No matter, her heart was beating like the crazy *batucadas* of the Ngoma, and her nightclothes were soaked in sweat. Mjusi was cooing at her ear and licking her with his rough forked tongue.

"I'm all right," she told him, caressing his head. "Just a bad dream." Which soon, she knew, may turn to reality.

***

Sleep didn't come easy to Jaali that night. In his dreams, he saw Milenda picking someone other than him for her consort. It didn't matter that she was so strongly against the idea and so dead set at picking him. They had talked in urgent whispers under the shelter of the trees and in the shadow of his *hema*. Promises of eternal love were exchanged in between the kisses and the cuddles. But he knew in the end, she wouldn't have much choice. She would be honor-bound to choose one who had fought for the honor, not one who had stood on the sidelines safe and sound in the knowledge she loved him.

These nightmares had tormented him, and he was fed up. He wanted to do something about it. Just as he had felt helpless and used during the time of his indenture, he now felt hopeless and lost. Jaali refused to be controlled by fear and doubt again. He was going to do something about it.

That morning, an idea had taken root in his mind, and as the day went by, the idea bloomed and grew until it was a fully grown plan, rich with branches and leaves of its own. Milenda would never agree with it, so he would have to keep it secret for as long as possible. Now that he had made the decision, he felt oddly light, as if an awesome weight had been lifted off his chest, and he was able to breathe freely again.

Classes seemed to linger and drag like giant slugs on an enormous leaf. He hadn't seen his Jewel yet that day. Her classes had taken place on the other side of campus, and he couldn't wait to meet her afterward. With a lighter heart, he would be able to enjoy her company fully, instead of fretting about the future. When the bell to the last class rang, he flew rather than walked to their usual meeting place in the jungle.

As soon as he saw her, draped in a soft gray *kanga*, he knew something was wrong; she never wore somber colors. Milenda was bent over, her head resting on her knees and arms cradling herself. As he approached, her face popped up to look at him. Eyes swollen with tears, she hastily wiped them with the back of her hand and straightened herself.

"What happened?" he asked, rushing to her side, taking hold of her hands. "Are you hurt?"

Her voice came out in little sobs. "No, I'm fine," she said, allowing him to rub the top of her hands with his thumbs. "I just can't shake off a nightmare I had last night."

Searching her face for permission, Jaali pulled her to him in a protective hug. "It was only a dream," he whispered. "It was only a dream."

Silence enveloped them for the next few minutes. Milenda's heart, beating against his chest, eventually slowed, and her breathing evened out. "I dreamed about the Trials," she said, raising her eyes to his. "It was awful, Jaali, truly awful."

"But just a dream, *msichana*. It's all right." He hugged her tighter, trying to banish all her fears away. "We don't have to talk about it if you don't want to."

Milenda pushed him away gently and stood up. "I want to talk about it," she replied. "I want to discuss it and analyze it… try to figure out how to prevent it from happening." Her bright green eyes were wet and her voice shook as she paced in front of him. He fought the urge to reach for her and shelter her within his embrace. "I've got to do something, Jaali. I don't know what, but I have to do something."

Jaali stroked her hair, and she leaned into the caress. "It will be all right," he said. "I promise. It will be fine."

His gaze darted from her emerald eyes to her full ruby lips, taking in her ragged breath. She cupped his face with her hands and smiled. Hesitant. Sad. Their heads inched closer, and their lips met in a soft, gentle kiss. Her mouth tasted like honey, soft and warm. Exciting. Bodies touching, his arms encircled her form, his hands tightening around her waist, pulling her closer still. He couldn't get enough of her taste and her warmth. His left hand climbed up her spine to cradle the back of her head as she yielded to his deepening kiss.

Their faces came apart and their hungry eyes met. Speechless, Jaali caressed her silky face, tracing the trail of her *matangazos* down from her ear to her neck. There was a yearning growing alarmingly fast in his heart. In his body and soul. He needed her to be even closer. He pulled her to him again for an urgent, intense kiss. Their lips moved against each other in a silent conversation, tongues touching and dancing together. As if in a frenzy, their arms tightened around each other, pulling and pushing, advancing and ebbing in a wave of desire.

Afraid of losing control, Jaali gently pushed her away from him. "If we don't stop now, I won't be able to stop ever," he said, his voice low and hoarse. Still unable to completely let go of her, his hands rested on her bare shoulders, relishing in the connection. "We better stop before we do something we both will regret."

Dating a royal was forbidden before the Choosing, before all the traditional and political formalities were finished and done with. Deflowering a princess meant death. Milenda knew it, and so did he. As much as they loved and wanted each other, they were both wise enough to know not to play with fire. Despondent green eyes rose up to meet his in reluctant acceptance.

He noticed the intense glow of her *matangazos,* and even

though he was not certain of its meaning, he guessed it had something to do with the way they both felt at that moment—exhilarated and frustrated all at once. Whatever reason made them glow like that, they made her look even more radiant, giving her a halo of otherworldly beauty.

"You are so beautiful, Milenda," he said, not able to contain his awe. He couldn't understand how such an amazing creature, and a princess to boot, could love him.

He was nothing. A twenty-seven-year-old academic who had spent ten long years of his life in captivity, doing other people's bidding, not having a will of his own and having to forgo his human dignity. It had taken him almost two years to rebuild his confidence and his will to move forward. After having earned his freedom from his last owner, Jaali had spent the first few months curled into a human ball under a concrete beam of the capital's main bridge, hardly eating, hardly living. Yet, this creature of beauty found something worthy in him. He couldn't understand it; hell, half the time he couldn't believe it. But he was infinitely grateful and happy that she did.

Milenda laughed, and the jungle was suddenly filled with her sounds of happiness. Her hand caressed his pale face. "You are the one who is beautiful, Jaali," she said. "You are one of a kind in this land of ours."

He could have refuted that assumption, for he knew it to be false. There were lots of people like him in Natale—mostly hidden in factories, private homes or hovels, but definitely there. However, the pleasure she gave him with those words was rare, and for once he accepted the fact that she really thought him to be so.

Their secret spot in the jungle offered them shelter from the outside world. Only Mjusi came to visit every so often. Jaali was certain they were being watched by royal bodyguards, but from afar, far enough that the details of their meetings were not immediately obvious. He also suspected that Milenda bribed the guards—or threatened them—in some way. All in all, these were moments of true privacy and peace.

Reclining together in the arbor seat, after finishing a book Milenda had to read for a class, Jaali felt the stirrings of desire begin again.

"Am I your first boyfriend?" The question came from the need to self-distract rather than real curiosity. He really didn't care whether he was her first love or not. All that mattered was she loved him.

Milenda, leaning against him, twisted her neck slightly to look up at him. "Why?"

He smiled. "Just curious," he said. "Someone as beautiful as you must have had many suitors."

"I had a few," she said, obviously uncomfortable. "But not because I am beautiful, as you say I am. Just because I am a princess and many would like to ascend to the throne any way they can. No boyfriends though."

"You never kissed a boy before?" He was sincerely surprised. He would have thought that even a princess, with all her social and political limitations, would have had some romantic experiences by her age.

"I kissed a distant cousin once when he came to visit the realm," she said with a comical frown. "He was only seven then, and his face was covered in dirt from playing in the yard. It was like kissing a blob of mud—which I have done before, by the way." Jaali burst out laughing, and after a moment of indignation, she joined him. "I also kissed a monkey once, but I think that hardly counts as a real kiss," she added, much to his amusement. "What about you, Jaali?" she asked him when their laughter died down. "Have you ever had a girlfriend?"

The remaining laughter abruptly died on his lips. This was not an easy subject for him to talk about. "I was an *indent*, Milenda," he said, lowering his voice to a whisper. "*Indents* don't have lovers. Not that way."

Jaali felt her stiffen against his chest. "Oh gods! I'm so sorry. *Nasikitika*," she said, her hand seeking his. "I wasn't thinking."

"Don't apologize, *msichana*," he said. "As hard as it is to talk about, I can't avoid it. It is part of who I am, who I was…."

"It makes me angry to think that Natale still tolerates such practices," she exclaimed, passion in her voice.

He slipped a loose strand of her hair between two fingers. It was so different from his—thick and curly, coarse compared to his satiny white hair, yet soft to the touch. "Not just 'tolerate,' Milenda," he said, still musing about the texture of her hair.

She twisted around, propping herself up on his chest with a hand. "What do you mean, 'not just tolerate'?" she asked, her eyes ablaze.

Surprised by her reaction, his head jerked back a little. "I mean, Natale profits quite a bit from the trade, you know?" he explained, shocked she didn't know. "They don't just tolerate it. They encourage and sponsor it."

Her chin fell slightly and her eyes opened even wider. "Does my father know about this?" she asked, as if he, a common man, would know.

"I would think so, considering that the Crown has its own head hunters," he said. Her *matangazos* were now a bright red, and he feared that, if he touched them, they would scorch his skin. "You didn't know?"

Milenda's body was outrage incarnated. Trembling, she sat up and turned her back to him. "Were you caught by one of the royal head hunters?" she asked, her voice muffled by the hand covering her mouth.

"I'm sorry, *msichana*, I thought you knew." He reached out to touch her shoulder, but she shrugged it away. "Yes, I was hunted and caught by the Crown's men. There is real big money in the slavery game." He reached for her again. "Why won't you look at me?"

He thought he heard her cry. "I'm ashamed of my own family and people." Her voice trembled. "I'm so ashamed."

In a swift move, Jaali pulled her toward him, hugging her close. He felt the wetness on her skin as his face touched hers. "You don't have to feel ashamed," he assured her. "You had nothing to do with it."

"But my family does," she said in a small voice that betrayed how young she really was. "My family is profiting from hunting humans like animals and keeping them captive for their own advancement. It's disgusting, immoral—"

"When you are queen, you'll be able to do something about it," he said, his mouth in the crook of her neck.

"Not if the Elders have any say in it," she said, turning her face slightly to his. With a spin, she turned her whole body to face him and smiled, her face still stained with tears. "But I will surely try."

Smiling, Jaali took hold of her hands. "That's the spirit," he said. "Until then, don't worry too much about this. Let's enjoy our time together." *Because it may soon be over.* He had a plan to make sure that didn't happen, but it was a risky one that offered no guarantees of success. No matter the risks, he wouldn't give up. If there was something slavery had taught him, it was to never give up hope and to never give in to fear.

The Elders

The room was not very large, but it featured ceilings that stretched so far upward, it was easy to imagine them touching the heavens. In spite of his nervousness, Jaali couldn't stop staring at them, his neck bent painfully backward, eyes following the seemingly never-ending laced beams up to the top. He almost expected to see an angel perched at the top, staring at him in curiosity. As an artist, he couldn't help himself; the ceilings in that room were a thing of beauty and wonder with their delicately carved arches and buttresses, laced woodwork, and gravity-defying height. The reason for his presence there melted into the background, a mere afterthought, at such a sight.

A muted clanking woke him from his reverie. Someone had opened the massive wooden door and was now standing in front of it, waiting for Jaali to acknowledge his presence. With a quiet clearing of the throat, the newcomer made himself known. "I beg your pardon, *mheshimiwa*," the small man said. "The Elders are ready to receive you."

Jaali swallowed the bile that had suddenly risen in his throat. *Gods protect me.* His legs were not cooperating with his will to move forward, so he had to take a moment to collect himself before following the little man through the open door.

At the end of a short hallway, there was an even bigger door—wood and metal working together to impress any onlookers. The nameless man opened it with apparent ease and signaled Jaali to enter. Mindlessly, he obeyed. He half expected a room of titanic size, considering the magnitude of the antechamber, but he was disappointed to find a plain room instead. It was a simple square with stone walls free of any adornments and with high ceilings of bare stone. A row of large, high-backed chairs lined the facing wall; three of them were empty.

"You will forgive us, *tukufu*." A deep voice reached his ears before he even realized one of the Elders was speaking. "Some of us had urgent dealings and were not able to be here today."

Jaali shifted from one foot to another, unable to stand still, his hands tightening into fists. In all his years in Natale, he had never once faced the Elders. These were respected figures, feared even, and only a select few had been given the honor of a face-to-face meeting.

"I thank you, honored ones, for hearing me today." Not sure whether to bow or just stand, he did nothing other than twist the knitted cap he held in his hands.

"I understand you come to volunteer?" It was not really a question but a statement of fact. Jaali had had to fill out an abundant pile of papers with information about himself and the reason why he was asking for an audience. Still, the Elders in attendance seemed to expect an answer.

"Yes, honored ones, I came to ask to be added to the pool of candidates at the Trials," he said, voice shaking like a leaf on a windy day. His hands shook just as intensely, and he tried to hide the fact by twisting the cap even further.

"And what, prithee, do you offer to the traditional ceremony that we may consider to include you?" The Elder sitting in the middle of the row spoke for the others, who seemed content to sit and listen quietly.

"Genetics, honored ones," he replied simply. "The heirs to the Crown of Natale have long stemmed exclusively from within the native people. Natale is not and never was a large nation in terms of population. After centuries of inbreeding, the royal line would benefit from a totally new gene pool."

"What authority do you have to speak of genetics thus?" the Elder asked, his voice denuded of any emotion. "Are you a scientist?"

Jaali shifted again. His feet tingled as if a million ants had made their way inside his shoes. "No, that I am not," he said, head bowed down for a moment. "I have studied history and science, however. I am a scholar at the university, and I have long been interested in the field of genetics. Sometime after I was freed, one of the deans in the university decided to hire me because of my knowledge of the northern languages.

Being an academic gave me ample chances to research the fascinating world of genetic science."

There was a moment of silence, quickly broken by the Elder. "Go on, you have my ear."

With a little cough, Jaali cleared his dry throat. "Well, you cannot get more of a diverse gene pool from Natalians than Fjordens," he said, hoping it was a self-explanatory statement. "Should I survive the Trials and win the Jewel's heart, I would bring—as a Fjorden—new blood to the royal line of Natale."

The Elders turned and looked at each other, as if conferring in some secret silent language. Then the middle Elder turned his attention back to Jaali. "We have heard you, and we will consider your proposal," he said. "Would you wait in the antechamber as we convene to discuss it?"

Of course, this was not a request. The veiled order had brought the small man back to the door, and Jaali saw himself being escorted out of the audience room quickly and efficiently.

He waited in the antechamber for what felt like an eternity. Provided with a comfortable chair and refreshments, the young Fjorden waited, refusing to allow his feelings for Milenda to cloud his determination. She would be livid if she knew what he was doing. It was not a fail-proof plan, of course. After all, if they did allow him to be one of the contenders, there was no guarantee he would be a survivor. He hadn't been around for a Trial, since the last one had taken place many years before he was born, but he had read the accounts at the university. He knew they were grueling tests of determination and strength that few men survived unscathed.

The great door opened again, and out came the same man,

shuffling his feet as if exhausted—it couldn't be easy to run around all day like that. He came to a stop in front of Jaali, and with a short bow of the head, he said, "The Elders would like to request a series of blood and DNA tests from you before deciding whether to allow you in the Trials. Will you comply?"

Stupid question. Why wouldn't he comply if he wanted to be considered as a possible royal consort? "Of course I will," he said, standing up. "When?"

The little man wiped his brow with a kerchief and then stuffed it in one of his many pockets. "Now," he told Jaali. "I will escort you to the royal labs here in the palace. It shouldn't take more than an hour or so."

Jaali was not expected at the university that day. Not certain of what this whole process entailed, he had requested a full day's leave. The dean had no trouble allowing it, considering Jaali had never once missed a workday even for illness.

The man shuffled his way through the many corridors of the palace and Jaali followed, feeling numb and strangely excited at the same time. He might be getting himself into a serious mess, but at least this time he was the one making the choice, not like in the past when he had been thrown into danger through no fault of his own. He felt in control, even though he realized he was not. Not really.

***

The Elders put their heads together and spoke in urgent whispers. This was an unheard of situation, and even though their first instinct was to laugh at the young Fjorden's impertinence, the truth was that he had made a very good point about the genetic issue. The Crown of Natale was showing signs of inbreeding problems. The Jewel's father himself had been infertile, the first royal male to be born like that. Even though this was not a commonly known fact, people were not blind; they all knew that Milenda was of Nyota stock so unlike anyone else in the family. Both her father and mother were Wazis. It didn't take a college degree to deduce that someone else had donated that sperm.

With time, things would probably just get worse. Rumors had the tendency to grow into incontrollable monsters that could potentially destroy a kingdom and a way of life. They needed to inject fresh blood into the royal line to prevent future problems. On the other hand, the fact that the Fjorden was so ostensibly different from the Natalians would provide the populace with fodder for harmless conjecture for years to come. Jaali had given them much food for thought, and their discussion had gone on for hours before they could come to a decision.

In the end, it was decided unanimously that if Jaali passed the medical tests, he would be accepted as a contender in the upcoming royal Trials. They knew the young man had once been enslaved; he was then tougher than he looked and was used to adversity. The odds of him surviving were very good, the Elders thought. Pleased with themselves and their wisdom, the Elders retired to their private chambers for a well-earned nap just as Jaali was being scanned by a giant machine down the hallway. The medics wouldn't find anything wrong with him.

Fjordens were well-known for their good health and strong bodies. Jaali would pass those tests with no problem at all. It was what would happen after the Trials that worried them.

***

The news came in the shape of a palace guard ceremoniously carrying a sealed letter. Jaali couldn't stop shaking and dropped the envelope several times before managing to get it open. The contents were not a surprise; the Elders had indeed decided to accept him as a contender for Milenda's hand. For a fleeting minute, he wondered if they would have come to a different decision had they known about their relationship.

It didn't matter. He was in, and for that he was infinitely happy and grateful—almost as much as he was terrified. His body shook convulsively, and he could do little more than just curl up on a chair. That's the way Milenda found him a few minutes later.

"Oh gods!" Her eyes opened wide as she rushed to crouch by the chair, her hands reaching out to hold him. His body, still wracked by tremors, was cold and clammy. "What happened, Jaali? Are you sick?"

The sound of her panicked voice snapped him out of his delirium just enough to realize he was not alone anymore. His eyes zoomed in on her graceful face. She looked so worried. "Milenda?" he uttered.

"What's going on?" She rubbed his arms, as if trying to instill some blood circulation into them.

But he was not numb. In fact, much the opposite; his whole

being was alive with nerves, fear and, strangely enough, hope. He actually had a chance now at becoming Milenda's husband. No matter how slim that chance was, it was there. It was a reality. His shaking subsided and his breath regulated to a normal rhythm. As crazy as it sounded even to him, things were looking up.

"Please talk to me, Jaali," she begged, her hands now warm and comforting on his knees. "Say something. You're scaring me."

"I'm fine, *msichana*. I'm fine." His voice was nearly back to normal, and he found he could talk without stuttering. "I just felt a little sick, that's all." To prove he was feeling better, Jaali stood, stumbling a little at first as his legs grew accustomed to his weight again. "See? I just need to walk a little."

Milenda slid under one of his arms and supported his weight with her tiny body. "I'm not sure that's a good idea," she said, noticing how wobbly his legs still seemed to be. "You may want to rest a little more."

Grateful for her slim shoulders to lean on, Jaali took a few steps forward. He was feeling better. The blood was circulating through his body again, and the shock he had suffered was quickly fading away.

"Let's walk," he said. "Fresh air and a little exercise is all I need."

Milenda obliged. As they walked around his *hema*, he gave a silent thank you to the gods for the fact he lived so isolated from everybody else in town. Tongues would wag dangerously at the sight of their Crown Jewel walking around with a man glued to her side.

Jaali snapped back pretty quickly. After a few minutes of walking around, he was able to move with no physical support from her anymore. Soon afterward, one couldn't tell he had been sick at all.

"Sorry, *msichana*," he said, stopping by his door and looking at her. "I had some shocking news and it caught me by surprise." The truth—or part of it—was always better than lying.

Her eyes dropped to her feet. "I'm afraid I have some more bad news," she said, her voice little and unsure. "This is the last time I can see you before the Trials."

A ball of mixed feelings formed inside his chest. On the one hand, not seeing her until the Trials was a godsend; it would be too hard for him to hide such a secret from her. He didn't want to lie to her, but he also didn't want to give her the chance to fight him on this. On the other hand, his heart broke at the very thought of going almost a month without seeing her. The next time they would be face-to-face was when he introduced himself to her as a contender. He cringed at the thought. Undoubtedly, she would feel betrayed and helpless. Gods! He did not want her to feel that way. He didn't want to hurt her in any way.

Gently, he pulled her just inside his doorway, far from any curious eyes, and held her close. He could feel her heart beating against him and was certain she could feel and hear his own heart beating against her face. "*Msichana*, I want you to know that no matter what happens, my heart is yours forever," he said, picking his words carefully. "Everything I do from now on is with you and your happiness in mind." And maybe a little bit of his, too. "Tell me you believe me, please."

Her head tilted upward, so she could look him in the eyes. Milenda smiled. "I believe you, *wimbo wa moyo*, my heart's song. I'll always believe you."

His heart twitched. She was so trusting, and he didn't deserve her trust. Not now. To appease his own guilt, Jaali put a smile on his face and said, "Let's go do something fun then. Gods only know when we will be able to do it again." *Or ever.*

The jungle had been a good refuge for them both. With Mjusi at their heels, they headed there, anxious to put all their fears away.

Jaali sometimes forgot Milenda was as young as she was. There was a maturity about her. Maybe the knowledge that the future of the nation was her responsibility had made her mature earlier than most. But at times like this, when she let herself relax completely, and he thought, even forget who she was, her youth showed through her layers. It was a beautiful thing to see.

He leaned on a tree trunk, long legs stretched in front of him, to watch her. Her sparkling laughter echoed through the forest like the chime of a million tiny bells. The blue *iqhiya* that covered her head had fallen off, and her springy coils of hair bounced and flew over her face as she raced Mjusi in a losing game of tag. Tiny and light-footed, she looked like a forest fairy with the loose ends of her *kanga* flying behind her like wings, her brown feet stained green from the grass below.

Mjusi was obviously used to this kind of play and squealed happily between trees, sometimes flying, other times scrambling on all fours. Winded from all the running, he had his long forked tongue hanging outside his mouth, drooping over his chin, at times actually skimming the ground. Jaali thought he saw him trip over it once when the creature took a sudden turn around a tall elephant-ear plant. Their game went on for so long, he was exhausted himself even though he had only participated in the first five minutes or so. It was a lot more enjoyable to just watch.

Milenda, shiny with perspiration and out of breath, dropped by his side, still giggling. "I think I have worn him out," she said, pointing at poor Mjusi trying to cool himself by burrowing into the mossy ground.

Her hair was flying in every which way, making her look wild and free. Jaali felt the urge to draw her to him and kiss her.

"You wore me out," he said instead. Her proximity was playing havoc with his senses. "And I was just watching." She giggled again, too tired to say anything, and laid her head on his shoulder. Not for the first time, Jaali wondered what madness was coming over him, where his body took control and only an extraordinary amount of mind power prevented him from giving in. His hand unwisely traveled to her face in a gentle caress that sent him spiraling and wanting so much more.

She's so young still. But he loved her. He loved the whole that was her; her face, her puffy hair, her small delicate hands, her haunting green eyes. He loved the way she laughed, the way she voiced her outrage, the way she had her guards wrapped around her little finger. Most of all, Jaali loved the way she made him feel. Complete and free, two things he had not felt since his childhood in the Outerlands.

Fighting to keep control, Jaali kissed the top of her head. "You are my *magiska fen, älskling*," he whispered, unwittingly falling into his native language. She purred into his shoulder. "You're like a magic creature, and I feel I don't deserve you. I am nothing and you are everything."

Her head popped straight up. "Don't say that," she told him, her young face twisted into an angry frown. "You are everything to me, *wimbo wa moyo*, everything. Thanks to you, I'm actually looking forward to the future. Instead of dreading a long, boring life burdened with responsibilities I do not want, I'm now looking forward to it with you by my side."

A smile lit up his pale face. Her soft brown hand was lying across his very white arm. "You brought color to my world. Obviously." He giggled as he caressed her hand.

Milenda's face relaxed into a wide smile. "I love how we complement each other in every way," he added. "Your color to my lack of it, your noble birth to my indenture…. We are so different and yet so alike."

Mjusi, finished with rubbing himself in the forest moss, crawled his way close to them, and curled himself into a scaly ball. After a gentle growl, he closed his eyes and fell blissfully asleep.

Jaali laughed. "You even brought a *msitu* to my life, a creature of myth. I love you, my princess, and I always will." He meant every word.

The Contender

The world faded in, one atom at a time. First she was aware of colors, then the blurry edges of shapes, the worried look in someone's eyes hovering over her. She had a foggy memory of standing as the contenders presented themselves to her. As the blood restarted its normal flow through her body and brain, Milenda became aware of her guards and faithful Asha fussing around her, touching, cooing, fanning her, as if the movement of air could bring her back to the world of the living. A quiet moan escaped her lips as the return of awareness also brought back her memory; the otherworldly face of her love introducing himself as a contender.

How did that happen? When did it happen, and why hadn't she known about it?

Painstakingly slowly, she sat herself up, the world spinning around her as she did. Young Asha held her by an arm, and an old woman she didn't recognize held the other. With their help, Milenda was able to sit on her throne-like chair with a modicum of dignity. Her heart bled when she spotted Jaali's worried face among the small crowd that had collected around the royal dais; she hadn't dreamed it. He was indeed a contender.

"Are you feeling all right, Your Royal Jewel?" the unfamiliar old woman asked her, checking her pulse. Was she a doctor? Asha looked at her, brown eyes suspiciously moist.

Milenda glanced at the woman. She was tall, thin, and ancient. Her parchment skin had been carved by the many rivers and rivulets of heartache and worry, and her dark, piercing eyes seemed to shine like black diamonds within its landscape.

"Who are you?" Milenda asked, her voice hoarse and unsteady.

The woman straightened her bright red *kanga* and voluminous *gele* and smiled, further wrinkling her face. "I am Mama Nyeusi, your *iyalorixá* here to make sure you are well. The orisas wouldn't be too happy if the Jewel was to get sick and die on them." Her voice was deep and exuded authority, yet it was also strangely comforting, like that of a mother.

"The orisas?" Milenda said, shaking her head gently to disperse the fuzziness in her mind. The orisas were minor gods of Afrikan mythology, both well-loved and feared by the people of Natale. "What do the orisas have to do with me?"

A chuckle escaped the old woman's lips. "Child, you are the Jewel of the Crown. The orisas have great plans and hopes for you."

Her wish to further interrogate the cryptic woman had to be put aside, for her royal father stepped in and ceremoniously held her hands in his. "Child of mine." He uttered the formal words with no real emotion in his voice. *For once, Father, I wish you really cared.* "How are you feeling? We were worried about you."

With a wave of her hand, Milenda dismissed the problem. "I'm fine, Father," she said, unable to hold the bitter edge from her voice. "I just got overheated, that's all. We can continue with the proceedings." For that, she knew, was all he was worried about, getting the ceremony under way and having one more thing off his royal plate.

The staff around them swiftly cleared up any mess while Asha busied herself making sure every fold in Milenda's *kanga* was straight and tidy. The Jewel sat, her back straight as a board and her breath ragged and choppy. She ignored all the movement around her and focused on the only thing that really mattered to her at that moment—the transparent blue eyes of her love, his ceremonial veil discarded at his feet, an expression of overwhelming longing on his paler-than-usual face.

She didn't understand why he was there. He knew she would have chosen him no matter what. Was he pushed into competing? Milenda couldn't imagine the Elders picking an ex-*indent* for a contender, but he was healthy, young, and fertile. There weren't many men like that around anymore. The danger of extinction was a very real threat hanging over the heads of her people.

Jaali's lips moved, forming silent words that she guessed

rather than understood. Her eyes, never leaving his, blinked away stubborn tears, and her lips mouthed words back. *I love you. Why are you here?* His sorrowful eyes were apologetic as they studied hers.

She wished she could telepathically talk to him. Her people were rumored to have been able to do it once upon a time. Even if there were any truth to that old wives' tale, she was not pure Nyota, just a mutt with no other connection to her fabled ancestors than a couple of stray chromosomes. A sad little smile would have to do.

"Let the festivities resume," she heard the commanding voice of her father say from behind her. On cue, all the contenders returned to their previous positions. Jaali picked up the veil and walked to the end of the carpet to place himself in front of the royal throne.

"Your most exalted Jewel," he started, his eyes appropriately and demurely lowered, "I pray thee accept me as a contender to your royal heart. I promise to fight with all my might to deserve the honor of your hand." He had changed the ritualistic words just enough to make it personal.

In spite of her worries, she smiled at him and accepted the veil he offered her. As she brought the veil first to her lips, then to rest upon her heart, she heard the sudden whispering of surprise from all watching. Was the princess showing favor this early in the Trial? A little flutter of concern was quickly replaced by her ever-growing need to let her blue-eyed love know he was, and always would be, the chosen one. Milenda watched with a heavy heart as Jaali backed away, slightly bent in a respectful bow, to join the rank of the other contenders.

May the gods have mercy on you.

Milenda stood, her legs still wobbly beneath her, and took a few steps forward to the edge of the dais. Standing erect and defiantly, she faced the crowd and the contenders. "May your journey be swift and the glory be yours."

With those words, the Trials had officially started.

***

Woeful eyes followed Milenda's progression back to the royal palace. The contenders were expected to stand quietly and respectfully by their chairs while the palace staff and government officials accompanied the Crown Jewel. This year, the procession was slower than usual, for the princess required help to walk and was now bookended by two servant girls supporting her weight.

Jaali bit his lip. Hard. Was she all right? He hated the fact that he was not able to run after her and offer her the comfort of his voice and his shoulder. He feared the next time he saw her she may not even want to speak to him. Doubts about his decision plagued him as he watched her painfully slow progress along the stone path.

Once the royal group vanished around the corner, the guards relaxed their stance and approached the contenders.

"Let's move it!" The captain barked the order, the time for niceties now solidly gone. "Back to the contenders' citadel."

The men obeyed, unenthusiastically marching in the opposite direction of the palace. The contenders' citadel was not as grand as the name suggested. It consisted of a series of tiny, spartan rooms where the men slept, an equally small refectory where they ate, a kitchen and pantry stocked with healthy, but unexciting foods, and the training rooms. The contenders would receive some training in fighting, basic survival skills, and a cursory education on life in the desert.

Upon arrival, Jaali and the others were allowed to retire to their rooms for a short rest and to change from the ceremonial robes they were wearing. He changed into their simple, beige training clothes and stretched his long, slim body on the bed. His mind wouldn't allow him to rest.

The desert didn't scare him like it did the other contenders. He had spent some time there when he had attempted to escape from his last owner. Anything seemed better than the life he had at the hands of Master Mnyama. Jaali had sought refuge in the desert because he knew nobody dared stay there for long. There were stories, told to children at night to make them obedient and told to friends as cautionary tales. He had hidden there with the full understanding that he may not come out alive. Unfortunately, he had underestimated Mnyama's thirst for him, and his men had sought him out and found him within a week.

A week in the desert was more than enough to realize the stories were strongly based on reality. Jaali knew what he was about to face out there. But that didn't scare him half as much as the idea of living the rest of his life without Milenda.

He dozed off for a few minutes. A loud knock on the tiny square window high above the bed wrenched him from his fitful sleep. Even with his tall stature, Jaali had to stand on the bed to peek out the dirty glass.

Mjusi was hovering in front of the window, flapping his wings like a mad bat. The window was stuck from disuse, and it took Jaali a couple of minutes to prop it open just enough so the winged creature was able to stick its long beak-like muzzle inside. Jaali backed up a little to avoid being pushed by Milenda's friend and noticed a piece of paper sticking from his fanged mouth.

"Is this from Milenda, Mjusi?" he asked, prying the paper from the creature's mouth. Mjusi shook his head as if to say yes and flew away before being noticed by the guards. "Thank you," Jaali yelled after him before closing the window.

Instead of reading the message right away, he hid it in the pocket of his pants for fear the guards may have been alerted by the booming noise Mjusi's wings always made while flying. But after a few minutes of waiting patiently and lying on his bed, no one came.

He could smell the lovely scent of shea butter on the white paper and he smiled. Images of beautiful Milenda took shape inside his mind. As he unfolded the torn paper, his hands shook. What if she was so angry at him she didn't want him for her consort anymore?

Why, Jaali, why? Why did you volunteer to be a contender? I wanted to make sure you were safe, and now you won't be. I love you and hate you right now. My heart hurts.

The Orisa

"Yemanjá doesn't grant wishes just because you asked," the old woman said, her voice quiet but firm.

Milenda squirmed in her seat. "But these are special circumstances," she protested. "Surely the mother would take that into consideration."

The *iyalorixá* busied herself pouring a pungent tea into two brightly-colored cups. "The orisas don't dance to anyone's tune but their own," the woman said unhelpfully, while handing one of the cups to Milenda. "However, you are special to them, and I may be able to persuade Yemanjá to help you in your hour of need." She sat down, spreading the large, poufy folds of her overdress around her.

Milenda straightened on the chair, teacup burning her hands. "So you think she would help me?" Her hopes had just swelled to double the size.

"It is possible, precious one," the old woman said, blowing at her tea daintily. "But Yemanjá will ask for something in return."

She had heard of that. She had also been told many fairy tales in her lifetime. "As long as she doesn't ask me for my firstborn." She chuckled, wrinkling her nose at the terribly strong scent of the tea.

Mama Nyeusi laughed softly. "You have always had a good sense of humor," she said cryptically. *Always? Had they met before the contenders' presentation ceremony?* "No, it won't be your firstborn, but something equally difficult and precious."

That piqued the princess's attention. "Like what?" She leaned forward on the chair and decided to forgo the hot brew altogether.

A big sip was followed by a loud, satisfied sigh. "Not for me to guess," Mama Nyeusi said, setting the teacup down on the side table. "I will tell you what the mother decides, child."

Dismissed, Milenda stood and took the still-full cup to the sink. "What is this brew we're drinking?" Even though there was no way she would drink it, she was curious. The smell was like nothing she had ever experienced.

"*Gotu Kola*, for clarity of mind," the woman said, following her to the sink. "Pity you didn't drink yours."

Milenda's *matangazos* shone brightly in embarrassment. "Sorry, Mama," she apologized. "The smell is a little off-putting."

The old woman led her to the door, one hand between

Milenda's shoulder blades. "Like in most cases, sometimes things that are ugly on the outside are beautiful on the inside. Remember that, sweet girl." Mama Nyeusi closed the door between the two of them.

With a shake of her head, Milenda began the long walk back to the palace. "Strange woman," she mumbled, kicking dust with her shoes.

In spite of her quick dismissal, she was happy. Hope had now swelled to fill her whole being; Yemanjá was going to help her and Jaali in his Trials. She just knew it. And with the mother's help, Jaali could not get hurt. Yemanjá was the Orisa of all creation, the great divinity of the sea. She protected those who sought justice and fairness, and she exacted punishment on those who did not.

The road forked, and Milenda stood at the junction for a moment. She really should go right, the path to the palace. The Elders were expecting her for yet another boring and useless guidance session; a whole lot of hullabaloo to keep her distracted from the real horror about to take place. On the other hand, if she went left, she may be able to take a peek at Jaali, maybe even be able to sneak in a word or two. Very unprincess-like, of course, but her heart was begging her.

Her feet made the decision for her, and left she went, picking up speed as she approached the contenders' citadel.

As she got closer, her heart jumped inside her chest, as if trying to get out. She scanned the area, looking for the lean form of her heart-song and became quickly discouraged when she couldn't find him. A tree provided her with a place to hide while she scanned the compound again.

In a group of men, all hanging out at a corner of the main building, she thought she recognized Jaali's tall figure, and her stomach filled with butterflies. It was him! She could never mistake his long, slender, yet muscular build. Milenda watched as Jaali, standing shirtless and in training pants, stretched his arms over his head. Tiny jolts of electricity ran up her legs and her arms at the sight of his beautiful, lithe body. Even though she couldn't see it, she could certainly feel her *matangazos* burning like fire alongside her neck and shoulder. Nobody had ever made her feel like that.

One of the trainers yelled orders, and the men all filed away toward the main building. Whatever they had been doing was finished. Most of the contenders looked exhausted, but Jaali— she noticed with a considerable amount of pride—walked easily and youthfully. His skin shone with perspiration, and his gray pants hung low enough on his hips she could see the lines of his bones V-shaping from his waist to…

She shook her head. Such improper thoughts should never enter a young lady's mind, she reminded herself. It couldn't be helped, though. In her eyes, he was the picture of physical perfection, and she yearned to know every inch of him in spite of the voices in her head telling her otherwise. With a quick stop by the water pump to spray some water on his face, Jaali went inside, and Milenda felt as if part of her had gone with him.

Thankfully, the area was surrounded by tall, lush trees that concealed her from prying eyes. Following the information she had bribed off one of the guards at the palace, she circled around the main building until she found the small window of

Jaali's room. Nobody was around. This side of the building faced the back and did not seem to warrant any interest from the guards. She was able to run to it and crouch on the grass without being seen. Her hand, shaking like a leaf, reached out for the window as she stretched on her tippy-toes, but she was too short.

A quick scan of the immediate area told her it was going to be impossible to reach the window. She grabbed a handful of pebbles and proceeded to throw them at the glass, hoping Jaali would hear it.

"Jaali. Jaali." She didn't dare raise her voice above a whisper.

The window opened. "Who's there?" Jaali's voice poured out. "Is that you, Milenda?"

A huge smile burst onto her face. "Yes, it's me. Are you all right?" Her voice was shaking, and even though she couldn't see him from where she was standing, his warm voice melted her heart and made her day brighter.

"Milenda, you shouldn't be here," he said, worry permeating his voice. "If they catch you, you will be in all kinds of trouble. We are not allowed visitors."

"Nobody knows I am here." *Hell, I didn't know I was going to be here.* "I needed to hear your voice."

There was a silence, and she feared someone might have caught him, but his voice wafted over to her again. "You know I love you, don't you?"

Those words filled her heart to the brim. "Then why did you volunteer for this?"

Silence came from the other side of the window once again.

When he spoke, his soft, warm voice made the butterflies inside her stomach go berserk. "It was the only way, *msichana*. The only way to guarantee I had a chance."

In spite of the warm feelings his voice brought to her heart, she felt anger rear its ugly head inside her core. "I promised I would pick you. Don't you trust me? Don't you think I would keep my word?"

"Of course I trust you." The protest came out louder than intended. "I trust you with my life, but I also know you are honorable and that you will do what you need to do to keep your nation going."

Realization sank in. "And I would feel obligated to choose one of the contenders in order to keep the peace and be fair," she completed the sentence. Her toes were starting to hurt under her weight, and her heart had started to bleed a little. Jaali was right; she would have to choose a contender for her consort. If she didn't, there would be public discontent, which could very well lead to a national crisis. She wouldn't do that to her people, no. matter how much she disliked the archaic traditions they followed. Sometimes tradition was all that held a people together. Pull that thread, and the union would unravel. "I'm sorry, *wimbo wa moyo*. I put you in this situation. You were happy and safe before meeting me."

"Maybe safe, but not happy," Jaali whispered from the other side of the window. "I may be in danger now, but I am infinitely happier. For the first time in my life, I feel loved and wanted. For the first time, I have hope. You gave me that, *msichana*. I love you."

Milenda sighed. Why did this have to be so complicated?

Why couldn't they just love each other and be happy? What difference did it make whether he risked his life for her or not?

A sudden rustling of leaves warned her of approaching people. She straightened, swallowed the tears that were threatening to pour out, and resigned herself to leaving. "I've got to go, Jaali," she whispered, her throat burning from unshed tears. "There are people coming. I love you. Don't forget it. You're my *wimbo wa moyo*."

She barely had time to hear him utter her name from the other side of the wall before fleeing into the tree-covered area adjacent to the building to hide. She crouched under the shelter of some large bushes and waited until the two guards cleared the area before heading back to the palace. Halfway there, Mjusi came out of nowhere and flew by her side the rest of the way, growling low as he perceived her emotional turmoil.

"It's okay, my friend," Milenda said, petting his scaly head. "I will be okay."

***

The journey was not long. All of Natale was a stone-throw away from the ocean, but it was hard to tell. The massive jungle surrounding and invading the city kept the blue of the ocean and the sounds of the crashing waves muffled and hidden away. Once Milenda was out of the thick body of trees, the white sand of a never-ending beach greeted her feet and the fresh briny air filled her lungs. She removed her slippers and ran toward the ocean barefoot. She had always loved the sea.

Near it she felt a sense of freedom she could not feel anywhere else—a sort of familiarity, as if she were finally home.

Mama Nyeusi watched her from underneath half-closed eyelids and smiled. "Milenda, my child, stop fooling around, and come over here," she yelled out.

The young princess turned around, feeling positively crestfallen. "Yes, Mama."

The old woman smoothed her ballooning skirts as Milenda dragged her feet up to her. "Now, child, you must make an offering to Yemanjá before we even attempt to ask her for anything," she explained, frowning at Milenda's hair. "Fix yourself. You look a fright."

Suddenly self-conscious of her looks, Milenda straightened her beaded collar around her neck and smoothed down her wild hair, giving up on looking for the *iqhiya* she had dropped somewhere on the beach. "What should I offer her, Mama Nyeusi?"

"Have you learned nothing during your classes at the university?" The disapproving scowl softened as Milenda raised her eyes to her. "And don't you look at me with those big green eyes. They may work with your subjects but not with me."

Milenda let out a generous laugh. "Subjects? You are a funny woman, Mama," she said, hugging and folding in on herself across the waist.

"Enough shenanigans," Mama Nyeusi said, sucking in her lips as if struggling to keep her composure. "We have to get busy."

The young princess stopped laughing and straightened her

back, waiting for instructions. "Go into the jungle over by that big rock. Pick some flowers and some greenery, and make a crown to offer Yemanjá."

Milenda frowned. She had always been hopeless with crafts and flower arrangements, even though she was expected to learn it as a young royal woman. "What if I can't do it?" she asked, biting down on her lower lip.

The older woman rolled her eyes. "Do I have to teach you everything? Go pick flowers and bring them to me. I will show you how." She waved her hand impatiently. "Go!"

When Milenda came back with an armful of flowers and greens, Mama Nyeusi was sitting on the sand, her ample skirts spread out around her in waves of folds and creases. The young woman sat down beside her and laid her gatherings between them. "Is this enough?" she asked, looking at her *iyalorixá* anxiously.

"It will do," the woman said.

Under Mama Nyeusi's tutelage, Milenda was able to put together a pretty, colorful crown of orchids and wiki. "See? Not that hard, was it?"

Milenda smiled, pride filling her with joy. "It looks beautiful," she boasted. "Perfect even."

The *iyalorixá* shook her head disapprovingly. "Let's not go that far."

Both women walked to the edge of the water where the gentle waves came crashing one after another, like children playing a game of tag. Under the direction of the older woman, Milenda raised the crown above her head and uttered a prayer. "You who rule the waters, pouring over humankind your protection, O Divine Mother, with your water, wash my body and my mind. I beseech thee, powerful Yemanjá, Queen of the Waters, to receive this prayer. With love and justice, give me the necessary strength to withstand the trials ahead. In your sea of nature and harmony, I want to live. Protect my loved one from all harm and danger. Hail Yemanjá, Queen of the Sea."

Taking a few steps forward until the water covered her feet, the Jewel lowered the crown of flowers to the waters and let it go. The flowery circle floated back and forth as the waves came and went. Mama Nyeusi slid her hand in her pocket and collected a few coins. "Here, child," she said, offering the money to Milenda. "Throw these coins into the ocean and pray for Yemanjá's gift."

At first hesitant, Milenda threw the seven coins as far as she could into the waves and said a silent prayer. *Yemanjá, mother of all things, give me a way to help Jaali. I beg you. Give me a way to protect him and be with him during this awful trial. I beseech you in the name of all that's holy. In the name of love.*

She opened her eyes and wistfully stared at the horizon, half expecting the great Orisa to jump out of the water to come and bless her with some superpower, which, of course, didn't happen. She looked at Mama Nyeusi, her green eyes opened wide in question.

The old woman smiled, forgetting to be stern for a moment. "The impatience of youth," she said as her hands lifted to the skies. "*Haraka haraka haina baraka[11]*. You must be patient, child. Yemanjá will let you know when she decides it's time. Do not question the way of the o"

Milenda noticed that Mama Nyeusi had lost most of her formality around her. Sometimes it seemed like they had known each other forever, when in fact, Milenda didn't recall a single occasion on which they had met before the contenders' introduction ritual.

The Trials would start in a little over a week. Milenda was anxious to find out how the Orisa was going to help them and nervous about what she would be asked for in return. Yemanjá was as famous for her motherly love as for her uncontrollable wrath when betrayed by those she protected. It was more than a little unsettling.

The two women, one just beginning her adult life, the other closer to the end, walked together through the jungle to the palace.

Transportation in Natale was tricky. There were many different vehicles, some running on electricity, others on fossil fuels. The jungle, however, had its own ideas and had grown fast and wild through streets, making it difficult to drive anywhere. The people of Natale regularly cleared the thoroughfares of invading branches and roots, but it was a losing war. It was preferable to just walk or ride a bike than to risk coming upon an unexpected obstacle on the road. Milenda loved the way the trees imposed their supremacy over humans. She was fast and, even though small in stature, had strong legs that could carry her to the ends of the earth if she so chose.

As she turned around a bend on the stone-paved road, the palace appeared like a giant peacock strutting its colorful feathers on top of the hill. Milenda supposed it was a beautiful example of local architecture, but mostly she thought it ostentatious and out of place. She much preferred the organic architecture of Jaali's *hema* to this work of excess.

The thought of Jaali made her chest tighten. What was he doing right now? Was he all right? Were they training him properly, so he would be able to withstand the hardships of the Trials? She so longed to see his face, to look into his ghostly eyes and touch his warm skin. Why did life have to be so complicated?

"Mama Nyeusi," Milenda said, stopping suddenly. "I have to see Jaali."

The old woman turned around to face her protégé. Her wrinkled face twisted into a sad smile as she offered her arms for comfort. The Jewel didn't have to be asked twice; she practically jumped into the motherly arms, relishing their warmth and support.

"I must see him, Mama," the young woman said, her voice muffled by the voluminous fabric of the *iyalorixá*'s dress. "I miss him so much, it hurts."

The Gift

His arms cocooned her in warmth and safety. With her face buried in the crook of his ivory-white neck, Milenda inhaled his scent, a heady mixture of wood and cinnamon. It was perfect. His long, hard body stretched beside hers while he whispered. Why couldn't she hear what he was saying? His mouth was right by her ear.

"What did you say?" she asked, reluctant to move her lips from his skin.

The sound of more unintelligible whispering reached her ears and she lifted her head to look at him. His full lips were moving, but she couldn't make sense of his words.

"What? What are you saying?"

Much to her distress, his whole being wavered like a curtain of thin smoke rising from a bonfire, and before she could reach out for him, he vanished.

Sweat covered her from head to toe. She sat upright in bed, horrified at her vision. Or was it a dream? Was there a difference? He had felt so real, so solid. She couldn't shake the feeling he was trying to tell her something from afar, that it had really been him on that bed with her just a few seconds ago.

"It felt real, didn't it?" A female voice rose from a dark corner of her room, making her jump off the bed. "Don't be afraid, *kidogo moja*. Yemanjá is here to protect you."

Milenda's eyes opened wide. "Yemanjá?" Her back was flush against the wall, and she was afraid that if she moved away from it, she would lose control of her shaky legs and fall. "Is it really you, Mother?"

From the shadows, a tall, beautiful woman appeared. She wore a tall *gele* and a plain golden *kanga* that seemed to shine on its own.

"*Kidogo moja*, favored little one." Her voice was soft and melodic, but authoritarian all the same. There was a strange, almost palpable power radiating from her, body and voice. "I came to answer your prayers. You please the Orisa and we expect great things from you."

"I am nobody, Yemanjá," Milenda protested, her voice suddenly tiny, like that of a child. "How can I ever do anything great?"

A gentle laughter followed a click from the Orisa's mouth. "You don't know your own strength, *kidogo moja*. You are not only the heir to Natale's throne, but the rightful one."

As Milenda had expected, Orisa seemed to speak in riddles. The rightful one? What did that even mean? She decided not to argue or ask any further questions, lest the mother get annoyed with her and retract the offer of help. "Yes, Mother," she said instead. "What can I do for you, holy one?"

"I like you, Milenda," the stunning woman said with a smile. "You ask the right questions, too. Wise beyond your years."

Milenda didn't feel wise at all, but she was not going to say so. She bowed her head respectfully and waited for her instructions.

Orisas were creatures of myth that, until a few minutes ago, represented a faint hope of a miracle. She had wanted it to be real with all the strength of her young heart, but deep down, she had never truly believed in the myth. She'd always considered them a figment of people's need to believe in something larger than life.

But Milenda had just been proven wrong. Yemanjá was very real and standing in her room, a magnificent creature of beauty and power.

"I will bestow a gift of great worth upon you, lovely *kidogo moja*," the mother said. "You have this gift dormant in you, one which you have inherited along with your Nyota roots. Your people were once powerful seers, capable of seeing what can't be seen, hearing what no one hears, feeling what they are not feeling."

Holy shamans! Could she be any more cryptic? "What gift did I inherit from the Nyotas, Mother?" she asked cautiously, not sure it was a wise thing to do. "I am not gifted in much, other than being able to mess up people's lives by being a princess." Bitterness dripped from her words.

"You are right to feel as you do," the Orisa agreed. "The

traditions of old should have been abolished long ago, but we cannot blame you for something you don't have control over. However, you will one day. Then you will be able to make a difference in the lives of the people of this land."

Milenda stared, not sure what to say or do.

"The gift is in you," Yemanjá continued. "All I am going to do is wake it up. Like a sixth sense, the gift will be part of who you are, indistinguishable from your other senses." *More riddles.* "Use it well and keep it a secret. People have trouble accepting what they don't understand."

"What about Jaali?" she blurted out, afraid that Yemanjá would leave without helping her.

The Orisa fell silent for a moment. With a couple of smooth steps, she approached the young woman and reached out to her cheek. Her touch was cool, like the morning breeze, and just as light. It lingered there for a second, and then it traced Milenda's *matangazos* from her ear all the way down to her shoulder. As her elegant fingers brushed against Milenda's skin, a tingling erupted from the spots. First, Milenda could barely feel it, but soon the intensity rose in a crescendo, not unpleasant, but unsettling all the same. Just as quickly as it started, the tingling stopped as the mother removed her hand.

"The gift will be yours to help him. Sometimes the only help people need is to know they are not alone." She smiled as if amused by her own riddles. "I bid you farewell now, *kidogo moja.* I will come back when the time comes to retrieve my favor."

Her favor! Milenda had totally forgotten that she must give something in return, and now it was too late to ask what that might be. No point in worrying about that now. As the Orisa made a sudden and mysterious exit, Milenda shook herself off and decided a shower may be what she needed right then.

A fluffy towel in hand, Milenda left her room and walked down the hallway and through the back courtyard door. This was an enclosed outdoor patio surrounded by the walls of the palace, but large enough to look like a small jungle. The showers were almost at the center of this lush, green area.

She opened the glass doors and entered the crescent-shaped space. The floors were covered in richly colored tile imported from the very north of the continent, but the walls were all made of glass, darkly tinted on the outside and totally transparent from the inside. The whole area was designed to make the bather believe they were showering outdoors amongst the giant jackalberry trees and sweet-smelling Natale mahoganies. Milenda loved the room and often lingered under the rain-like shower longer than necessary. The soothing feeling of cool water dripping and running over her head and her shoulders allowed her to forget she was a princess... for a few minutes, at least. It gave her a few moments of peace of mind, of guilt-free pleasure.

With the water running at its highest setting, she undressed and slid under the stream, closing her eyes as the liquid peace washed over her.

The peace didn't last long, for a few seconds later, she felt something touch her—a light and startling brush of a hand on her arm. Her eyes popped open in panic, but to her surprise, there was nobody there. Gingerly, she stepped out from under the stream of water and looked around. No one was there.

There really wasn't any place to hide.

I must be going crazy.

The shower beckoned her, and she slipped under the water again. A few seconds later, there it was—a definite brush of someone's hand along her right arm.

There's nobody here. Get it together, girl.

What was that she was hearing? Sounded like words uttered from a distance, getting louder, approaching….

She jumped out of the shower, covered herself with the towel, and turned off the jet of water.

She could hear it more clearly now—a male voice, a familiar voice. "I love you, Milenda," it said over and over again.

"Jaali," she called.

But where was he? Around the bathhouse, there was only the small jungle. She opened the door and called his name, thinking he may be hidden in the trees. That was crazy, of course. She was inside the royal residence. Jaali would never be able to enter it unless invited by her father.

The invisible hand was now traveling along her shoulders, but it was no longer frightening. Somehow, she knew it was Jaali's hand, caressing her as only he could. A small frisson of pleasure ran through her. "Your skin is so soft and warm," she heard his voice say, and she melted. She was not sure what was going on, but having him there with her was comforting. His hand continued traveling along her *matangazos* in a maddening caress that set her on fire. A soft sigh escaped her lips as she felt his mouth touch her shoulder.

Suddenly aware that she was naked under that towel, inside

a bathhouse alone with an invisible Jaali, heat rose to her face and her *matangazos* burned alongside her neck. "Your spots are beautiful," Jaali said, as she felt the unmistakable warmth of lips on her neck, trailing along her markings. She moaned in pleasure. "I just want to kiss you all over."

As much as her body longed to let him do just that, her sense of propriety and those annoying voices in her head startled her into reality. "I can't, Jaali. I can't."

Silence. The hand was no longer there, the lips no longer teasing her sensitive skin, the voice gone. Jaali had left.

She stood still as a statue, afraid if she moved, the magic of what had come to pass would be gone forever. What had just happened? How could she have heard Jaali? How could she have felt him? She could still feel the lingering heat from his fingers caressing her skin, the silkiness of his voice in her ears.

Firmly wrapped in the towel, Milenda made her way to her room as quickly as her legs could carry her. She sat at her small desk to write Jaali a note, but the words wouldn't come. What could she ask him that wouldn't make her sound crazy? *Were you in the shower with me today?* No matter how she worded it in her head, it sounded insane. She dropped her pen, then her head.

A faint knock from the window brought her back from her stupor.

"Mjusi," she exclaimed, her eyes blurry. Her old friend was at the window, gently knocking with his big wings, his wet green eyes peering through the glass. As soon as she opened the window, Mjusi squeezed himself through it—not an easy feat for a creature with his wingspan. Milenda scratched the top of his head, and he moaned gently in gratitude. "What are you doing here?"

The scaly lizard stretched his beak-like muzzle toward her, and she noticed he had a note between his fangs. Hastily, almost ripping the paper, she tore the note from his teeth and unfolded it. It was Jaali's unmistakable penmanship, and she let out a sigh as she sat down on the rug. Mjusi curled himself into a big ball by her and promptly fell asleep.

Msichana, I had a strange and beautiful dream today. I dreamed of you. It was such a vivid dream I could have sworn I actually felt the heat of your matangazos under my fingers and the silkiness of your wet skin on my lips. You were in this strange place, wrapped in a towel, and I couldn't resist; I had to touch you, to feel you.... What a beautiful dream it was. I can't wait for the Trials to be finished, so we can finally be together as husband and wife.

Her heart skipped a beat—what was going on? He, too, had felt what she had felt, seen what she had seen. How was that even possible? She tried to remember what exactly had happened in the shower right before she felt his presence there, but all she could remember was that she had been relaxed under the jet of water....

No, she remembered her thoughts wandering to her love and how he made her feel. As soon as she'd had those thoughts, Jaali had materialized in the shower with her. Could she have unwittingly summoned him there? But how? She had no magic powers. Other than being a princess, she was nothing special.

Or was she? Mama Nyeusi had hinted at something to do with her heritage. What was it exactly? She really needed to start paying more attention to what the old woman told her. Milenda was starting to think Mama Nyeusi's sudden appearance in her life had not been accidental.

Whatever the reason for the strange events of the morning, she couldn't help but rejoice it had happened. Whether it was real or a figment of Jaali's and her vivid imagination, it had been wonderful. She found herself craving more, a feeling that filled her with just as much apprehension as wonder; the censoring voices in her head didn't like it a bit. Maybe one of these days she would ignore her fear of sounding ignorant and ask Mama. She would undoubtedly be a lot more honest—and blunt—than the zoom-zoom of her conscience.

Changed into a more formal *kanga* and matching *gele*, she headed to the Elders' chambers, where she was expected for further "orientation." Of course, she couldn't tell exactly what she was being oriented to, since all they really talked about was what she was not allowed to do during the Trials.

You shall not get involved in the Trial. You shall not show favoritism. You shall not talk about the Trial to anyone until it is completed and a winner is chosen. You shall not… and on and on and on. Why didn't they actually give her information that would be helpful, or at least clear up some of the many questions she had about the process?

The Elders looked particularly solemn today. Unlike in previous sessions, when a few of them were always absent, the full body of the council was present.

Her heart faltered. As she stood in the center of the chamber waiting to be told to sit, Milenda felt sick.

Uh-oh. What's going on?

"Sit, child." The invitation finally came. "We must talk about something important today." She snickered a little. Was that an admission that they had been neglecting the vital information and focusing on the superfluous?

The chair they had for her today resembled a throne rather than just a chair. They obviously wanted her to be fully aware of her royal status for this conversation. Try as she might, she couldn't relax, and she sat uncomfortably straight, hands resting on the lightly padded arms of the chair.

"What might that be, honorable ones?" Her voice quavered, much to her annoyance. She didn't want to let them see her unsettled.

"It has come to our attention that you have had," the Elder paused and cleared his throat for emphasis, "dealings with one of the contenders, a young ex-*indent* called Jaali."

Instead of upsetting her, this filled her heart with hope. Maybe they would now forbid him to be part of the Trials. He would be safe at last. "Yes, I knew him before he became a contender," she said carefully and emotionless. "Is that a problem?"

"No, not a problem," the Elder continued, nodding toward his peers. "But it changes the procedures a little."

Milenda's eyebrow arched upward and her *matangazos* pinched, as if contracting in fear. "What do you mean? How will it change it?"

"Because he may be viewed as a favorite—" Anticipating a protest, the Elder held his hand in the air "—no matter if he is or isn't, loving Jewel, people will think you wish him to be the winner. If so, he will have an advantage over all others."

"How's that? No one is going to help him one way or another." Her voice had gone up an octave, and her markings felt as if connected to electricity, lightly shocking her at regular intervals. "How is that an advantage?"

The Elder lowered his hand and sighed deeply. "Calm yourself down, my child." It was an order. "The other contenders will view him as the winner no matter how well they may do and morale will be low amongst them. That is a huge psychological advantage."

Her outrage didn't totally blind her to the wisdom of his words. It was well-known that if you believed someone to be a favorite in a competition of any kind, your mind would sabotage you, and chances were, you would truly lose. "Nobody else is aware we know each other from the university," she protested feebly. "He is a professor there. I go to classes…." Her voice trailed.

"We are not accusing you, or the boy, of any wrongdoings." The Elder's voice had regained its composure. "However, we must adjust the rules to accommodate for people's perceptions."

Her heart sank. Certainly this was not going to be a good thing. *Oh gods, what have I done?*

"May I respectfully ask what the changes will be?" She hoped the formality of her speech would put her in their good graces again, so they might go easy on Jaali.

"The Trials will be different for him," the Elder said in a quiet voice. Was that elation she heard in his voice? "Regrettably, he will have to endure harder challenges if he is to prove himself worthy of his place in the Trials."

"Harder?" It was a shrill voice that she barely recognized as her own. Her heart was racing in her chest, and the electric current that seemed to go through her *matangazos* was now running through her whole body. "But the Trials are already incredibly dangerous. You will kill him."

"That was always a possibility." The logical tone of his voice grated on her nerves more than anything else. "It hasn't changed."

"What if I refuse to pick anyone? Will that cancel the Trials?" In her mind, she had her hands wrapped around the Elder's throat. The hate she felt at that moment was indescribable and frightening.

"You are not the ruling Jewel yet," the Elder said with infuriating calm. "You don't have that kind of power."

Later on, she couldn't recall how she had left the council chamber. She must have run for miles, though, because by the time she returned to the palace, it was early evening and the soles of her feet were raw and bleeding.

Inside the privacy of her room, she threw herself on the bed, buried her face in the pillow, and cried bitter, angry tears. Why couldn't she be just a peasant, a girl from the lower city who could live without the responsibility of a nation on her shoulders, who could pick her own husband and love whoever she pleased?

Jaali, wimbo wa moyo, I'm so sorry.

A wisp of a touch on her hair made her turn her head, and she saw him—not totally materialized—half man, half mist. Jaali, lying across the bed, worry in his translucent eyes, caressed her hair. His lips moved, but no sound came out. And yet, she knew what he was saying.

I love you, too, sweet Jaali. I love you too.

***

Tomorrow it would all change. Life as he knew it would be no more. As worthy as what was waiting for him at the end of the imminent journey was, he knew he would be changed; the world would be a different place for him. Fear had paralyzed him many times before, but he had learned that he could control it, that he could replace it with a more urgent need or desire. At that moment, the need to prove himself was overwhelming, and it diluted his fear to the point of nonexistence. The fear of losing Milenda was so much stronger and deeper than of whatever he would have to face in the next weeks. Well acquainted with hell, he deemed himself properly equipped and prepared for this dangerous journey.

Jaali sat with his back against the wall, his feet covered in a mix of animal fat and shea butter, enjoying the warmth of the sun on his naked torso and face. In preparation for the long hikes across the desert, he had been consistently preparing his feet and his hands to handle the abuse. One of the Elders had visited him the day before to let him know his journey would be rougher than the other contenders'. Even though he knew he should be worried, he wasn't. In fact, the idea of being out there in the wild by himself, free and relying only on his own wits, pleased him. After all his years as an *indent*, always relying on others to feed him and dependent on others' whims and desires, this was so close to what he used to dream about as a young man, he couldn't help but love the idea.

"Is that edible?" His eyes popped open. Milenda stood there as a shadow between him and the sunlight. "Well, is it?"

Was she really there, or was this another of those very vivid dreams he had been having lately? He squinted up at her. "Is that really you, *msichana*?" Her smile competed with the sun as she sat next to him on the grass. "I can't believe you're really here." His hands itched to touch hers, but there were others around.

"They allowed me to come and see you before the Trials start tomorrow," she explained, her fingers surreptitiously touching his. "I will have to visit with the other contenders as well, but that's a small price to pay to spend a few minutes with you."

A comfortable silence lingered as they gazed at one another. She had such big green eyes, like round pieces of malachite, and her lips... Gods, he wanted to kiss those lips! "Thank you," he whispered. "This is the best gift."

"How are you doing?" Her voice, soaked in concern, caressed his ears with the softness of silk. "Are you eating well? Sleeping?"

A chuckle escaped his lips. "Yes, Mom. I am being well-treated." She laughed with him. "You? Are you all right?"

Fingers overlapping his on the grass, she smiled. "I'm well, but worried," she said. "Did the Elders tell you?"

"About the Trials? Yes, one came to see me yesterday." One of her fingers was caught between his, and he delighted in how that simple touch could bring him such pleasure. "No reason to worry. I'll be fine."

A look of outrage took over her face. "Fine? You will be fine? Do you understand that this makes a dangerous situation that much more dangerous?"

"I have been through worse," he said. Well, maybe that was not 100 percent true, but there were dangers out there worse than something that may kill you. Dangers that destroyed you inside were so much more frightening, and he would choose dying over being exposed to such things any time. "Don't worry, *msichana*."

Appeased, at least for now, Milenda stared at his feet. "What in gods' names is that on your feet?" Her mouth twisted into a grimace. "It smells bad."

"Animal fat and shea butter," he said with a chuckle. "It does reek, doesn't it? I learned this trick years ago. It helps toughen your feet to avoid cracks and blisters on long hikes."

"I think I would prefer blisters," she replied, seriously. "I'm surprised it hasn't attracted any flies yet. If you wash that gunk off, maybe we could go on a walk and have a more private talk."

He liked the sound of that. Ever since he had dreamed of her in the shower, he had been dying to touch her skin for real.

In no time, his feet had been released of all the fatty substances covering them, and Jaali jumped upright. Milenda took the hand he was offering her and stood as well. They walked at an appropriate distance from each other in the direction of the jungle, glancing around every so often to make sure they were not followed. Once under the cover of the thick trees and greenery, Jaali curled an arm around her waist and pulled her toward him.

"I have been dying to do this," he whispered. With her face buried in his bare chest, her warm breath stroking his skin, he shivered. "*Msichana*, you've been in my dreams." Her normally shy hands had flattened themselves over his naked skin, and he could feel her heat radiate into his body. "Tell me you feel it, too. This need, this yearning…"

"Jaali, the other day when you had that dream…," she started, too embarrassed to look him in the eye. "I had it, too."

Pushing her gently away from him, Jaali looked at her in surprise. "The same dream? The one where you were in the shower?"

Resolutely, her eyes met his before wavering away again. "I was in the shower."

Jaali's body loosened against her, and he narrowed his eyes to a slit. "What do you mean you were in the shower?"

Milenda's chin dipped down, and her feet shuffled close to his. "I don't think it was a dream," she finally said in a nearly inaudible voice.

"Look at me." His hand cupped her chin and tilted it up, so she would look at him. "It wasn't a dream? I am pretty sure I never left the citadel."

"Yemanjá came to see me." Her voice quavered under the weight of his gaze.

"Yemanjá? The mother?" His mouth fell open. Was she talking about the Orisa? Was she even real?

Milenda let go of him and, hands on hips, stared at him. "Yes, the Orisa. She came to see me and told me I had inherited a gift from my people. She touched my *matangazos*, and ever since then, I have been having these… dreams."

Jaali's eyebrows arched upward. "Only I don't think they are dreams. I think I can somehow see and feel across distances."

"What about me? I don't have such gifts, and yet I could see you. I could feel you." His stomach tightened at the thought. "How is that possible?"

"It seems I can also project…" She sighed deeply. "I don't understand it myself, Jaali. I just know it's happening."

She looked so bereft and confused, he slid his hands over her hips and smiled at her. "Does this mean we will be able to see each other during the Trials?"

A faint smile appeared on her lips as she nodded slowly. "It looks like it."

Suddenly, his smile turned wicked and his eyes sparkled in the darkness of the forest. "So…" he dragged the vowel sound longer than he had to. "That means, if I want to, I can kiss you no matter where I am?"

Giggling quietly, Milenda nodded. "Only if I want to. I am the one with the gift, remember?"

Jaali looked at her *matangazos* and smiled. "Oh, you want to," he said, noticing her markings glimmered. He pulled her closer and wrapped his arms around her shoulders in a tight embrace. "I know *I* do." His voice came out hoarse as he lowered his face to hers.

Her lips opened up to his, and as his tongue danced with hers, the fire within him flared and raged. With a jolt, he realized he had slipped one hand inside her *kanga*. This was neither the place nor the time for this, no matter how much he craved it. His thirst for her had to wait. "*Liten häxa*, I love you."

Milenda's eyes opened slowly, as if waking up from a wonderful dream. "*Liten häxa.* What does that mean?"

With a big smile, he kissed her forehead. "Little witch. You've put a spell on me, *liten häxa.*"

A voice called out from the main house. It was time to go.

He didn't want her to go. What if he didn't make it? Not that he was afraid of dying, but he was scared of losing her to someone else. "Wait for me," he whispered into her hair, breathing in her scent. "Promise me you will wait for me."

A tear fell on his bare skin. Milenda was crying. "Promise me you will get out of it alive," she stuttered. "Promise."

"I will, *msichana.* I will."

The Trials

————————————————

The wake-up call came at first light. The sun hadn't even broken through the morning clouds on the horizon, and the dusk hung on as if reluctant to allow the cruel spectacle of the Trials to begin. The contenders were yanked out of bed by their trainers and quickly prepared for the weeks ahead.

Washed, fed, and fully awake, Jaali followed one of the trainers into the open area of grass out in the back of the main house. Most of the contenders were already there, bleary-eyed and anxious. Their eyes all moved to Jaali as he positioned himself among the ranks. The Elder had not been wrong; as soon as the fact he was an acquaintance of the princess was common knowledge, he had become a pariah. No matter. He would be on his own during the Trials anyway. Cooperation didn't seem to play any part in the process. In fact, it was highly discouraged.

Better to keep his eyes on neutral ground and wait for the directions from the trainer. Strangely, no one was talking. The trainers themselves seemed to be waiting for instructions. Both the contenders and the staff stood in attention stance for what felt like an eternity.

Jaali's feet and legs were starting to itch for movement when the voice of one of the trainers broke the silence.

"Attention, contenders. Today you are honored with the presence of her Royal Jewel, Princess Milenda."

Jaali's head jerked up, and his eyes met the tiny figure of his beloved princess.

A blue *kanga* was wrapped around her body, and today she wore no *gele*. Her hair, puffed up in a wild profusion of kinks and curls, was simply adorned with a blue water lily. Around her neck, she was wearing promise rings, a traditional collection of metal and beaded adornments worn by brides before their wedding. For a moment, he thought he was dreaming again because he could have sworn he had seen some sort of rainbowed mist wafting off from her as she walked toward the men.

"Contenders," she said in a quiet but commanding voice, "I came to wish you all the best luck in the world and to beg you to be careful and keep safe. I do not wish any of you harm of any kind. Come back safe and sound, so your families can enjoy your company for many years to come."

The men's eyes were transfixed, stuck on her beautiful, earnest face. Not one moved, not one talked, as if afraid to break whatever spell they were under. Jaali was no different.

He breathed her in like precious oxygen he could not live without, and it intoxicated him. In his veins, the blood ran hot and wild. Lightheaded and giddy, he felt his lips stretch into a wide smile.

"The Jewel of Natale wishes you all well," she continued, her green eyes not meeting his. "Please, do not forget this. If I could, I would save you from the cruelties of the Trials, but I can't. My heart goes out to and with you."

Jaali's heart jumped. She was moving slowly toward them. Starting at the end of the line, she moved to stand in front of one of the men. All eyes were on her, surprised and curious about what was about to happen. Milenda held the contender's hands in hers and brought them to her lips for a kiss. It was a gesture used by the king's subjects when swearing fealty to him. So, that's what she was doing; with a simple, formal gesture, she was promising her loyalty to all of them, letting them know she had no favorites and that she wished them all to succeed. His heart swelled with pride. She was a true princess, compassionate and loyal to her people.

Unhurried, she worked her way up the line until she was standing in front of him. For the first time that morning, her emerald eyes met his and it was electrifying. A current of energy went through him, reinforcing his resolve to make it out alive for her, for them. Milenda held his hand in hers, one sliding underneath to press a small, hard object to his palms. Careful not to show the surprise he felt, he scooped the object and held it tight between his fingers. Her hand was now caressing his as she brought them up to her lips. Something warm and electric invaded his gut as her warm lips met with the skin of his knuckles in a longer-than-necessary kiss. With her lips still on his skin, she raised her eyes to him. "I love you," she whispered against his hand. "You are my beloved. Come back to me."

.The moment was over too soon, and she moved to the two other men left in the line. There was so much energy coursing through him, he was afraid he was going to take off like one of those carnival rockets, all the way to the clouds and back. Instead, he stayed rooted to the same spot, holding his jittery happiness in like a coveted secret.

Milenda, finished with honoring all contenders individually, moved to her original spot on the field and scanned over all the men, her eyes pausing briefly on his. "Honorable contenders, I bid you farewell for now," she said, her voice trembling slightly. Were those tears dancing in her eyes? "Be safe and come back to us. May the gods and the orisas shine their graces on you." She licked her lips, and just as she moved to leave, she turned her head to the men again and said, "And thank you for thinking I am worth it."

Jaali watched her walk away, her back a little slumped, her step just a bit heavy, as if carrying the weight of these men's fates on her shoulders. He wanted to yell out his love for her, but he knew it was better if he didn't. Milenda, of all people, wouldn't expect it. For a crazy moment, he wished for her gift, so he could tell her without being heard by the others.

As soon as the thought was formed, he felt her presence beside him. "You want to tell me something?" she seemed to say, as her lips moved soundlessly.

Jaali smiled and whispered the words burning on his lips.

"I love you, and you are so worth it." A smile hovered over her mouth as her ghostly presence wavered and dissipated like the morning mists over the lake. He could now focus on the task at hand.

***

The desert stretched out in front of him in blurry waves of sand and sporadic low-growing bushes. Lonely and foreboding, it held such beauty of its own; it reminded him of Milenda. The lonely, young princess who everybody was afraid of getting close to, who was forbidden to most, and who was the owner of untamed beauty that rivaled nature itself. A deep sigh escaped his dry, cracked lips. Unreasonably, he wished the Trials were over and he was again reunited with his Jewel.

"No point in wishful thinking," he said out loud into the warm, dry air. It had only been a day since they had dropped him in the middle of the *Jangwa Pori*. He had never seen a blade-runner before, much less traveled in one. For a few hours, he almost forgot where he was heading with all the excitement of being lifted up in the air in a noisy flying machine, the clouds laying beneath him, and the city shrinking before his eyes.

His journey to Natale as a young *indent* from the lands of the north had not been so exciting. Back then, they had loaded him like cattle, along with many others, in the hull of a small ship. They sailed for more days than he could keep count, seasickness and fear threatening to make him lose his sanity. Once in Afrika, they had all been packed into small land vehicles, very different from the ones he was used to in his homeland. The drive had seemed to last forever with rare stops. The *indents*, females and males, were resigned to relieving themselves off the side of the moving machines. Unaccustomed to the furious heat of the jungle, most of them had become violently sick. Some died and were disposed of by the side of the road, fodder for wild animals. Jaali was able to survive the heat, the dehydration, even the loss of dignity.

Jaali shook his head and tried to focus on the hot sand burning the bottoms of his unshod feet. The trainers had not given him much: a backpack with some strange potions that he had been instructed not to touch until told to, a blanket that barely covered his long body, a small knife, a container with water, and not much else. At the last minute, they had removed his shoes and the hat he had brought to protect himself from the unmerciful sun. The soles of his feet, which he had carefully prepared for a rough hike, were already burned red and punctured by the small, sharp-edged rocks hidden in the desert sands.

He scanned the horizon, hoping to find shelter of some kind. A tree or a bigger bush, but nothing was visible other than the never-ending undulating sands and the bright, hot sun. Temptation was strong; it would feel heavenly to pour some of the water over his aching feet, but he knew he needed the water to survive. Not being certain when or where he would be able to refill his meager supply of the life-sustaining liquid, it was wise to ration it and stretch it as much as possible.

The sun, high in the sky, told him there were still quite a few hours to go before the land was immersed in darkness and coolness came to rule over the red-hot earth.

"I better keep going," he said. A smile crept up to his lips as the image of Milenda laughing at him and wondering about his sanity came to his mind. Leave it to her, even from a distance, to make him feel better.

The decision to keep moving made, Jaali shielded his eyes with his hand and kept going. His sense of direction told him he must be heading the right way. Everyone in Natale knew that, to get to the city, you must always move west. He had no reason to believe otherwise. The walk was made so much harder and longer by his loneliness. His mind wistfully went to Milenda and the honeyed voice he loved so much. He could hear the nuances of her voice as she either teased him or chided him about something she didn't like. Her voice in his head was so real, he caught himself looking around, certain she was right beside him.

"How do you feel, Jaali?" she asked him in his daydream.

Who cared if it was just a fancy of his overheated brain? "Feeling lonely, sweet Jewel," he whispered.

"I will keep you company." He couldn't see her, but the hair on his neck stood on end when the breeze of her breath touched it. "I am a princess. I have nothing better to do."

The sound of his laughter didn't travel far in the emptiness of the desert, but his heart felt lighter. Was she really talking to him, or was he going crazy already? "Is that really you, *msichana*?"

"Of course it is!" He smiled at the annoyance in her voice. "Who else would be talking to you in the middle of the desert?"

"I thought I may be hallucinating from the heat." Burning

feet forgotten for the moment, Jaali sped up his step. "I am so happy we can talk."

"So, tell me, what are you doing exactly?"

The scorching heat created ghostly waves all around him. "If I didn't know better, I would think I am in a dream. The air around me seems to waver and fade in and out." His dry throat was starting to hurt, and he wished for a soothing tea or even a chunk of ice. "It's miserable here, Milenda, but I will be okay. What are you doing?"

There was a slight pause, and he could tell she was thinking. "Well, let's see… the Elders made me get all prettied up to address the nation tonight in a gathering on the palace's grounds. The whole city is in a frenzy of preparation, because apparently I am going to tell them something really smart and worth leaving the comfort of their houses for."

Sweat dripped from his forehead, but for once he didn't notice. "Well, are you? Going to tell them something amazing?"

"Not that I know of." He could hear the clicking of her tongue. "Mind you, the Elders often give me speeches to read at the last minute. Good thing I'm an excellent reader. What if I read something wrong?"

His feet slid down the giant dune he had been climbing. "That would be disastrous, I'm sure."

"It could be." Clearing her throat a bit, she continued in an overly formal voice, "Ladies and gentlemen of the royal coop—oops, I mean royal court. I come today to offer you a good stick—oops again, I meant stake."

Laughter rolled over the never-ending dunes.

"Or, I came to propose that shepherds should stop the bleeding of their sheep—I meant, bleating." Their laughter joined together in a cacophony of snorts and high-pitched squeaks.

"What can I do to help you?" she asked, once her laughter subsided. He felt a faint brush of fingers across his face and smiled.

"You have already." Jaali's hand caressed the spot she had just touched. "By keeping me distracted, I forgot about my burnt feet and"—his eyes scanned the horizon again, and this time they zoomed in on a small patch of green ahead—"I just found a place to spend the night and rest."

A whoop of triumph reached his ears. "Yes! Now I can go deliver my fantastic speech in peace. You will be all right, won't you?"

"I will be fine," he assured her. "Will you come back soon?"

The dry skin of his lips felt moist suddenly. With surprise, he realized her lips were on his.

Too soon it was over.

"I love you." She was gone even before he could respond.

The small oasis beckoned him like a light at the end of a dark tunnel. He continued his descent, quickening his step and managing to ignore the nagging pain shooting up his legs.

It was indeed small, with only two squat trees and a few flanking bushes, but trees meant shade and water. Maybe even some sustenance. Too afraid of losing the few supplies he had with him, Jaali sat with his back to the gnarled trunk of a tree, keeping the backpack glued to his side. He planned to rest first and then to look for a drinking source to refill his water skin. Instead, he fell asleep almost immediately.

Nothing seemed that different in the realm of his dreams, except he was not hot, and his feet didn't hurt. The oasis where he stood was the same—the trees, the bushes. As far as dreams went, this one was pretty strange, he thought. He had never once dreamed about the same exact place or situation he was in during his waking hours, and yet here it was. Curious, he looked around, seeking an inkling of a difference, a clue as to why he was dreaming about this. After a few minutes of contemplation, he finally saw it—the tall, forbidding figure of an Elder standing directly in front of him. Jaali tilted his head, confused. The Elder advanced toward him, as if floating on air. What was he doing in his dream and what could he possibly want?

"Contender, the implant you have on your shoulder was just activated," the voice boomed. "This implant will allow us to give you instructions throughout the Trials and will also allow us to keep track of you at all times."

Jaali cringed. He had worn a locator as an *indent*, implanted under his arm. It had provided his owner with precise information on his whereabouts any time of day or night. The thought that they had implanted him with another gadget left a sour taste in his mouth, and for the first time in a long while, Jaali felt angry.

"Listen carefully to the following directions." Indifferent to Jaali's emotional upheaval, the Elder continued, "In this oasis, there is a creature, small in bulk, but fierce and dangerous in temperament, a *shetani*. You must capture it and kill it, or it will kill you. It lives under one of these Acacia trees. After you accomplish this mission, you must walk to the next oasis and drink the potion from the red bottle. May the orisas be merciful."

The image faded and Jaali woke up.

Confused for a moment, he looked around, not sure of where he was or what he was doing. His heart, galloping in his chest, slowly calmed and his breathing evened out. Anxiously, his hand went to his side to check if his bag was still there. His muscles relaxed when his fingers touched the rough surface of the backpack. What had he just dreamed about? Was it even a dream? Almost involuntarily, his mind called out to Milenda, but she didn't respond. Belatedly, he remembered she had an event to attend and would be unavailable until afterward.

Standing, he stretched his long legs and arms before opening the bag and removing the only personal item he had been allowed to carry with him, a couple of *buugengs. Buugengs* were objects that resembled snakes, with their S-shapes carved out of wood or metal and painted in mesmerizing patterns and colors. Jaali's were made out of hardwood. He had carved them himself, then sanded to silky perfection and later edged in metal protectors. Along with his mother's blanket, this was all he had left from his homeland—a tiny slice of his own cultural background. In the northern lands, young men and women were taught at an early age the art of the *buugengs*, sometimes called *magie slangen*, the magic snakes. Expected to have it mastered by the time he was in his early teens, Jaali had instead excelled in the art by the time of his kidnapping. Not sure of what to do with the strange and unfamiliar contraption, the slave hunters had allowed him to keep it. He had since then sharpened the edges to a fine, lethal point and used it more than once as a weapon.

The air had cooled substantially. Night was coming and with it, cold air, a double-edged blessing for anyone stranded in the desert. While providing welcome relief from the heat of the day, it also often killed. Hot and dehydrated human bodies, suddenly exposed to what felt like arctic air, became hypothermic as body temperatures swiftly fell. Jaali was well aware of this. The small blanket he was provided would not offer the protection he needed to survive the night.

He took a deep breath, delighting in the coolness he inhaled. Then, he opened and clicked the two longer pieces of the *buugeng* in place. Stretching his arms in front of him, he began his routine. His arms had been mostly inactive all day, and he could now feel the blood flowing through his veins, heating up as the muscles tensed and relaxed with each twirling of the *magie slangen*. Other than his arms, his body stayed still, enjoying the feeling of total control, something often lacking in his life.

Around him, all was still and quiet. The few animals that lived in the desert were mostly underground during the day, but they would soon come up to feed. Jaali wondered in his half-meditative state whether the *shetani* would come looking for him or if he had to seek him out.

It was not a totally unfamiliar creature to him. During the training at the citadel, the name had been brought up a few times and met with shivers of apprehension. Killing any living creature was not something Jaali liked contemplating, but survival came first and he would do it if necessary.

The movement of his arms slowed and the *buugeng* stopped. It was time to prepare for the next leg on his Trial.

Water was not hard to find. Not far from the tree he had slept under, there was a small puddle that in turn led him to a shallow underground well. He drank with total abandon, refilled his water bottle, and washed off the sandy layer that covered his whole exposed body. Slowly and carefully, he removed the tip protectors from his *magie slangen* and began his search for the little devil of the desert.

It didn't take long. The sound of scratching claws told Jaali the *shetani* was just behind the next tree. He couldn't believe his eyes when he first saw it. The *shetani* was no bigger than a house cat, but it looked more closely related to Mjusi than any other animal he had ever seen. Its small, lizard-like body was covered in an armor of dangerous-looking scales the color of the sand, and his armor was composed of sharp spikes that protruded from every inch of it, including its wide mouth. At the end of its short legs, claws that resembled scissor blades were busy digging through the roots of a bush.

Jaali accidentally stepped on a twig and alerted the creature to his presence. The *shetani's* head popped up, red, beady eyes focusing on Jaali, a strange low growling sound coming from its throat. It was going to attack.

Jaali didn't hesitate and attacked first. With his right arm, he swung the *buugeng* in a wide circle while charging toward the dangerous creature. Just as the *shetani* hissed and swung his spiked, long tail to strike him, Jaali impaled it with his weapon.

The creature squirmed and snapped its jaws a few times before lying still and lifeless. After a few minutes, Jaali poked him with the *buugeng,* making sure it was indeed dead. Only then did he dare touch the strange creature with his own hands.

The growling of his stomach reminded him he had not eaten in over a day, and he wondered whether the dead animal was edible. It had never been mentioned among the poisonous creatures during his training, so he decided it wouldn't hurt to try.

Jaali collected some pieces of wood from the sandy ground and started a small fire. Once he had removed all the scaly armor from the *shetani,* he cut it with the small knife and put it over the fire to roast.

The sky was studded with stars and Jaali tried to recall the details of a story his mom used to tell him as a child. Remembering only fragments, his frustration grew and sadness took hold of him. It had been years since he last remembered really missing home. In spite of the reason why he had turned up in Natale and all the bad things that had followed his arrival, this was his home now and he loved it as such. Now, however, sitting by the fire alone and gazing up into the night skies, tears of bereavement pooled in his eyes, and a sense of loss echoed in his soul.

"Why do you cry?" Milenda's voice caressed his ear. A gentle flurry of fingers across his face, wiping the tears and leaving behind a tingling of pleasure, told him she was there with him again. "Are you hurt?"

In the dark, it was easier to see the faded contours of her body, the shine of her big green eyes. "Just remembering my family in the Outerlands." Could he touch her like she touched him? Raising his hand, he hesitantly reached out to touch her. She felt solid under his fingers and he smiled. "I can feel you."

"What's that on the fire?" Milenda had sat down beside him, facing the fire, the side of her body warming up his.

"Long story." A chuckle escaped his lips. One day into the Trials and he already had a story to tell.

Milenda demanded to be told, and for a while he painted the story of his hunt in every gory detail while she inundated the silence with a barrage of questions. Once the lizard-like animal was cooked, he was surprised to find it tasty and satisfying.

By the time he had finished eating, a heaviness had started settling in his eyes. He had not planned to sleep any more. Traveling during the night would have been more comfortable and easier on his feet, but his body seemed to have other ideas.

"Sleep, Jaali." Her voice was like a lullaby. "Lie down."

Reluctantly, he slid all the way into the now cold sand, pulled the blanket up as far as he could without uncovering his naked feet, and felt his eyes closing of their own accord. Milenda had stretched herself alongside him, and as he drifted off to sleep, he wondered as to how strange it was that he could feel the comfort of her heat even when they were miles and miles apart.

***

A smile had, unbeknownst to her, settled on her lips. Cuddled up against the faraway body of her Jaali, Milenda couldn't think of one single thing she would rather be doing at that moment. Earlier, she had to stand in front of a crowd of hundreds and deliver a speech she had not written nor been consulted for. As the future ruler of Natale, one would expect her to have a little more say in national matters, but the Elders thought differently. Used as a figurehead—and a popular one at that—the Jewel had resigned herself to go along with the flow until she gained some real power.

The speech had been long and boring, full of nothing. Her words were meaningless to her and to anyone listening in. Whoever wrote the speech was a master at avoiding the real issues, focusing only on insignificant problems and making them out to be what they were not. By the time she had finished, and the crowd had dutifully, but unenthusiastically, applauded and cheered, she felt as empty as the words she had just uttered. With a strong yearning to run out of there and go lock herself in her room, instead Milenda stood on the dais, smiling graciously at her people, who had all dressed up and taken time out of their busy lives to come and listen to nothing more than hot air. Being able to hold on to Jaali, whom she loved and loved her back, was like a salve for her aching heart.

Jaali looked so peaceful. All his worries and exhaustion had been washed off his face as slumber took hold of him. She had never seen snow, but she imagined it looked like his skin—white, soft, and untouched by the stains of evil. Her hand reached out to touch his satiny hair spilling over his face. How could he be hers? This exotic creature of light that even the dark of the night could not totally hide. Leaning forward, she bestowed a kiss on his cold forehead.

He was shivering, she realized. From the distance, she couldn't feel the cold air, but she could feel it in his body, in the way his body jerked underneath the thin blanket. With a scoot, she spooned his trembling body, her chin buried in the crook of his neck, breathing warm air into his cold skin.

"Stay warm, love. Stay alive," she whispered in his ear, wrapping her arms tighter around him. Lulled by the sense of comfort and safety she always felt in his presence, she fell asleep.

A little dazed, she opened her eyes and realized it was morning already. She was in her bed alone. Jaali was gone— or was she who was gone? A whole long day of official ceremonies awaited her.

Before Asha could come to help her dress, Milenda jumped out of bed, opened the window, and said prayers to her Orisa. It never hurt to show gratitude for divine favors. "Thank you, Mother, for your favor. Steer me in the right direction to help Jaali, to protect him, to love him. Yemanjá, benevolent mother of all earthly creatures. Thank you."

Her mind reached out to Jaali, but couldn't find him. Now that she had done it a few times, she was starting to realize that it often took both of them thinking of each other at the same time in order for it to work. Or just one of them needing the other.

She sighed and closed the window just as Asha came in, a yellow-hued *kanga* in her arms. Milenda lifted an eyebrow. "Hospital?"

Yellow was the traditional color worn by Natalians when

visiting the sick. Tradition dictated that yellow, being the color of the sun, brought joy and health for all of those who displayed it and for those who gazed upon it.

"Yes, Jewel, we are visiting the children's ward of the National Mercy Hospital today." Asha hurried to spread the sunny *kanga* across the bed.

Milenda's spirits lifted a little. Visits to the sick, especially the young, although sad were also full of hope and joy. Unlike with most of what she was obligated to do on a daily basis, this made her feel useful and worthwhile.

She hurried to wrap the fabric around her, not bothering to bathe. After returning to her room from her awful public speech the night before, she had carefully washed before reaching out for Jaali. Even though she had slept in the desert for part of the night, there wasn't a speck of sand or dirt on her.

From her collection of *geles,* she chose the most extravagant one, knowing it would amuse the children in the hospital. It reached at least two feet high, made of stiff gold and orange fabric and rich with ornate bows. She giggled in front of the mirror. Asha gave her a disapproving look, but she knew the young girl thought the *gele* as ridiculous as she did herself.

It was a long morning, yet satisfying. The children at the hospital had, just as she had predicted, loved the headdress and the much needed and healing chuckles went on for hours. She had brought sweet treats and some of her own toys to give away. The hospital officials hovered around, but mostly allowed her the space and the freedom to act like the silly girl she often felt she was. No speeches were made, and the Elders never made an appearance. It was heavenly.

On her way back to the palace, she floated rather than walked, her heart singing for joy. On her way, she stopped for an iced treat, and as she paid for it, she realized she was just minutes away from the university and the spot where Jaali and she had so often met. On a whim, she decided she was going to enjoy her *barafu* there. She hadn't been back since Jaali volunteered for the Trials, and she missed it.

To her great delight, the place had not been touched at all. Her guards must have been making sure no one else used it. She reclined in the arbor seat, arranged the cushions behind her back, and took a big lick of the iced dessert in her hand. It tasted of coconut and mangoes with a hint of mint, she thought. Eyes closed, head on the side of the curved seat, Milenda reached out to Jaali… and met chaos.

Nothing made sense. Jaali was there, but everything else was blurred, almost as if she were watching it underwater. "Jaali," she called, suddenly nervous. "What's happening?"

There was no answer. A confusion of blurred images, nauseating in their movement and coloring invaded her mind. Was Jaali sick? Drunk? How could that be? He had nothing but water to drink. Her stomach couldn't take it anymore; she broke the connection and ran frantically to a corner to throw up.

Mnyama

Upon arrival at the next oasis after a long, arduous walk in the scorching desert, Jaali slumped against a tree and closed his eyes to restore his strength. The second day was almost over, and he had no idea of how far he had really gone or even if he was going the right way.

Before he could follow the instructions of the Elder, he had to find a water source and something to eat. He had finished what was left of the *shetani* throughout the day, and although the heat stunted his hunger, the challenging walk brought it back.

This oasis was bigger than the previous one, and water was easily accessible. The water cooled his scratchy, dry throat. Food was harder to find, but eventually he was able to secure some succulents and edible insects. Not a royal meal, but a meal nevertheless.

Hunger satisfied, he opened the bag and removed the small red bottle. Inside was a thick liquid that reminded him of blood. His stomach protested against it, but he pressed on. Removing the stopper, Jaali brought the bottle to his nose for a whiff. The contents had a sweet, pleasant smell that thankfully didn't match its looks.

For a moment, he wondered what the potion was and if it would hurt him. Were the Elders trying to get rid of him by poisoning him? After all, he was just an ex-*indent*, a stranger from a foreign land, who would bring totally different DNA to the royal gene pool should he win. Not everyone would see that as a good thing. What if they wanted him out of the race? Would they go so far as to kill him?

With a shake of his head, Jaali threw caution to the wind, and in one smooth move, he swallowed the whole contents of the bottle. The potion left a warm trail down his throat all the way to his stomach, but it didn't taste bad. He sat still, not sure what to expect.

It hit him like a punch. The world quickly began losing its contours, one thing fading and blurring into the next in a sickening dance that made him heave. He couldn't lose the contents of his stomach, so he closed his eyes to bar the images, but they kept coming. He realized his brain was the culprit, not his eyes.

What was in that potion? The closest he ever remembered feeling like this had been during his indenture. His owner, Mnyama, had made him drink too much *muwa pombe*, an alcoholic mix made from sugar cane. It was an unpleasant memory. He remembered being aware of what was happening to him, but unable to do anything to defend himself.

Eyes opened again, Jaali tried to stand, but the whole oasis moved around him as if the sand had become liquid under his feet. With a heavy thump, he fell back down, his hefty head lolling backward and hitting the trunk of the tree.

That's going to leave a mark.

What was that noise? Unfocused and reeling from the effects of the unknown drug, Jaali tried to identify the noise coming toward him.

Steps! How could that even be? From amid the fog of his mind, he realized how ludicrous the idea of hearing steps in the sand was, and he chuckled drunkenly to himself. Yet… there it was again, definite steps, someone heavily treading across a wood floor.

Mustering strength he was not sure he had, Jaali lifted his head and opened his eyes. Horror filled his heart as his body tensed at the sight.

Mnyama, all six feet five of man, walked across the oasis toward him. "No, no, no!" His voice exploded, dripping in fear. As his feet scrambled to move him closer to the tree, he felt a desperate scream growing in his throat.

The massive, dark man approached, a cruel smirk on his lips, and stood mere steps away from Jaali who had curled up into a fetal position, crammed against the tree trunk.

"We meet again, little white boy." The slaver's booming voice echoed through the oasis like thunder. The man swept one hand over his massive, bald, brown scalp as he licked his lips. "It's been a while since I had a taste of that milkiness."

Jaali's body jerked in terror, and a whimper left his lips as the big man reached down to grab him by one arm and pull him up. His legs failed and Jaali fell to the ground again.

The slaver dropped to his knees right beside Jaali and laughed. "Lying down will work too." Jaali felt Mnyama's sweaty hand sliding under the waist of his pants. His skin shrank away from the touch, but there was no place to go, no place to hide.

"You know how this works, boy," the cruel man said, pulling on the fabric of his pants. "The more you fight it, the more it will hurt."

Jaali bit his lip and tasted blood. In a terrified stupor, he realized Mnyama was peeling off his clothes, denuding him of his dignity. Again. Hot, disgusting fingers worked their way along his chest and belly, quickly descending; further down they went, and Jaali's body tensed in revulsion.

No. No. You are not doing this to me again.

He was no longer a child. Mnyama may be much bigger and stronger than he was, but he was a man now, and he would fight him to the death if necessary. He could no longer be intimidated by an older, mightier man.

With a leap, Jaali jumped away from the other man's grasp. His trembling hand pulled his clothes back in place and his eyes locked with the devilish brown eyes facing him.

The slaver growled like a lion in distress. "So, you want to fight me, little boy?"

Legs as thick as tree trunks moved threateningly forward. Jaali stepped back, widening the space between them, eyes scanning the ground around him in search of a possible weapon. They locked onto a small, thick, broken branch.

"Don't even think about it. First, I am going to have some of that exotic body of yours, and when I'm done, I'm going to pound you into a fine white powder."

Jaali remembered those same threats from when he had been a terrified, sixteen-year-old boy, alone in this world with nowhere to run to.

"I am not a boy anymore, Mnyama." His voice was steady, and his legs held him. "I will fight you, *duivel*. I will fight you until both our bloods run in the sand. You will not break me again."

In a single swoop, Jaali bent and took hold of the branch. When his eyes looked up again, the slaver was gone. Confused, Jaali looked around him, eyes darting in every direction, but the big man was nowhere to be found.

"Where did you go, *duivel*?" As he turned around, he felt his legs growing weak again, buckling under his weight. He fell onto his knees, arms too tired to buffer the fall, head lolling backward again as the adrenaline rush subsided.

"You did well, young Jaali." The voice of an Elder echoed through his mind. "You faced your biggest fear and won."

"You did this?" Shocked, but too weak to react, Jaali allowed his body to slide all the way to the sandy ground. His head was swimming again, lights flickering in his eyes. "You did this to me?"

"The potion you drank brought on a fear-induced delirium," the Elder explained, his matter-of-fact voice grating in Jaali's unbelieving ears. "The test was to see if you would be able to face your biggest fear. You passed. Rest well, and may the orisas be merciful to you."

As he did the night before, the Elder vanished, leaving Jaali prostrated on the ground, unable to move.

Too tired to feel angry, he felt his eyes close. A pair of thin, warm arms wrapped themselves around him.

"Msichana, stay with me," he whispered. "My heart hurts."

Air and warm lips fluttered over his cheek. "I will be here, sweet Jaali. Sleep in peace." Like the wings of an angel, her arms cocooned him in softness and safety, and he fell asleep.

***

The night was cold. She felt it on his skin, in the way he shivered in her arms, but that was not why her insides froze and her blood ran cold. The fear she had felt in Jaali's mind and the things she had witnessed through his eyes chilled her to the bone. What horrors had he faced as a young man? How was it possible that such things still happened in her beloved nation, otherwise so advanced and tolerant?

Smoothing his hair with her hand, Milenda studied his handsome features, now at peace. The images of just an hour ago flashed through her mind; the wild look in his normally calm eyes, the rasping of his breath, the uncontrollable tremors. What had that man done to her Jaali? And why would the Elders put him through such a cruel memory?

He was guarded about his past as an *indent*, but she was starting to realize there was a lot more to the story than she had been led to believe. There was so much she did not know about Jaali, about her nation, about the world. Growing up in the palace had sheltered her from reality. How could she be expected to be a good ruler when she knew so little about life outside the protective walls of the royal home? Without knowing what her people had to go through in their daily lives, how could she rule over them, make decisions that would affect every life in her realm?

A movement under her head startled her. Jaali was waking up, gently at first, then with a sudden jerk.

"*Tulia, tulia,*" she cooed, trying to keep him calm. His startling blue eyes opened and blinked away the sleep as he adjusted to reality again. Milenda watched him as his expression quickly changed from confused to terrified. Like a coil of wire, he jumped to his feet and brought his arms defensively in front of him. He was ready to fight.

"Mnyama, leave me alone!" His voice shook, and the fear and anger in it broke her heart.

"Jaali, sweet Jaali." She realized that in his state of terror, he couldn't see her standing right in front of him. The drug-induced delirium was still clouding his mind. She stepped forward and touched his face, hoping he wouldn't flinch away. Instead, he immediately leaned into her hand and his breathing slowed.

"It's me. Milenda. Can you see me?"

Jaali relaxed, and his hands dropped alongside his body. His unfocused eyes cleared, and the frown on his face gradually turned into a promise of a smile.

"*Msichana*? Where are you? I can't see you."

Her fingers slid down his arm to hold his hand. "Can you hear me?"

He nodded and smiled broadly. His features had relaxed into the serene Jaali she knew and loved. "I can hear you, but why can't I see you?"

"The drug you took must still be confusing your senses," she explained, a little unwilling to bring it up for fear he would regress into a state of fear.

A frown twisted his face for a moment. "The potion in the red bottle." He was beginning to remember. "Nothing I saw was real?" It was a question rather than a statement.

"They had you drink *homa*, a drug that induces hallucinations." She bit her lower lip, struggling with the decision of bringing up something obviously so painful to him. "It feeds on a person's worst fears and makes them seem real."

Jaali's body tensed up. "Did you see it all?" His watery eyes were still searching for her.

"Most of it," she admitted in a small voice. She didn't want him to be embarrassed. "I was able to channel into what you were feeling, if not totally into what was really happening."

His face relaxed a little. "Did you see *him*?" He emphasized the pronoun as if it were a proper name. "Did you see the beast?"

"If you are referring to the big, bald man, yes, I did see him." She had felt the man was the source of Jaali's terror. Something he had done to her beloved had been so traumatic, Jaali still felt it as if it had never gone away. "I could tell you were terrified of him."

His voice went down to a whisper. "Did you see what he was doing?"

"No, I just felt your reaction to what he was doing, not the actual act." How would he feel if she asked him about it? Would he shut her out? Would he block her thoughts from reaching him again? She couldn't lose him now. "I know that whatever he did was traumatic and criminal. I am hoping one day you will share that part of your life with me."

Jaali chuckled—a bitter, sad laugh. "Not something I like to reminisce about," he said. "Nor do I want to drag you down into the mire along with me."

She stood behind him and hesitantly wrapped her arms around his chest, her head resting on his shoulder. "I know you don't want to remember it, but if we are going to be husband and wife, I need to know. No matter how dark, how horrible those memories may be, they have shaped you into the man I love. Like it or not, they are part of you. And I need to know all of you, Jaali, not just the pretty, easy parts."

He covered her arms with his. "There is a light inside of you, Milenda, an innocence I don't want to ruin." He twisted his head around to lightly touch his lips to her face. "I don't want to be the one to bring you darkness."

"I already live in darkness," she protested. "I am the future ruler of this country, and I am largely ignorant of what my people go through in their daily lives. I am an involuntary accomplice to all the bad things that, as a kingdom, we tolerate and condone. I'm part of the darkness already. You didn't take me there; my heritage placed me right in the middle of it."

There was a moment of silence while Jaali processed what she had said. Her body, glued to his back, felt at home; she didn't want to move, and as tired as she was after spending the whole night keeping vigil over him, she didn't want to sleep either. This was where she belonged.

"One night, when I was twelve, they came into my house." Jaali's quiet voice startled her. He dropped to his knees and she followed him, sitting next to him, her legs still touching his, their hands still entwined. "They gagged me before I even realized what was happening, and they spirited me out of my home in the Outerlands and into the cargo hull of a ship. I was not alone. They had kidnapped dozens of young boys and girls that same night. I was so scared I wet my pants and didn't even have the time to be embarrassed about it. All I could think of was that I was being taken away from everything I knew and loved."

Milenda gave his hand a reassuring squeeze. Her heart shrank a little at the thought of Jaali as a young boy being stolen away in the dark and taken into an even darker place.

"We had heard stories about kidnappings," he continued, "but we thought they were just stories told to children to keep them obedient and out of trouble. But the monsters were real after all." He paused, lost in thought for a moment.

"It was a long, horrible trip. We were barely fed, kept in too small of a space for our numbers, and not allowed fresh air or the dignity of relieving ourselves in private. The air reeked of urine, feces, and fear."

Milenda scooted closer. His hands shook—in anger or pain, she couldn't tell which—and she wished she could comfort him.

"After we landed somewhere off the coast of Afrika, we were put into bush vehicles and taken on a trip I never thought would end. Lots of us died from illnesses, dehydration, heartache…. I wanted to die with them, but my traitorous body kept me going."

The first few years had not been too terrible, considering he had been taken away from his homeland and family and thrust into slavery. Once he was sold to the furniture manufacturer, he was treated fairly by his corporate owners and overseers. He had been well-fed, comfortable, kept in clean housing, and given adequate resting time. He had even been given some small freedoms such as the opportunity to go to school or to walk among the free. During those years, he made friends among the other *indent*s and had lived, if not a happy life, at least a bearable one. When the fire had consumed his workplace and everything within, his life took another nightmarish detour. He was sold to Mnyama, a slaver who specialized in a very particular trade. A man without morals or understanding of common decency. A beast.

"I had just turned sixteen when I came to be one of his *indents*." Jaali's body shook like a leaf as he closed his eyes. "Mnyama was not human. There is no way a human being could act like him. He was known for taking great pride and enjoyment in taming his belongings. He was also well-known for his unsavory appetites." His voice choked in his throat. "He took an instant interest in me. My coloring was like a spark that inflamed every disgusting, immoral desire he had. He just couldn't get enough of me…"

Milenda's stomach sank. Was he saying what she thought he was saying? "Did he… oh, my gods Jaali! Did Mnyama rape you?"

His chin dropped to his chest. His hands on his lap, still holding hers, twitched. Milenda felt the wetness of tears falling on them. Jaali was crying, and her heart bled for him.

"Over and over again." The silence was broken only by his quiet sobs and her increasingly agitated breathing. She pulled him down until his head was resting on her lap. *No wonder he had been so terrified last night.* She had thought of beatings, but this? How could anyone do that? It was just too awful to even process.

Then, his voice rose again. "When he wasn't using me to satisfy himself, he sold me out to other men and women who, like him, had the moral stature of desert crawlers." He sat up and looked her straight in the eyes. Tears flooded the sky of his eyes. "I can see you now Milenda, and I hate that I made you cry." Her hands went automatically to her face. She hadn't realized she had been crying too.

"It's all right, Jaali. You didn't make me cry." She wiped at her tears and then wiped his. "The knowledge that you, and others like you, went through this makes me so angry. It's horrifying, inhuman, and must be stopped."

"How can you look at me the same way knowing what I did? How I was used? Broken and devoid of any dignity or pride..." He was sobbing, his chest rising in stutters, tears running freely down his cheeks. A pool of tears gathered in Milenda's eyes, and her heart pounded in her chest. "How can you love me? I'm a nobody, a thing to be used and thrown away. I have no family, no country, no identity. How can you, a princess, a woman of pure heart, love me? I don't deserve you."

Milenda threw herself in his arms, desperate to comfort him and be comforted in return. "I love you, Jaali. Don't you ever say that about yourself. You're not a nothing. You're everything. You're everything to me, and I can't imagine a world without you anymore. Please, don't ever think I am better than you. I am better because of you."

Pulling away just enough to look at him, Milenda kissed his wet face and his lips in a desperate frenzy. His cold lips opened to hers, and she felt his tongue flicker across them. She drank in his taste, the salt of his tears, the sadness of his heart—and a fire exploded within her.

Her hands slipped under his shirt to feel the skin and the hard muscle underneath. The desire to make him feel loved and worthy just heightened her yearning for him. "I love you."

Surprisingly, Jaali pushed her away gently. "No, Jewel, not now, not like this." She looked at him, disappointed, forlorn. "It wouldn't be fair to you or me. We are both vulnerable right now, hurting. I'd never be sure you didn't do it for pity, and you'd never be sure I didn't take advantage of the situation."

He tucked a loose strand of curly hair behind her ear and kissed her nose. "I love you, *msichana*." A smile lit up his face. "Go home and sleep. I better move on, and you have some princess-ing to do."

She giggled.

"Go! I'm glad you know… I want you to know me, even the bad bits."

Nodding, she hugged him again. She was indeed exhausted, physically and emotionally. "Until later, *wimbo wa moyo*. Be safe."

The oasis was no more. She was kneeling on a rug in the middle of her room within the protection of the royal palace, while Jaali was out there alone in *Jangwa Pori*, fighting for his life and for her. It didn't seem fair. She curled up on the rug, not bothering to get into bed, and fell asleep with the flavor of Jaali's kiss still dancing in her mouth.

On Fire

A loud knock woke her from a blissfully dream-free sleep. She jumped to her feet, not taking time to wonder why she was sleeping on the rug, and ran to the door, her slippers flip-flopping on the stone floor.

Blurry eyes met the face of Mama Nyeusi looking not a bit too happy.

"Child, you will be the death of me." Not waiting to be invited, she sashayed into the room with the authority of the old. "We thought you had died or something."

Milenda looked at her, baffled by her attitude. What was she talking about? Why would anyone think she was dead? "I have been here since I came back from the hospital yesterday."

The *iyalorixá* clicked her tongue and nodded her head. "Child, that was two days ago. You haven't been seen or heard from since then. Asha was in a panic thinking something bad had happened to you."

Two days? She must have been more tired than she'd thought, and had slept through the day and following night. "Asha is a baby," she said, deflecting. "I just slept longer than usual."

"Asha was correct in being worried. Don't pin this one on her. The girl did the right thing, coming to fetch me."

Properly chided, Milenda shrugged her shoulders defiantly and sat on the edge of her still perfectly made bed. "You obviously did not sleep in your bed. Where were you?"

For a moment, Milenda felt like a child again. It was not an altogether bad feeling. "I was here. I slept on the rug. I was exhausted!"

The woman's eyebrow shot up in a high arch. "Exhausted from visiting a few sick children? You have told better lies." Her arms were crossed in front of her generous breasts, and her voluminous skirt's movement betrayed a tapping foot.

"I'm not lying, Mama Nyeusi." There was no way around it. She was going to have to tell her. "I was here, but with Jaali, as well."

The *iyalorixá*'s foot stopped tapping, and her eyes crinkled with curiosity and surprise. "With Jaali? How is that possible? Even the tracker cannot place exactly where he is."

Milenda scooted further up on the bed and tucked her legs under her. "I didn't have the chance to tell you that Yemanjá came to see me about a week ago."

For the first time, the old woman seemed truly shaken. She grabbed hold of a nearby chair, as if to prevent herself from falling, and the other hand went to her heart. "What are you saying, child? Yemanjá came to see you? What for?"

"She said some stuff about being pleased with me and Jaali and that she was going to wake up my family's gift." Why was Mama Nyeusi so surprised? Yemanjá visited her charges all the time, didn't she?

"The gift of the seer."

The statement surprised Milenda. Mama Nyeusi seemed to know more about her family than she had led her to believe.

Not sure how to proceed or how to tell her what had happened without revealing some very private events, Milenda chose to run with the truth and just try to omit certain details. "Yes, the seer thing. At first, I was not sure what that meant, but then one day I realized I could see Jaali even when he was far away. I could feel him, talk to him, and he could see me and touch me as well."

The woman wavered on her feet, and after a moment's hesitation, pulled the chair closer and sat on it. "Child, are you telling me that you can see, touch, and talk to each other even at a distance?"

Milenda rolled her eyes. Isn't that what she had just said? "Yes, exactly. The gift of the seer."

Mama Nyeusi shook her head and waved her hands in front of her. "No, no, you don't understand. The gift of the seer gives you the skill to be able to see and feel through someone else's eyes. It's a rather abstract gift. It is up to the seer to interpret that feeling. With practice, a skilled seer will be able to master that gift. In time. But what you are telling me is so much more than that."

Milenda crinkled her brow in a frown. "What do you mean? I thought that was normal for someone with the gift."

"Young Jewel, the gift you speak of is a thing of myth, of legend." Milenda had never seen the old woman so agitated. "The books speak of a woman over a thousand years ago with that same gift, but other than that, it's unheard of."

She stared at Milenda who seemed to be more confused than ever. "Don't you get it, child? You have been given a gift we didn't even know for sure existed."

Milenda thought about it and quickly dismissed the idea. She was not going to spend too much time dwelling on it. She was just happy she had been given this gift and that she was able to be with Jaali during this difficult time.

"Well, whatever it is, I have been able to keep him company. That's where I was. I spent the whole night watching over him after a particularly tough trial and then part of the day talking to him about it. But I have been here all along."

A peal of laughter escaped the old woman's lips. "Milenda, you are special. I just told you you've been given a gift that is legendary and you just blow it off as if I told you someone gave you a new *gele*." Her chuckles were contagious, and Milenda soon joined her, laughing until tears popped in her eyes. "Child, what am I going to do with you?"

The young princess shrugged again. "The question is what are we going to do about the terrible things that have been happening under my family's rule?" Her face had turned serious. She felt older after finding out the horrors that Jaali had gone through as a young man. "We can't allow that to go on in this land of ours."

Mama Nyeusi had stopped laughing, and her face showed a new expression of admiration. "Not sure where this is coming from, but you make me proud, young one. Yes, things must change, and you will be the one doing it once you become the monarch."

Milenda shook her head. "No, this must be done before then. We can't just allow these atrocities to go on. What Jaali had to go through as an *indent*, no one should have to experience." Her voice was firm, and she almost didn't recognize it herself.

The old woman smiled and folded her hands on her lap. "So you shall. Once you're married to Jaali, nothing will stop you. As an official royal adult, you won't have your father's powers, but you will have the voice."

The young woman smiled, filled with pure joy, and Mama Nyeusi laughed again.

A shadow suddenly clouded Milenda's heart. "Jaali went through hell, Mama, and I don't know how to comfort him." The burning in her eyes hinted at the tears that pressed to come out. "I want to make him happy, to make him feel proud of himself again, to help him find the boy he lost in all the abuse and humiliation. How do I do that?"

The *iyalorixá* smiled sadly. "Child, I think you are already doing that. He was willing to go through hell again, so he could have a chance at marrying you. I would say he loves you, and just having you love him back must be a source of great joy and hope for him."

With some difficulty, she stood and walked to the bed to place a hand on Milenda's head. "The orisas are on your side, my child. May they bless you and guide you in this journey."

A thought stirred Milenda into movement again. "My gods! I need to check on Jaali. It's been over a day since he left that oasis. Who knows what new horror awaits him in the next one?"

Jumping off the bed, she ran to the bathroom. "Could you tell Asha to bring me some clean clothes? I need to get ready quick." She vanished behind the door. Anxiety had suddenly taken over her, and she desperately wanted to reach out to Jaali.

The shower was quick, and by the time she stepped out, young Asha was waiting for her with a blue *kanga* in her hands and a matching *iqhiya*.

"Quick, Asha, I must go somewhere fast. Help me get dressed." With the help of the servant girl, she wrapped herself in the *kanga*, arranged the *iqhiya* over her freshly washed, half-tamed hair, and slipped into her silk walking shoes.

"Done. Go now, Asha. I won't need you until tonight."

The young girl stared at her, confused, as Milenda led her to the door. "But where are you going, exalted one?"

"You really must stop calling me that, Asha. My name is Milenda," she protested, while opening the door and gently pushing the servant girl through it. "Good-bye, Asha."

"Aren't you going out? You got all dressed up…"

"Gracious no, I'm not going anywhere." She was already closing the door on a very bewildered Asha. "I'm staying in with a good book."

Not wasting any time, Milenda ran to the center of her room, closed her eyes, and reached out for Jaali. At first there was nothing, but soon she started feeling something; a sense of uncomfortable heat crawled up her arm into her neck. It became hard to breathe, and everything around her blurred as if she were looking at it through water.

What's going on, Jaali? What have they done to you now?

***

Fire. He was on fire. His hands, arms, and shoulders burned with the intensity of a raging fire. He heard a guttural scream, and it took him a few seconds to realize he was its source. Gods, the pain was unbearable as the heat spread to his chest, his neck, his face. The cool sand of the oasis offered meager comfort as he rolled around, trying to extinguish the invisible flames. He knew there was no fire, even if all his senses were telling him otherwise. The wave of devouring heat was the effect of something just as destructive.

Less than an hour ago, he had received directions from the Elders as to what his next trial would be. It had seemed so simple and innocuous, it made all of Jaali's internal alarms go off.

Something is not right. Knowing that didn't do him any good, however; he had to follow the Elders' instructions if he was ever to finish this journey and be eligible for Milenda's hand in marriage. Clenching his jaw and taking a deep breath, he approached the place he had been directed to—a small hole in the ground, about two fists wide, but seemingly much deeper. Crouching by it, Jaali took a look inside. It was deceptively dark, with nothing extraordinary about it. The

Elders would not have asked him to do what he was about to do if this were just a plain hole in the ground.

Bracing himself for what was to come, Jaali thrust his arm down the hole as far as it would go and flinched; something was moving on the bottom. His instinct wanted him to remove the arm, but the directions were clear; he must keep the arm in for at least one full minute. Sweat beaded on his forehead in anticipation of whatever was about to happen.

A tingling started on the tip of his fingers, crawling up his hand and his arm. Ants! He had just stuck his arm inside an anthill. The question remained: what kind of ants?

The answer came when the minute was up, and he pulled his arm out from the hole. The tingling quickly changed to the feeling of many stings. He had been stung by ants before, but this felt different. The stinging pain was quickly followed by a burning sensation. His white arm, now outside the hole, had turned black with crawling ants. He watched them, half fascinated, half horrified.

"For søren!" Bullet ants! Those were bullet ants, the most dangerous creatures of the desert. Tiny and harmless-looking, the ants bore very little in common with their kin. Bullet ants were highly poisonous and aggressive.

He forcibly stuck his hand in the sand, trying to rub them off, but it was too late. They had already started their attack in earnest, and the pain was quickly becoming intolerable. As he rolled around on the sand, fighting against the tiny enemy, he felt his muscles go stiff. It became harder and harder to move his arms, and his legs weighed him down like anchors. Paralysis was taking hold of him as the pain grew in waves of pure agony.

Another scream escaped his lips. "Milenda!"

"*Wimbo wa moyo.*" His beautiful princess knelt beside him, her face twisted in a frown and her arms reached out to him. He could feel her fingers examining his arms, now bloated and bloody. "What happened? What's wrong? Are these bites?"

"Bullet ants." The words came out as a groan. "I can't move…. It hurts."

Milenda scanned the oasis around her. Standing, she ran to a bush of succulents partially hidden by a tree. She broke one of the thick leaves and hurried back to Jaali's side.

"This is a *dawa* leaf." She talked as she swiftly broke the leaf in half and began rubbing the moisture insides over his bites. "It soothes pain. It's an anesthetic the surgeons in Natale's hospitals use. Of course, they prepare it better than this, but—is it helping?"

Jaali's breathing was ragged and shallow, but the pain was subsiding just enough to offer some welcome relief. "Yes, better." Managing a smile, the young Outlander gazed up into her big green eyes. "You are my salvation, a *malaika*, an angel from heaven sent to help me."

Still spreading the juices of the plant over his bitten arm, Milenda smiled at him. "Nobody ever accused me of being a *malaika* before." She reached out to touch his face, still distorted by pain. "You are the angel, *wimbo wa moyo*. I'm just glad I can actually touch things here. I wasn't sure my gift would let me do that."

Just like the previous two nights, she stretched out beside

him in the sand, soothing him with words, and tonight, with the salve from the plant. When he shivered uncontrollably from a fever brought on by the poison in the ants' stings, she wrapped her arms around him and anchored him. She brought water to his lips when he found it hard to swallow and fanned him to cool him down when sweats assailed his body. By dawn, the pain had toned down to a bearable degree and he began to move again.

"Does it still hurt?" They were lying side by side, noses almost touching, hands entwined. He couldn't get enough of her eyes.

"A bit." His eyes traveled to her lips. "Must I always be in pain of some kind for you to lie with me?" A teasing smile lifted the corners of his lips.

She smacked his shoulder playfully. "It's your fault. You keep getting yourself in these binds. Someone has to rescue you."

"I'm supposed to rescue you, not the opposite." It was a feeble protest. He knew she didn't need rescuing. She might be young and innocent, but she was far from helpless. In this story, he was the damsel in distress. He giggled at the thought.

"What's so funny?"

Her mouth was so tantalizingly close to his. He could smell her subtle jasmine scent. "What's that scent you're wearing? It's intoxicating."

"That's the fever talking." With a chuckle, she threw her head backward and her *iqhiya* fell off, revealing the raven-black kinks of her unruly hair. A stir of desire grew within him, like the fire that had consumed him earlier.

Tilting his head toward Milenda, he touched his forehead to hers and breathed her in.

"I want you, my jewel." The whisper left his lips and met hers with the effect of a kiss. His body shook with yearning. "I want you."

With her eyes closed and her breath quickening, the young princess inhaled his scent as if it were perfume. "I'm not really here, Jaali." There was a sadness in her voice he couldn't quite place.

"I can feel you, you can feel me." As if to prove it, Jaali brushed his hand along her neck, tracing her *matangazos* all the way to her exposed shoulders. "It doesn't matter how far we are from each other. We are here together now." He lowered his mouth to her lips and sighed as they parted for his kiss.

The fire in his gut grew stronger. He nibbled gently on her lower lip and touched it with his tongue. The kiss became deeper, more frantic, and her little moans of pleasure further fueled his desire.

"I am not supposed to…" Milenda kissed the corner of his mouth and then his chin. "I'm a princess. Princesses don't do this." She seemed to be talking more to herself than anyone else.

His hands slipped under the bodice of her *kanga* and he felt the heat of her soft skin close to her breasts. Desire erupted, and he wasn't sure he could control himself anymore.

"Gods, you feel so good, Milenda." With his lips, he left a trail of kisses along her *matangazos* all the way down where they met the top of her *kanga*. He traced her skin along the blue fabric with his tongue and trembled at her reaction.

"Jaali, my love." Her eyes were closed, and her face bespoke of ecstasy. It was Milenda's turn to slip her hands under his shirt. He shivered with pleasure as she explored his abdomen and chest in a flurry of curious fingers while her lips melded into his again. She was becoming bolder, and her tongue teased the corner of his mouth until a groan of both frustration and yearning escaped him.

"Contender, focus!" The voice came out of nowhere and shocked him into a near paralysis again. The Elder was talking to him and here he was, body wrapped around Milenda's, lips glued to hers. Could they see it? The last thing he wanted to do was get Milenda in some kind of trouble. "Jaali, do you hear us?"

Pulling himself from Milenda, he cleared his throat and uttered a little prayer under his breath.

"Yes, Elders, I hear you." There was silence, and Milenda looked at him with dreamy eyes, as if waking up from sleep. "I did what you asked me. I survived." The last words dripped with bitterness. He was becoming more and more convinced the Elders were indeed trying to kill him.

"Well done, contender." The voice was neutral, no feeling at all. "A new trial awaits you in the next oasis. Until then, may the orisas have mercy on you."

The Elder's voice was gone and Jaali exhaled a sigh of relief. "He didn't see you."

Milenda sat up and was looking at him with curiosity. "Who did not see me?"

Jaali shook his head. Of course she couldn't hear the

Elder's voice. The device was in his body, and only he could hear it.

"The Elders just sent another message. They are pleased with me, I guess." From the sand where he was still lying down, he smiled up at her. She had sand in her hair and a twinkle in her eye that he had never seen before. "You look beautiful."

"You're still feverish." Reaching out her hand, she helped him sit up. His muscles were still uncooperative after so many hours of paralysis. "The sun is setting. I should go if you're okay. You need a good night's sleep to recover."

"I'm sorry, Milenda." His pale eyes sought hers. She looked up at him uncomprehending. "For—you know, the kissing and…"

A generous smile illuminated her light-brown face. "Are you really sorry?" she asked. "I'm not." With a scoot, she leaned against him, her head on his shoulder. "I wish…"

Jaali tilted his head a little so he could kiss her neck. "I know. Me too." Her perfume tickled his senses once again.

He sighed. "Soon… but I shouldn't have touched you like that." Jaali sought her eyes for reassurance. "You're young and innocent, and I am… stained." The last word was uttered in a barely audible whisper.

Jaali lowered his eyes in shame. How dare he touch someone as pure as Milenda when he had been marked as spoiled goods for so long now? Suddenly, he wanted to cry; instead, he began scratching his face in anger. "I don't have the right to ask you for anything. I'm no good. I'm less than that."

Milenda watched him, eyes wide in alarm.

"Stop, Jaali." She took hold of his hand before he tore at his face again. Already, several bleeding scratches were etched into his extraordinarily white skin. He fought her without much conviction and then gave up, eyes lowered to the sand, his breathing sputtering.

"Stop, please, *tukufu*. How can you say that? How can you even think that? You are important to me. More than important. You are essential to me like air is to breathing. Without you, I would shrivel up and die."

He shook as Milenda brought his hand to her lips and kissed his still-sore knuckles. "I want you as much as you want me." It was her turn to lower her eyes in embarrassment, her *matangazos* shining red. "I want you so bad it hurts, Jaali. No matter how much these voices inside my head tell me it is not the proper thing to think or do, I can't help it. Every time we are together, it's like a fever takes over me, and I lose track of all common sense."

The glow of her green eyes seemed to illuminate the night as she raised them shyly to him again.

"I love you so much, Milenda, and sometimes I have to wonder whether I'm doing the right thing by you." He swallowed hard. "Wouldn't you be better off marrying some other man, one of your own race and nationality, rather than having to settle for an ex-*indent* Outlander? My coloring, my background, my sins—"

The princess shook her head, sending her tightly curled hair flying around her face. "Can you imagine the children we'll have?"

Jaali's eyebrows shot up.

"My brown skin, your whiteness. My green eyes, your blues, my matangazos… gods, they will look like nothing anybody has ever seen."

He burst out laughing. Sweet Milenda rescuing him once again from a dark place.

She joined him with her laughter. "Good thing they will be royalty, or they would be bullied their whole lives, poor babies."

When the laughter finally ceased, Jaali held her hands and gazed at her in gratitude. "Thank you, Milenda. You yanked me out of the abyss again. See what I mean? I need you. You're my sanity, my hope, my joy."

For a few moments, they sat in silence, holding hands and staring into each other's eyes, oblivious to the passage of time. Milenda broke the silence. "So?"

Confused, he dropped her hands. "So what?"

"Aren't you going to kiss me good-bye?" Her eyes twinkled with mischief. "I thought you loved me."

A smile widening his lips, Jaali pulled her to him and kissed her. "I love you. Until next time, remember me like this." He gently nibbled her bottom lip before fully melding his mouth to hers. Sighing, he allowed himself to give in to the exhilarating madness her touch always caused.

The Flight

Disbelief washed over him. He could not have heard it correctly. It was sheer madness. The Elders could not be serious. Yet, wasn't that exactly what they had just told him through his implant?

The message was as simple as it was insane. "Go to the nearest cliff and fly off it." Fly? How could he fly? He was human, not a bird or an angel. If he had any doubts as to their wishes to kill him off, they had been totally washed away. Obviously, they did not want him to finish the Trials alive.

Dejected, he dropped to the hot sand and rubbed his head, trying to make sense of his last directives. Unless the Elders knew something he did not, Jaali was pretty sure he was not endowed with the hollow bones and feathery wings that would allow him to glide over a cliff safely.

He shook his head and jumped to his feet. No point in dwelling on it too much, since there were no cliffs in sight as yet. The journey must continue. Soon, the sun would be dipping into the horizon and shelter would be virtually impossible to find in the dark.

With a long, strong branch he had collected from an oasis in one hand, Jaali began making his way westward. He was alone today. Milenda had another of her royal events to attend to and couldn't keep him company. Just as well, he thought. It was getting harder and harder to control himself around her, and he didn't want her to see the beast inside him. Better to keep some distance and give himself time to cool off.

In spite of his resolve, he couldn't help wondering what she would say about the crazy trial the Elders had just dropped in his lap. Knowing her, she could very well come up with some equally crazy idea that just might work. She had come up with the idea of ripping part of his shirt and using the shreds to wrap around his feet in order to give them a little more protection from the heat. For someone brought up within the protection of the palace, she sure had a knack for the practical.

He was not sure how long he had walked. The sands of the *Jangwa Pori* appeared the same, no matter where he looked. There were no landmarks, no vegetation outside the oasis, just a never-ending expanse of beige, thin sand that found its way into everything. His skin, his hair, even his mouth felt gritty from invading grains of sand.

After climbing a particularly high dune, he saw it. Sprawled just a few yards away from the bottom of the dune, a steep, rocky cliff opened up like the giant toothless jaws of some alien creature. Jaali stood and stared, imagining what it would feel like to go over the edge. He didn't like what his imagination came up with. He liked what reality was telling him even less. There was no way he would survive a jump off that cliff.

The darkness was coming fast. Jaali started the downhill descent, heading toward a large oasis that seemed to hang over the chasm like a big bird of prey. He would spend the night there and make some kind of plan for the next morning. What those plans could possibly be, he had no idea.

By the time he was sitting against a tree, drinking from the fresh water he had just collected in a small pond, the night had blanketed everything in black, punctuated by the light of a million stars. Jaali looked up at the sky and was immediately taken by an overwhelming sense of awe.

The universe was too amazing and too immense to wrap his head around. To think that same sky had awed millions of others throughout time and space made him feel less lonely. Somewhere, somebody was looking at that same sky and wondering the same thing.

"This is so beautiful," he said out loud.

"Does that mean you don't need my company tonight?" The familiar voice tore him from his contemplation.

Milenda was sitting next to him in a bright red *kanga* and an elaborate *iqhiya,* looking beautiful and annoyed. "Because I can leave. In spite of what you may think, a princess has lots of things to do."

He chortled at her expression before throwing his arms around her neck. "I always need your company." He nuzzled her neck, chuckling at the little groan he extracted from her. "I just didn't expect you tonight. How did the event go?"

The touch of her moist lips against his face made him quiver. "Boring as usual." Seemingly oblivious to the effects her lips were having on him, Milenda continued to trail light kisses along his jaw.

Drawing on strength he didn't know he had, Jaali pulled away. "Are you all right?" The surprise in her eyes was quickly replaced by worry.

He took a deep breath to collect his thoughts and to regain control of his body. "I have another trial tomorrow morning. It's not good."

Was she aware that, when she looked at him with her big, beautiful eyes, his insides melted like wax on a windowsill?

"When were the Trials ever good? What cruelty did they come up with this time?" Her hands suddenly bereft of his touch were drawing circles in the sand. He longed to cover them with his own.

"I have to fly off the edge of that cliff." It sounded even crazier when he said it out loud.

Melinda's eyes opened wide, and her hand came to rest on her chest.

"What? Fly?" She rose to her knees. "What are they thinking?"

Jaali sighed as he leaned back into the tree again. "They're thinking they can easily get rid of me." Hearing it from his own mouth made him feel depressed. How was he going to do this?

The silence emanating from Milenda told him she was thinking. He was both scared and excited about what she might come up with. Her mind worked in mysterious ways. Jaali's eyes wandered to her face, now tight in concentration, her bottom lip caught between her teeth.

So lovely.

"We must build you some kind of flying contraption," she said, finally breaking the silence. For a moment, he questioned her sanity. Flying contraption? Out of what? Leaves and branches?

"Milenda, we have nothing to build it with, even if we knew how." His protest came out as a cry of disappointment. He had really been hoping for one of her fantastic, wild ideas. Not a flight of fancy.

"But we do. We certainly do."

What was he missing? There were no parachutes in his backpack or hang gliders.

"We have Mjusi."

"Mjusi? He is not a contraption—and wouldn't that be cheating?" Trying not to sound too outraged, Jaali lowered his voice and his eyes.

It was Milenda's turn to be outraged. "Please! Cheating? What do you call asking a human being with no building materials or tools to fly off the edge of a cliff? I call that cheating. You either give up the Trials and stay alive or jump to your certain death." She stood and paced frenetically. "The Elders are the ones doing all the cheating." Her voice had gone up several octaves as she worked herself into a tiff.

"It's okay, Milenda." He tried to soothe her with words, still reluctant to touch her. It was not working.

Obviously agitated, Milenda was wringing her hands

as if they were a couple of wash rags. "No, it is not okay. They are being dishonest by giving you trials they know you can't possibly accomplish. They are setting you up for failure because they're scared."

Looking up at her moving figure, Jaali scratched his head. "Scared? Of what?"

She stopped and faced him, her youthful face twisted in a frown. "Don't you see? They are afraid you will win the Trials and that our children will be a totally different breed of people. They fear change, because it is in tradition and habitual norms that their power lies. If we change things even a little bit, they will lose their relevance, their authority. They will be powerless."

Jaali was in awe of her. Of course, she was right. It hadn't occurred to him that he was indeed a threat to the Elders as an institution of power. He was not used to thinking of himself as anything other than a nobody who wasn't going anywhere.

Milenda was right. They were scared of the changes that would no doubt come from such a union. He stood and walked the few feet that separated them and slid his hands around her shoulders to pull her close to him.

"I never thought of that, *msichana*. You're a genius."

Milenda laughed, her body shaking in his arms.

"I mean it. You're amazing." He planted a kiss by her ear and made her laugh again.

"I have to go, Jaali." She pulled herself from him gently. "I have to prepare Mjusi for tomorrow morning."

Dropping his arms alongside his body, he stepped back. "How? How is he going to fly me over the edge? He is not that big, and I'm not tiny."

"He's a lot stronger than you think," she protested. "Properly geared, you have a very good chance of flying off and not killing yourself in the process." Jaali couldn't help but admire her determination and creativity. He smiled and she frowned.

"What are you smiling about? This is serious."

"Sorry, but it is amazing what you come up with to solve problems." He opened his arms invitingly. "What would I do without you?"

Accepting the invitation, Milenda cuddled into the cocoon of his arms. "By now you would be a piece of beef jerky, dry and dead." He laughed into the top of her head. "You better never forget it." The threat came out sounding like a plea, her voice muffled by his shirt.

Later, alone and tired, Jaali stretched on the sand under the flimsy blanket, unable to sleep. Far from worried about what was to happen the next morning, he was kept awake by the memory of Milenda's body inside that red *kanga*, her amber shoulders and her elegant bare neck, *matangazos* glowing in the dark.

What was wrong with him? He was almost twenty-seven years old, and he had never felt like this. His traumatic experiences as an *indent* were sure to blame, he knew. After all he had gone through, love and physical yearnings were not on top of his list of priorities or interests. He had buried his sexual being way down inside of himself to never see the light of day again, but Milenda had changed all of that.

With her youthful and innocent beauty, her purity of heart

and soul, she had managed to pry that forgotten part of him into existence again. Like a phoenix out from the ashes, his heart and his body had awakened with such intensity he was struggling to keep it under control. If on one hand he rejoiced in the knowledge that he was not totally dead inside as he had suspected for years, he was also terrified of bringing some of his demons down on the sweet princess he loved more than life itself. Was the darkness he carried inside contagious? Could he unwittingly transmit it to her lily-white soul?

*****

The bridle was not Mjusi's favorite part of the getup. He tossed his head left and right, trying in vain to bite it off his muzzle. Milenda was having a hard time convincing him to wear the small, almost ornamental saddle, on his back. She had it made years ago when she had first made friends with the lizard-like creature, in hopes he would eventually allow her to fly on his back.

That had never happened, of course. Milenda quickly realized Mjusi was too much of an independent creature to ever allow himself to be used that way. She had always respected him for it, but now it was a question of life or death, and she was not going to give him a choice.

"Sorry, friend, but you have to do this." She patted his scaly head, trying to calm him. "It's just one time, Mjusi, and it's to save Jaali's life. You like him, right?"

The beast stopped moving for a moment and looked at her with his two great big green eyes. "He needs you to be able to complete this trial. If you don't help him, he will either die or lose."

With a low growl, Mjusi gave his assent to the invasive addition of the saddle on his back. Milenda finished tying the buckles around his body as tight as she could while still allowing him to move freely.

Mjusi had instructions to fly to where Jaali was. The flying creature had the unique gift of being able to locate people and animals like no one else could. Milenda had this theory that some sort of device had been embedded in Mjusi's brains, but the truth was probably much simpler—nothing more than genetics.

It was almost morning when Milenda finally reached out to Jaali. He was still asleep, and Mjusi was not there yet. She curled up on the sand beside him and fell asleep.

A wet, cold nose woke her sometime later. She patted Mjusi's head. "Hi, my friend. Are you ready?"

In his sleep, Jaali had moved and had his hand over her now. By the looks of the sand underneath and around him, he had not slept peacefully. When a wet, rough nose prodded him awake from his fretful slumber, Jaali nearly jumped out of his skin.

"Gods, Mjusi! You scared me to death."

The creature whimpered as an apology and poked him with his nose again.

"Okay, okay, I'm up. Let's do this."

For the first time, he realized Milenda was right next to him, bleary-eyed and smiling. "When did you get here?" He kissed her cheek.

"A while back. Took a nap in the meantime." Studying him, the young woman reached out for his hand. "You didn't sleep well."

His eyes immediately dropped to the sand. "I'm just nervous about this whole thing." He was lying. Something else had been bothering him, but she was not going to pry. With a tilt of her head, she watched him as he bit his lip and shoved his foot into the sand. "Tossed and turned, but I will sleep better after this is done."

She pulled him closer, not liking the distance between them. "Will you look at me, Jaali?"

Eyes the color of a clear sky rose up to meet hers. She would never tire of flying in those skies, even when they were troubled as they were now.

"I'm afraid." The pause in his voice and the hesitation in his eyes made her heart clench in worry. She was scared, too, afraid he would fall to his death, terrified of having to spend the rest of her life without him. There were so many reasons to be scared, but she couldn't allow those bleak feelings to cloud her heart and take away her hope. In the end, hope was all anyone could claim to hold on to.

"I'm scared as well," she replied. He blinked, and she thought she saw the depths of an ocean in that instant. "But I love you, and I know in my heart we are going to be all right. Victory will be ours because the orisas are with us. They are watching us and rooting for us."

Jaali took a deep breath and smiled a tiny, hesitant smile. "What do I have to do?"

The next ten minutes were a blur of activity and preparation.

Reluctantly, Mjusi allowed Jaali to climb onto his back and harness himself to him. The creature looked as nervous as the young man on the saddle.

"Remember, you must hold on for dear life until Mjusi lands at the bottom." She fussed over buckles and belts, checking and double-checking. This had to work. "Mjusi is small but strong. You can do it, can't you, Mjusi?"

Her scaly friend gave her a nod as if to agree with her.

"I will see you both at the bottom."

As they exchanged a final look, Milenda felt the sudden urge to hold onto Jaali's neck and not let go ever again. With a heavy heart, she leaned forward on her tiptoes and kissed him lightly on the lips. "Yemanjá, don't fail me now," she whispered in a prayer.

The *msitu* glanced at her one last time and took off, gliding gracefully over the edge of the cliff. He dove toward the bottom at an alarming speed.

Oh gods! Is Jaali too heavy of a weight for him? Praying under her breath, Milenda hovered over the edge, watching as the two of her most precious treasures free-fell the dizzying height of the precipice. She wished she could close her eyes, but it was as if she were under some hypnotic spell, and she just couldn't break her visual connection from the potential disaster happening beneath her.

"Mjusi! Climb! Climb!" she yelled, knowing full well he couldn't hear her.

A few seconds before hitting the sandy ground, their speed faltered. Milenda reached out and found herself on the bottom, looking up at the plummeting duo.

Mjusi seemed to have finally slowed their descent. The flapping of his wings was more deliberate and focused, and their speed slowed considerably. She exhaled the breath she had been holding for the past few minutes. *It's going to be okay.*

Her eyes, glued to the flying pair, searched for Jaali's face and found it. His eyes were closed, and his skin was paler than usual. He seemed to be slumping to the side, sliding off the back of the creature. His hands were not holding on to the saddle anymore.

Jaali was unconscious and quickly falling off Mjusi. Milenda cried out in shock and desperation as her love dipped lower and lower, and eventually detached from Mjusi's back. From forty feet high in the air, he crashed to the ground with a sickening crack.

"No! No!" Milenda ran to his side and dropped to her knees. Jaali was stretched in an awkward position, his leg bent at an impossible angle, his head twisted and bleeding. She searched him for signs of life, but couldn't find any.

"No, you can't die on me. Jaali, don't leave me, please." Sobs erupted from her throat as she pressed her lips to his. Her breath, stuttering and dry, filled his chest with much-needed oxygen, but his heart still didn't beat. Tears now flowing freely down her cheeks, Milenda tried again. Her hand rested on his chest, but she couldn't feel his heartbeat.

"Come back to me. Don't you dare leave me now. Jaali!"

His heart was not reacting to her ministrations. Jaali's pale face remained lifeless. Milenda slid her hands under him and pulled him to her chest, crying.

How could this happen? Yemanjá had promised he would be all right. They had a deal.

"You promised me, Mother!" It came out as a primal scream, fierce with agony and anger. "You promised me!"

In her arms, Jaali moved. A tiny, almost indiscernible twitch. Milenda looked down at him and brought her head to his chest, listening for signs of a heartbeat.

There it was, faint and irregular, but there nevertheless.

A loud sob left her lips. "*Wimbo wa moyo*," she whispered into his lips. "I love you. Come back, come back to me."

Jaali's chest moved on its own now, inhaling and exhaling the life-giving air.

Milenda, tears still streaming down her face, checked his twisted leg. It was almost certainly broken. Her mind searched for what she had been taught about treating wounds and injuries. She felt along his leg, assessing the extent of the damage, and was pleasantly surprised to find there were no broken bones. The muscles and probably the ligaments had been twisted. Jaali wouldn't be walking any time soon, but he would heal.

The shade from the cliff offered some shelter from the desert heat. Milenda, with Mjusi's help, dragged Jaali closer to its walls to keep him cool. There was not much she could do other than sit by him, keep his lips moist, and wait until his body was recovered enough to come to. Dehydration and exhaustion, added to the free-fall, must have made him faint. She wiped her tears with the back of her hand, and then, ripping a piece of her *iqhiya,* she proceeded to clean his head wound. It didn't seem too severe or too deep—probably the result of his head scrapping against Mjusi's sharp scales.

"Come here, Mjusi. Clean this up for me please."

Msitus were well known for their healing saliva. At one time, they had been hunted for that very reason and almost completely wiped out as a species. Now, the few survivors like him were protected by law. Killing or imprisoning a *msitu* carried a steep prison sentence that few were willing to risk.

Mjusi stepped closer, his head lowered as if in shame. "Not your fault, friend. He passed out. You did all you could." She hugged him. "Thank you, friend."

The creature growled gently, and taking a further step forward, bent his head and licked the wound on Jaali's head.

"We'll just have to wait," Milenda whispered.

The landscape was different at the bottom of the crag. The ground was still mostly covered in sand, but there were more trees, and even a small stream just a few yards away.

Jaali must be getting closer to civilization. Closer to the end of the Trial. Closer to winning her hand in marriage. This accident would delay everything. Not being able to walk on his own, Jaali would have to wait it out.

"The important thing is that you are alive," she said out loud, caressing his face.

Not as pale anymore, Jaali seemed to be sleeping in peace for the first time in a long while. She would let him sleep. Gods knew he needed the rest. Tired herself, Milenda drifted off as well, her head nestled on his shoulder and Mjusi curled up against her legs.

The night had arrived when she woke up. Mjusi had flown home, and Jaali was awake and watching her in silence.

"Jaali, why didn't you wake me up?"

A smile lit his face. "I like watching you. You're so beautiful." Milenda sat up and helped him do the same. "What did I do to myself? I remember feeling dizzy, and then I woke up next to you. Not a bad dream, really."

She laughed. "You fainted and fell from Mjusi's back, still some ways from the bottom." His almost-white hair seemed to glisten in the faint light from the moon. "Your leg is badly injured."

He attempted to move his leg and groaned in pain. "Hell, what do I do now?"

"You wait." His eyes shot up to hers. She nodded. "You wait until your leg can carry you."

With a shake of his head, he dismissed the idea. "No, I can't wait. Anything can happen out here and you know the Elders, as soon as they find out I'm alive, they will make sure I won't stay like that for long. I have to move on. I have to finish the Trials."

"You need to think this through." She sat forward and held him back with one hand on his chest. "You can't put any weight on that leg, trust me. Your muscles are strained badly and the ligaments probably are too."

"We have to think of something. A crutch of some kind…" He looked around, but the advancing darkness didn't allow him to see much. "I guess we have to wait until morning."

The air had cooled considerably. Milenda retrieved the blanket from his discarded backpack and covered him. "You must rest. You fell from pretty high." She leaned forward and kissed him. "I thought you were dead." Her voice was low and shaky as she swallowed a sob.

"I'm not leaving you," he said, pulling her in for another kiss. "I promise."

They cuddled against each other under the relative protection of the crag wall and fell asleep.

Desire and Fear

Milenda spied Asha tiptoeing across the room, lighter than a feather, aiming quick nervous glances at her as she curled up on top of the bed. Milenda had been in a strange mood since that morning, and the young servant had found her in that sort of trance she went into when she reached out for Jaali. In a panic, the young girl had tried to wake her from whatever strange sleep-walking state she was in and had succeeded only in making the princess angry. Milenda had raved and cursed like a pirate, walking around in circles with her hands thrown upward. Not quite sure whether that anger was directed at her, Asha had left the room and was just now returning.

"Asha, you don't have to be so quiet." Milenda's voice startled the young girl, stopping her in her tracks. "I'm awake—thanks to you, I may add. I'm not mad at you. Just a little annoyed, that's all."

The princess sat up on the bed. The jagged shadows around her head caught in her peripheral vision told her, her wild hair was even wilder this morning. It wouldn't be easy appeasing such ferocity with a comb. Asha's eyes opened wide at the sight of her mistress still wearing the *kanga* she had worn the day before. Let the young maid make her own conclusions. She didn't care.

"I have decided I will visit the Elders this morning." Milenda swung her legs alongside the bed and stood. "Bring me the most royally exuberant *kanga* and *iqhiya* you can find. I want to appear before them as powerful as I possibly can."

The girl spun around and headed for the door.

While her maid was away in search of some ridiculously elaborate outfit, Milenda undressed, wrapped herself in a fluffy white bathrobe, and ignoring her slippers, left the room to go visit the outdoor showers.

The water was, as always, a mixture of warmth and coolness that soothed her aching muscles.

Asha had unwittingly pulled her out of her contact with Jaali in the desert. She had been so comfortable in his arms, sleeping the wee hours of the morning away when suddenly she had to return to her room, with no time for good-byes. Jaali probably thought she had abandoned him, bad leg and all.

Now that she was back, she had a crazy idea, and she couldn't wait to execute it. She was going to confront the Elders about the unusually cruel trials they were putting Jaali through. The only problem was how to do it without letting them know she was in contact with him.

The water fell on her face and her shoulders like a caress and she sighed, feeling her muscles relax. Without thinking about it, she reached out for Jaali.

Almost immediately, he was there, leaning against the tiled wall of the shower, leg bent at the knee and standing on his good leg. His azure eyes scanned her from head to toe, and yearning lit his face. "You're beautiful."

Milenda, standing naked in front of him, felt strangely at ease. The way Jaali was looking at her was exhilarating, and it made her whole body tingle. "You shouldn't be here," she said, her voice void of conviction.

"You called me here," he protested. "Milenda, you know I don't have that power. You wanted me here. Why?"

The princess moved a step closer to him and Jaali trembled. "I'm not sure. I should be embarrassed, but I'm not. I guess I wanted you to see me whole, no secrets, no unknowns. I have seen you in your most vulnerable moments. It's only fair you get to see me, too."

Soaked by the waters of the shower, Jaali's clothes were clinging to his body and making it clearly obvious how aroused he was. "Milenda, I shouldn't be here. Send me back." His eyes were as pleading as they were foggy with desire.

The princess smiled. "Sweet Jaali. What are you so afraid of?" She took another step toward him, raising her hand to come and rest it flat on his shirt. "I'm the one who should be scared. This is all so new to me."

Jaali exhaled loudly and leaned further into the wall. "I don't want to hurt you, Milenda," he whispered with difficulty.

"Please, send me back."

His body and his eyes belied his words, and Milenda felt a surge of a strange and intoxicating power. Mother Nature had given her this power in the shape of her female body, and for a moment, she drank it in. She wanted to test it, to see how far she could go. They were so close now, she could feel the panic in his breath as she began peeling the shirt off him. Why was he so nervous? Her tutors had told her that men were always willing and ready for this, but Jaali seemed almost terrified.

"Send me back, Milenda. Please." The plea was so heartfelt it stopped her. Veering her eyes from his cloud-white chest up to his eyes, she was surprised to find sadness and fear. Her hands fell alongside her body, and she tilted her head in question. "Please. I don't want to hurt you."

Frustrated and embarrassed, Milenda turned off the water and made a grab for her robe. It suddenly felt extremely important for her to cover herself, although she had been so pleasantly comfortable in her skin just a few minutes before. A sideways glance told her the young Outlander was grateful for the respite. He stood by the wall, dripping wet and shivering. The princess scanned the shower area with her eyes, and finding a towel on the rack, went to cover him up with it.

He was trembling so much, Milenda was suddenly afraid she may have gotten him sick somehow. Draping the towel around his shoulders, she helped him hobble on one leg to the nearest bench. "Sit. Jaali, rest." She rubbed his arms with the towel, trying to bring back some of the heat he seemed to have lost. *"Nasikitika,* sorry. I don't know what I did that got you so upset, but whatever it was, I'm sorry." Crestfallen, she risked a glance into his liquid eyes. They still wore a harrowing expression, panic and fear swimming in that blue ocean of peace.

A hand shot out from underneath the towel and held hers. His hand was ice-cold, and she automatically closed hers around it to warm it. "No, I'm the one who's sorry, *msichana*. You did nothing wrong." His voice was clipped as if he was still having trouble breathing between words. His lips and chin quaked convulsively.

Was he really that cold?

"I'll get another towel. You're freezing." She half stood before he pulled her back onto the seat. "Jaali, what's going on?"

The air in the shower room was warm and uncomfortably sticky, the excess of humidity brought on by the spilled water and the oppressive heat. However, Jaali didn't seem to notice it; rather, his body was raked by shivers. Milenda thought that maybe she should let go of him and allow him to go back into the desert where he would undoubtedly warm up, but she was too scared of letting him go like this. Maybe he was running a fever due to injuries she had not been able to uncover.

"I'm not sick, Milenda," he said, guessing her thoughts. "At least not physically. But I am terrified." His beautiful, silvery hair was plastered to his head. He looked so young and so vulnerable. Milenda felt an urge to hug him, but thought better of it. Her touch hadn't seemed to help matters earlier, and she was now embarrassed that she had, if only for a moment, indulged in the heady feeling of power over him.

"You are almost done with the Trials, Jaali." Who could

fault him for being scared? The Elders had put him through hell, and they were not done with him yet, she suspected.

"No, you misunderstand me." He rubbed a hand across his face, wiping some of the wetness still lingering on his skin. "I'm not scared of the Trials. I can easily handle that. What scares me is how I feel about you."

Milenda's heart sank. What did that mean? Her world would crash if he were to decide he didn't love her anymore.

"I thought you loved me." She had known very little love in her life, and she hadn't realized how much she needed and wanted it until she met Jaali. She couldn't lose that now.

"Of course I love you." With a shrug of surprise, Jaali let the towel slide off his shoulders onto the wet floor. "That's why I'm so scared, sweetheart. I don't want to hurt you, but I want you so bad I'm afraid I will end up doing just that."

Confused, Milenda blinked her eyes. "How will you hurt me? Do you have a secret fetish I don't know about? Do you like to beat up your lovers? Because I haven't seen any sign of that so far."

She had meant it as a joke, but his eyes clouded. "No, I would never lift a finger against you. There are other ways I can hurt you." He sounded so serious, her stomach churned in apprehension.

"What could you possibly do to hurt me, Jaali?" In spite of herself, she was afraid of the answer. "You're such a gentle creature. What could you do to hurt me?"

His eyes lowered again, Jaali rubbed his hands together as if trying to produce heat. "I could hurt you like they hurt me." The statement was made so quietly, Milenda almost missed it.

Reaching out, she held his hands to stop him from the compulsive rubbing. He was going to rub his skin, already so dry, raw if he continued. "Who is 'they' and how did they hurt you?"

His voice was but a whisper. "Mnyama, the *duivel*, and his friends."

Comprehension finally sank in. He had been raped many times over by the horrible men and women who had kept him in captivity. But why would he be afraid of hurting her the same way he was hurt?

"That was them. You're not like them at all. What makes you think you'd hurt me like that?" Milenda tilted his head up with a finger under his chin. "Look at me, Jaali. We're equals. You're not an *indent* anymore. You look me in the eye, you hear me? Tell me please, why do you think that?"

Her words, authoritative but also gentle and loving, were the motivation he needed to start speaking. It came out in a torrent of words, like a maelstrom of thoughts and feelings so long kept deep down inside they had trouble coalescing into something material. As he related to her his often-disconnected thoughts and memories, her heart began bleeding.

She was going to find these men and kill them with her own two hands. Since that first night in the desert, Milenda was aware of the horrors he had gone through during his long years as an *indent*. What she hadn't realized was that those horrors had left much deeper scars inside Jaali's heart and soul than they had on his body. Abusive sex was the only sex he had ever experienced in his life. He had been so afraid that was all sex really was, he had avoided all human contact once he was a free man. Now that they were together and in love, Jaali had started feeling the pull of sexual desire. For him, that meant one thing only—pain. With shock, she realized that Jaali believed he would hurt her if he ever gave in to his longing for her.

They had broken him, and she was going to break them.

"Sweet Jaali, no," she cooed, enfolding him in an embrace. "You would never hurt me, or anyone else for that matter. What those people did to you was unnatural, evil. You were just a boy, and they used sex as a weapon to keep you down and meek. Good, healthy sex is not like that at all." Or so she was told. Her experience in that area was limited, but her tutors had taught her well. "Sex can be wonderful and wholesome, magical really."

She felt him relax against her, his body not trembling any more. "Are you sure?" His voice was muffled by her robe.

"Well, I can't personally attest to it since I never had it before," she said, happy that he couldn't see her face flush in embarrassment. Her tutors would have flogged her for speaking like that to a man. "But that's what I have been told by many different people who have indeed had sex."

To her surprise, she felt him chuckle against her shoulder. "You have these conversations often?" he asked.

Their bodies separated, and they were finally eye to eye. "No, but... you know... I was curious so I've asked." Realizing she was stuttering, Milenda stopped talking. "Don't tease me."

Color returned to his face, and the smile he gave her illuminated the whole room. "And you trust these people?"

"Of course," she said, a little indignantly. "They wouldn't dare lie to their princess."

"I hope they are right, Milenda." His face was somber again. "I want you so much, but I'm scared of pulling you into my darkness."

She took another look at him and giggled. "We look pitiful. You soaking wet and shivering, me trying to decide whether to be grateful you are such a gentleman or offended for being rejected."

His face assumed a panicked look. "Gods, no. I'm not rejecting you at all. I'm just so—" Without warning, Milenda swooped him into her arms, muffling his last word.

"I know. I'm just teasing you, Jaali," she whispered in his ear. "I can't even imagine what you went through as an *indent*, but I'm hoping one day I can help you erase those fears and make you see things differently." She giggled again. "I thought I was the blushing virgin in this relationship, but you got me beat." He laughed with her.

For a while, they talked in whispers, sitting side by side on that bench, hands and gazes entwined. When it was time to go, Milenda remembered his injured leg and the fact that he wouldn't be able to move at all on his own.

"You stay put until I have a chance to come back," she told him, the royal authority seeping through in her voice. "I'm going to have a little chat with the Elders, and then I will come back and figure out what to do. Promise me you will do as I ask."

Jaali smiled broadly. "Yes, *bwana*, whatever you say." With a playful slap on his shoulder, she let him go and headed back to her chambers to get ready.

***

The desert looked lonelier now that he had been to her side of the world and enjoyed her warmth and company for a while. He leaned against the crag wall, stretching his legs in front of him. His clothes had dried almost instantly upon his return, but the burning in his leg still made him shiver. He was running a fever, he knew. It was not the first time he had been burning with a high temperature. As an *indent*, he had learned how to recognize the signs and how to treat them. Unfortunately, there was not much around him, and the fact he could barely move didn't help matters. He had plenty of water, so he could at least keep hydrated.

He remembered he still had some of the pain-relieving plant Milenda had used on him when he was stung by the bullet ants. He pulled it out of the bag, hoping it would at least help with the pain, which was quickly becoming acute. He rolled up his pants to his knee and cringed at the color and swelling around his ankle. With his knife, he made a deep cut on the plant and squeezed some of the moisture from the inside onto the surface of his inflamed tissue. The relief was almost instant, but he knew it was only a temporary solution to his predicament—just like that thick, long branch on the sand just within arm's reach. He was hoping to use it as a crutch so he could move, however slowly. Better than the alternative.

His thoughts wandered to Milenda and their meeting in the shower. With a heavy heart, he closed his eyes and hoped the princess was not hurt by his rejection. He was so confused and frightened of what he didn't know and didn't understand.

He was just a child when he had been taken into captivity, and by the time he was sixteen, he was little more than a sex slave for the evil man who had purchased him. Before that, he was pure as most children are, pure of heart and soul, but Mnyama had soiled him, had spoiled him. He did not want to do to Milenda what those men and women had done to him. Was there really another way? Was Milenda right? He hoped so, but his heart didn't dare believe it for fear of more heartbreak.

The Elders had not spoken to him since before his fall, almost as if they had expected him to either die or give up. Anger filled his heart. Why would they try to kill the one person who cared for their princess more than anyone else? But then again, he remembered the rumors about her mother's death. Popular belief held that her death had been a murder. He was now inclined to believe the stories.

As if on cue, the voice of an Elder exploded in his head. "Are you there, contender?"

"Yes, I am alive, if that's what you mean." He couldn't keep the bitterness from his voice.

There was a pregnant pause and a murmur of voices in the background. "What do you want me to do now? Throw myself into a fire? Or better yet, lay down in the sun for a few hours and let the heat mummify me?"

"There is no need for that tone of voice." The Elder sounded a little taken aback, be it by the fact he was still alive or that he had uncovered their real intentions, Jaali couldn't tell. "I trust that you have accomplished your trial."

"Yes, I flew off the cliff and almost killed myself in the process." A throbbing pain in his ankle reminded him of the so-called flight.

The Elder cleared his throat. "We're glad you are well." The insincerity in the voice was so obvious, Jaali laughed out loud. "Something amuses you?"

"What do you want?" Jaali's patience had run out, and he was getting tired.

"Your next trial will be announced later today. May the orisas have mercy on you." The voice faded away, and Jaali knew he was alone again.

What crazy task were they going to design for their amusement and his torment? And what exactly was Milenda going to talk to them about? His head burned as much as his ankle now, and his vision begun to blur. He thought of maybe taking a nap, but the idea of allowing himself to close his eyes during the day when danger lurked in every corner was not attractive at all. His body slid down further into the shaded sand. As his heavy eyelids threatened to close, Jaali fought to stay awake, but the fever was taking a firm hold on him. "Gods, Milenda, don't take long," he uttered as a prayer. He was like a sitting duck for any predator in the desert, but his traitorous body dragged him down into slumber anyway.

"Back so soon? You must really miss me." The deep, low voice made his heart clench in his chest.

Mnyama! No, it couldn't be true. It was the fever talking, an illusion created by the high temperature wracking his body and brain. Rationally, he knew this, but another part of him trembled in terror. "We were interrupted earlier, but it looks like you have backed yourself into a corner. You were never very smart, boy." The scathing words pierced his fragile ego like daggers.

His lead-heavy eyelids didn't budge when he tried to open them, to confirm he was just hallucinating again. He could smell the nasty slaver, a mixture of sweat and what he imagined evil smelled like.

No, his senses were tricking him. Mnyama was not there in the middle of the desert with him. The slaver was so scared of the *Jangwa Pori*, he had sent his lackeys to look for Jaali instead of coming after him in person all those years ago. Why would he risk it now? But that smell… Gods, he remembered that smell well. His stomach churned as bile threatened to empty it even more. If he could only open his eyes…

"I've had other boys from the Outerlands, but I have to say, no one compares to you, little Fjorden." The jagged voice reached Jaali's ears like teeth tearing at his skin. "There was something special about the way you whimpered and begged as I undressed you, it made my blood run faster and made it all so much more… pleasant." Mnyama punctuated his words with a mocking laugh that shredded the last thread of rational thought in Jaali's feverish mind.

"Remember the special days when I invited friends to partake of your snowy goodness? Those were the best. How you cried and pleaded before we took turns making you squirm. How you moaned afterward when we left you curled up on the floor, bleeding."

Jaali twisted on the sand, his nightmare too real, so real indeed he could feel the pain and the shame all over again—a pain so overwhelming he had frequently considered suicide. But every attempt was foiled by the slaver, who took great pains to keep him around, alive and available.

What was it about him that made him so special to this horrible man? What could he possibly have done to provoke such evil, such cruelty? Maybe he had evil inside, as well. Mnyama would often whisper in his ear after sodomizing him, "Deep down, you know you like it rough, boy. There is darkness in your soul just like in mine. Darkness attracts darkness, didn't you know?" Was that true? Had some strange wickedness inside of him attracted Mnyama's attention? Had he been born with a stained soul?

A loud sob escaped Jaali's throat. His face was on the ground now and little grains of sand made their way into his mouth.

"Why don't you just kill me once and for all, Mnyama?" Jaali asked.

"So much more fun to kill you from the inside out, one inch at a time. First your body, then your soul, and finally your heart. Break you one little piece at a time." The man's voice rang closer. "Well, do you undress yourself or must I do all the work?"

Weeping in hopeless abandon, Jaali pressed his face into the ground and held it there until he began inhaling the sand. With a strange sense of pleasure, he felt the gritty substance scratch the inside of his nose, his throat, and burn in his lungs. This time, Mnyama wouldn't stop him. He could feel himself going numb, his senses fading, his breathing becoming labored as the sand choked him.

"No, stop it!" The voice interrupted his falling into oblivion and he groaned. He was not going to allow Mnyama to stop him now. When he felt a hand grab him by the shoulder and pull him away from the sand, Jaali gathered the little strength he had left and, aided by the terror in his heart, threw his arm around and hit his attacker across the face. His eyes, still too heavy to open completely, blinked the sand away and glimpsed a figure dropping to the sand with a thud. He coughed convulsively and spat sand out from his mouth while trying to crawl away from the fallen man. Maybe he could make a run for it, except his ankle wouldn't hold him and his body kept collapsing.

He felt hands on him again, and he tried to kick Mnyama with his good leg. But the man was quicker than him, and soon he had Jaali pinned down under his body.

"Stop fighting me, please…"

Since when did Mnyama ask nicely? Something was off, he realized behind the fogginess of his mind. It didn't matter. His strength was totally spent, and he felt himself fade further and further into unconsciousness.

It was over.

Killing Demons

On the way to the Elders' chambers, Milenda met Mama Nyeusi. The old woman positioned herself between her and the door to the palace wing where the chambers were located. Winded and scowling, the *iyalorixá* placed her hands on her hips and gave Milenda a look that spoke volumes. "What are you doing, child?"

Like a true child, Milenda bristled at the woman's words. "None of your business, Mama. I'm a grown woman, and you're standing in my way. Please be so kind as to go away." Her petulant tone belied the sinking feeling she felt inside. She had been taught to respect and obey her elders. Doing the opposite, even for a good cause, killed her a little inside.

"Asha told me you were going to speak to the Elders." Mama Nyeusi scanned her from head to toe and clicked her tongue. "And by the looks of it, not a social call at that. What are you plotting, Milenda?"

The princess lowered her eyes to the floor, embarrassed at her previous tone of voice and frustrated her plan was being foiled. "It's nothing. I was just going to have a little chat about the way they are treating Jaali."

"And allow them to know you've been in touch with him?" Mama Nyeusi lowered her voice. She took quick glances around them. "Have you lost all common sense? What do you think the Elders will do if they realize you have that gift?"

Milenda risked a quick look at the older woman's face. She didn't look happy. "Be delighted and impressed?"

"Don't be daft, child. Stupidity does not become you."

The harsh words hit Milenda with the sting of a slap in the face. Tears immediately burned in her eyes.

The *iyalorixá's* expression softened. "Let's go somewhere private and talk, sweet Jewel. Please."

The fight gone from her heart, Milenda followed her to a room down the hallway. It was mostly empty, save for a couple of chairs, a basic cot, and a small table. It was a room the palace guards sometimes used when on break, to rest for a while or to take a quick nap.

The two women took the chairs, side by side, and Milenda prepared herself mentally for a tongue lashing. But Mama Nyeusi didn't look angry anymore. Her dark, wrinkle-framed eyes were sad as she let out a long, deep sigh.

"Child, I didn't mean to be so harsh," she said, her voice soft as the sound of a rain shower. "You can't let the Elders know about your gift. Never, you hear? You must keep it a secret from everyone including your father."

Milenda's eyes shone with curiosity. "But why? I would have thought they would be excited about it."

"That they would be, but not in a good way." She lowered her voice even further and scooted the chair closer to the young woman's. "Your mother lost her life for less."

The revelation made her heart explode in a crazed rhythm. "What do you mean?"

"What I'm about to tell you must never be repeated, do you understand?" The conspiratorial tone in her voice made Milenda agree immediately. "Your father was found barren shortly after they were married. A nation must have a royal heir or it will fall into chaos, so it was decided that a surrogate father would be picked so your mother could conceive a child. A pool of eligible males was presented to your mother, but she was understandably reluctant to pick one."

"My mother had to pick a lover? That's insane and degrading." Milenda's outrage was obvious in her suddenly strident voice. Catching herself, she lowered her voice to a whisper. "That's awful and so… wrong."

"Yes, I agree. However, it is not an uncommon practice among the royal families in Afrika. Our fertile male pool is dwindling fast, and the crown must protect their lineage any way they can."

Mama Nyeusi wiped a hand across her eyes. She seemed exhausted. "Your mother requested some time to think about it. During that time, she met a young man from Nyota lineage and fell in love. Nyotas are a vanishing race, as you well know. People are scared of what they don't understand, and

Nyotas are almost mystical for most. They have been hunted down, killed, or just plainly ignored for centuries now."

"I'm a Nyota. Does that mean I will be hated for it as a monarch?" Milenda cringed at the thought of her own people hating her because of her race. She was no different from anybody else, save for her *matangazos*. She bled like everyone else.

"Only time will tell, Milenda. I think your people truly love you, and you may be the one thing that will change the way they look at the Nyota as a race." Mama Nyeusi patted Milenda's hand. "Your mother kept it a secret, and when she became pregnant, she was scared. She knew that choosing a Nyota for the father of a royal child was not going to be taken lightly, and there was a very good chance the Elders would make her abort."

"They wouldn't dare!" A new, red-hot anger was blazing in her heart. Who did these Elders think they were, playing around with people's lives like that?

"Yes, they would. The Elders have held the true reins of power in Natale for far too long, and they won't hesitate in doing whatever it takes to protect that." The *iyalorixá* smiled sadly. "Your mother came up with a plan that saved your life, my child. She told the Elders she was ready to choose a surrogate and then pretended it was his seed. The Elders bought it and so did your father. You were allowed to be born. Once you were born, there was nothing they could do about it. Royal heirs are blessed by the orisas shortly after their birth, and no one—not even the Elders—dare to go against them."

"I don't understand. Didn't they see my spots as soon as

I was born? Why did they allow me to leave the birth room alive?"

"Nyota babies are born unmarked. Your *matangazos* didn't manifest themselves until you were about one-year-old. By then, it was too late to do anything about it." Mama Nyeusi's voice dropped another octave. "Unfortunately, the same couldn't be said about your mother and the man who had fathered you. No one ever found out the real story, but both your mother and the Nyota man she so loved met their untimely deaths soon after your first birthday."

A sob caught in Milenda's throat. She had always had her suspicions, and she had never trusted the Elders, but her innocent mind could have never suspected such a terrible thing.

Her Nyota genes had always been a mystery to her. She'd assumed her mother had some Nyota ancestors. It was not unheard of for certain traits to be skipped by generations, only to be picked up much later. "Did my father know about this? My mother's murder?"

"I truly don't know, child." The old woman's voice reflected her sadness. "I'm sure he was not happy about another man fathering his child, but would he willingly be part of his own wife's murder? I don't know."

Milenda realized she was crying. Drops of salty tears rolled down her cheeks and hung precariously on the tip of her nose as she hung her head. Her *matangazos* burned like they had never burned before, and the anger in her chest was coiled like a cobra ready to attack.

"How do you know all this, Mama?"

Mama Nyeusi licked her lips and sighed. "I was your mother's *iyalorixá*, as well. I was the one who came up with the plan to save you. Unfortunately, I couldn't come up with a plan to save your mother and father, as well." She smiled at the memory. "They were beautiful people, inside and out. Very much like you. They would have been so proud of the way you handle yourself and how you stand up to injustice. They would not want you to be a moving target for those who thirst for power and for those who don't mind who they hurt to protect that power."

Milenda licked the tears collecting around her lips. "But I must protect Jaali. They are trying to kill him, and they will succeed if I don't do something fast."

"You are already doing something, child." The woman leaned forward in the chair and held Milenda's hands in hers. "Be smart. They don't know what you can do. Your secret gift is the only weapon you have against their scheming. Do not give it away. Once Jaali gets to the end of the Trials, they will be powerless to do anything about it. The law says you can pick from any of the fertile males in the land. They can't stop you."

"Jaali's lying at the bottom of a crag right now, hurt and running a fever." Milenda's voice broke at the thought of her *wimbo wa moyo*, alone and hurting in the desert. "He may die. He has nothing to fight the fever with, and I can't bring him anything, just myself."

"Are you sure?"

The question surprised Milenda. "What do you mean? You think I could bring something with me?"

Mama Nyeusi straightened her back. "You said you can touch each other just as solidly as if you were actually there. It is possible that if you have something on you, that something becomes as material as you do. No harm in trying."

The Jewel jumped off her seat and wrapped her arms around the old woman's neck in a tight hug. "Thank you, Mama," she said, sobs choking her voice. "You just gave me hope again."

The *iyalorixá* laughed and got up. "You are choking me, child. Let's put some space between you and the Elders before they smell something is afoot. And let's take those awful clothes off you, as well. What possessed you to wear that?"

Milenda walked out of the tiny room, still holding on to the old woman. "I wanted to look very royal." She giggled. "They are awful, aren't they? So tell me, what can I bring with me to help with a fever?"

Milenda and her mentor walked the hallways, arm in arm, talking quietly about herbs and potions and plotting how to save the pale man who was to be her royal consort.

***

As her head hit the sand, Milenda allowed herself a moment to collect her thoughts. The right side of her face and her eye burned, and her vision was blurred. She had never been hit before. No one in the kingdom, her father included, would dare to lay a hand on her. Law dictated that physical violence directed at a royal heir was grounds for immediate imprisonment and possible execution.

After a few seconds, she sat up, shook the sand out of her hair, and searched for Jaali. He was not far, scrambling to get up and falling every time as his leg gave up under his weight. With a tightness taking over her chest, she watched as her future husband crawled on the sand, desperately trying to get away from whatever was haunting him.

Milenda had reached out shortly after collecting what she thought she may be able to carry with her across the space that separated her from Jaali; some herbs, a disinfectant, bandages. She had stuffed her pockets and even the inside of her *iqhiya* with the healing materials, hoping they would be carried along with her when she reached out to Jaali. She never had the chance to check it.

As soon as she arrived at the bottom of the crag, she watched in horror as Jaali tried to suffocate himself with sand. Without hesitation, she ran to him, grabbed him by the shoulders, and tried to pull him away. To her surprise, he mumbled something, his mouth spitting out sand, and swung his fist straight into her face. Hard.

She fell, momentarily blacking out from the impact and confused by his reaction. Something must have happened while she was gone. What had the Elders done now?

On slightly wobbly legs, Milenda got herself back on her feet and followed the frantic young Fjorden across the sand. He tried to kick her, but she was able to avoid his leg. Not knowing what else to do, Milenda sat on him, holding his arms down before he could hit her again.

"Stop fighting me, please…"

Jaali's belligerence seemed to suddenly ebb away, and his

body relaxed under her until it was completely still. He had passed out.

Worried, she slid off him and checked his mouth. There was still a lot of sand in it, but not enough to kill him, and she hoped he hadn't inhaled too much of it. He was breathing regularly when she turned him on his side so he would not swallow any more of the irritant. Only then did she sit beside him to check her pockets.

A smile stretched across her lips as she discovered the herbs and disinfectant were still there. Her *iqhiya* was laying some ways from her where it had fallen off her head, and she could see the bandages peeking from inside.

Gingerly, she touched her face and realized it was swollen where Jaali had hit her with his fist. Her eye was tender and so was the corner of her lips. She would survive, she concluded. Jaali might not if she didn't take care of his injury. He was hot to the touch, and his behavior spoke of hallucinations brought on by his high fever.

With great tenderness and care, Milenda cleaned his leg wound, treated it with some herbs, and wrapped it tightly with a bandage. Then she drenched another bandage in the cool water of the nearby stream and dabbed his forehead to cool him off.

In his frenzy, Jaali had moved away from the shade. With strength she didn't know she had, she dragged him slowly until he was under the protective shelter of the crag wall. With his head lying on her lap, she looked at him. Jaali still appeared tormented, his mouth twisted into a frown of agony. She wanted to wipe that frown off his lips just as she wiped his brow, but she knew she couldn't. He had lived through things she couldn't even imagine. His scars were deep, and undoubtedly had been reopened after what the Elders had made him go through. She hated them with all the passion of her young heart, and she vowed to herself and Yemanjá to make them pay for what they had done to her mother and to Jaali.

Jaali moved on her lap, and in spite of herself, she prepared for another attack. Instead, he turned his head to look at her, and his pale eyes filled with tears at the sight of her.

"Milenda, *msichana*. You're here."

Exhaling in relief, Milenda helped him sit up against the rocky wall and checked his forehead for fever. He was still burning up.

"Oh gods, what happened to you?" he asked, a hand reaching out for her swollen face. A cloud of fear covered the light in his eyes. "Did I do that to you? You're hurt..." As realization washed over him, tears began rolling down his cheeks. "I'm evil, Milenda. I don't deserve you. I will hurt you over and over again because that's all I've ever known. I don't know another way."

Making a mental note to hunt down Mnyama and make him pay alongside with the Elders, Milenda pulled Jaali to her. "Stop. You didn't hurt me. You were fighting your demons, not me. I was just in the wrong place at the wrong time." He coughed out more sand. "You are burning with fever, hallucinating. We need to get that temperature down."

She lit a small fire to make tea and made him rinse his mouth with water until most of the sand was gone. Mama

Nyeusi had taught her how to brew a special tea to fight a fever. She hoped it would work quickly. Seeing Jaali sinking into his nightmarish world was tearing her heart into small pieces.

She offered him a cup. "Drink this. It will chase your ghosts away."

He accepted it gratefully. After he finished it, he rested his head on her chest. With her hand soothing him, Jaali slowly relaxed and faded into what she hoped was the peace of a dreamless sleep.

"My ghosts will never really go away, *msichana*." His voice startled her. She thought he was already asleep, but he was watching her. "I'm afraid they will never go away."

"You are not alone anymore, *wimbo wa moyo*." Dipping her head a little, she kissed his forehead. "Remember that. I will fight your demons with you. I love you."

Jaali closed his eyes again. "I love you, my jewel. I love you, too." And he fell asleep.

As much as Milenda wanted to go back to the palace and talk to Mama Nyeusi about all that had transpired, she didn't dare leave Jaali alone. His fever seemed to be receding, but bouts of delirium still assailed him, and he barely gained consciousness in the eight hours she had been with him. Persistently, she dosed him with the healing tea and cleaned and treated his injured leg. Cold sweats had drenched his clothes, which now stuck to him like a second skin. She collected as much water as she could from the stream and washed him with some leftover bandage. Jaali's face relaxed as she wiped the cold, wet cloth across his forehead, his eyes, and his lips.

For a moment, she thought he was actually smiling.

Now I'm the one hallucinating.

Dousing the cloth again, Milenda wiped the skin on his neck, chest, and arms. She struggled with the heaviness of his inert body to remove his shirt so she could better reach his skin.

Even in his ailing state, Jaali was beautiful. His alabaster skin, so different from her own, seemed to glow in the impending darkness. He was slim, but strong muscles corded his arms, chest, and abdomen. A frisson of desire ran through her, much to her dismay. How could she feel like that when he was so sick and vulnerable? Hoping the coolness of the wet cloth on his skin would help bring the fever down, Milenda continued her ministrations, stopping only to take the shirt to the stream and rinse it off. Even though night was upon them, there was still enough heat in the air to dry it quickly and effectively. After draping the soaked shirt over a nearby rock, Milenda returned to Jaali's side and resumed the process of tempering him down.

The dark of night had rolled over and around them by the time Jaali finally moved. The light of a full moon gave the whole area a special glow, turning an otherwise desolate location into a watercolor painting.

"Milenda?" His voice was weak at first, hesitant, as if he were still not sure what he was seeing was real. "Is that you?"

Milenda brushed the wet rag over his chest again. "Yes, *wimbo wa moyo*, it's me. Everything is okay. Your fever is breaking, I think." Was his platinum hair actually shining?

Jaali's smile brightened the night. She helped him sit up

against her and checked his forehead for signs of fever. He was definitely cooler; his temperature was almost back to normal. "Have you been here all along?" He held her hand and brought it up to his lips. "Thank you, *msichana*."

Milenda carefully kept herself behind him, not wanting him to notice her badly swollen eye and face. She had been applying the salve from the *dawa* leaf to stave off the pain and cold water patches whenever she could to bring down the swelling, but her body was not used to any kind of abuse and had reacted viscerally.

"I'm so happy you're feeling better, Jaali. I thought I was going to lose you for a while. Do you remember anything?"

Jaali shook his head violently. "I don't want to think about it. It wasn't… pleasant." He kissed her hand again. "You must be tired."

He gently pulled on her hand to make her come around and face him. Afraid of his reaction, Milenda braced herself while allowing him to turn her.

The light on his face came to an abrupt death. The violent, swelling on her cheek must have been a sight, for his eyes grew somber, and his lips turned into a frown. "Gods! Look what I did to you. What is wrong with me?"

Determined not to let him go down that path again, Milenda wrapped her arms around him and whispered in his ear, "You didn't hit me. You hit whoever was attacking you in your nightmare. You would never hit me. I know you. You're a gentle soul who would not hurt anyone unless you were defending yourself."

Jaali sighed, his warm breath blowing shivers down

Milenda's neck. "You don't know this darkness I carry, my princess. Mnyama always said I was evil inside. Evil attracts evil, he said."

Pulling away, Milenda stared at him, her mouth set in a hard frown. "Mnyama is evil. Evil men relish in destroying what's good and pure. Don't let his deviant thoughts and words destroy the goodness in your heart. Don't believe him, because he lied to justify his cruelty. Promise me you won't heed his words."

Jaali's eyes softened and he raised his hand to her swollen cheek. "Let me take care of that. It's my turn to take care of you." He reached out for the wet rag she had been using on him and doused it in the water before gently patting her bruised face. "How are you going to explain this at the palace?"

Milenda giggled quietly. "I don't know. I'm pretty klutzy, everyone knows that. I'll tell them I had a close encounter with a door." The young Fjorden laughed with her, his nightmares now distant enough to allow him to breathe easy. "They'll believe me. I've told many a fib in my time, and no one has ever questioned me."

Side by side they rested, their bodies stretched on the sand, Jaali's hand underneath her neck. The magical, star-studded skies and the silence of the night enveloped them in a comforting sense of peace and safety. Milenda turned to him, and her eyes were drawn to his bare chest, now dry but still glowing under the moonlight. An overwhelming craving came upon her, shocking in its intensity.

As if pulled by invisible strings, her hand came to rest on his collarbone. Jaali flinched, glanced at her, and then relaxed against her touch. His watery aquamarine eyes seemed to emit their own light as they met hers. She spread her fingers across his upper chest and savored the contact along the sensitive skin of her palm. A jolt of excitement went through her when she felt Jaali's heart accelerate under her hand. His reaction emboldened her, and she slid her hand along the center of his torso down to the tight muscles across his abdomen. She felt him quiver at her touch.

Their eyes locked in a question as their breathing quickened.

"Milenda?" His question sparked the fire quickly growing inside of her. She sat up and then, bending down, she touched her lips to Jaali's, lightly, teasingly. "I don't know—"

Milenda cut him off with another kiss, this one deeper and more passionate. Jaali responded in kind. His tongue explored Milenda's swollen lips first, then her mouth, deepening the kiss and waking up every nerve in her body.

"Are you sure, *msichana*? It may not be safe. I may not be safe."

"Shut up and kiss me, you beautiful Fjorden." Her playful words were all the permission he needed. In a smooth move, he flipped over her. Supporting himself on one arm, Jaali stared deeply into her eyes. It felt as if he were looking into her soul, and her body melted into his, wanting more. "Love me, Jaali."

His mouth descended on hers again. With a moan, Jaali suckled on her bottom lip, making her body turn liquid. Hungry hands enveloped Jaali's body and pushed him against her. With a mixture of delight and wonder, Milenda noticed his body reacting to her, and her own desire grew exponentially. Jaali's hands inched their way up the inside of her *kanga* top until she could feel his fingers touching the bare skin under her breasts.

Pushing him away gently, Milenda pulled the top over her head and watched Jaali as he took her in with thirsty eyes. Suddenly fearful the sight of her bare breasts was displeasing to him, she attempted to cover herself by crossing her arms, but the Fjorden stopped her and slowly uncrossed them. His gaze warmed her from head to toe.

"You're beautiful, *msichana.*"

"You're beautiful, too."

Jaali brought his lips down onto one of her breasts. Her *matangazos* started their hot-cold dance along her neck and shoulder as she arched up against his mouth, hungry for more. The voices in her head were quiet for once, and she mouthed a silent thank you. Jaali's mouth moved to her other breast and played havoc with her senses.

Her inexperienced hands reached for the ties on his pants, and he followed her lead to unwrap her *kanga* skirt away from her body. Soon, only her undergarments stood between them. Jaali tried to straddle her, but his injured leg wouldn't cooperate. Milenda, rolling herself over him, sat on top of him, her legs bookending his hips. Heat rose to her face as she felt his arousal against her, and for a moment, she wondered whether she was doing the right thing. With her inside voices silenced, she couldn't be sure; but it felt so right, it just couldn't possibly be wrong.

Jaali groaned as she rubbed herself gently against him,

trying it out, testing the waters. "Gods, Milenda, I want you." His voice was husky with desire, his hands resting on her hips, guiding her as she gyrated on top of him. He sat up suddenly, wrapping her legs around his waist, his naked chest against her breasts.

Their lips met again in a hungry kiss, and Milenda felt his desire for her against the thin material of her intimate wear. Excited and scared all at once, Milenda pulled on her panties, trying to remove them.

As she stood up to do it, Jaali took hold of her hands and dropped them alongside her body. "I'll do it," he said, his head tilted upward to look at her. A nervous giggle escaped her mouth when the young Fjorden, his face directly in front of her belly, pulled down on her panties until they began sliding painfully slowly down her hips and legs. He whimpered and began trailing kisses down from her bellybutton.

Milenda couldn't handle it anymore. She straddled him again, shivering from excitement and pleasure as she felt his warmth meet hers. Nothing her tutors had ever taught her could have prepared her for this feeling of overwhelming yearning, this deep-seated need for something only Jaali could give her.

She looked into his sky blue eyes, darkened by desire, and smiled. "Make me yours, Jaali."

He was breathing heavily and looked divided between elation and fear. His gaze bounced from her eyes to her lips, as if trying to decide what to do next. With his hands on her hips, he pulled her up just enough to reposition her lower body on his, and she held her breath, waiting for what was about to happen.

But at the last minute, Jaali pulled her off him and sat her down beside him.

"I won't do it. I won't hurt you." He dropped to the sand, naked, eyes closed, punching the ground with his fists while she sat next to him, still shocked by his reaction, but also worried about him.

"What are you talking about, Jaali? You weren't hurting me." On her knees, she half crawled to his side. Afraid he was running a fever again, she checked his forehead, but he flinched away from her touch and rolled on his side.

"Stop it, Jaali. What are you so afraid of? I want you to make love to me, do you hear me? I want you to."

He lay there, his eyes still closed, his back turned to her. Milenda scooted closer and stretched herself along his back, molding her body to his, one hand coming around his chest and resting where she could feel his heart beat. This time, he didn't flinch away from her, and he allowed her to nestle her head on his shoulder, lips against his skin.

"What are you so afraid of, *wimbo wa moyo*? You would never hurt me." Her hand traveled down to his stomach and then lower. Jaali moaned, but didn't pull away. Her lips traveled along his neck and his shoulder, leaving a trail of light kisses in their wake. "You won't hurt me. I know that. Why don't you believe that?"

Jaali turned to face her. "How can you be so sure?" His transparent eyes were full of doubt and fear.

Milenda kissed his lips. "Because I know you. I've seen the goodness in you through your eyes and felt your generous heart beat against my hand." She kissed him again. "I know who you are, and you are not this wicked person you think you are. You need to believe it."

Hesitation reflected in his face for a moment, but the clouds vanished from his eyes soon after. Enveloping her with his arms, he rolled on top of her and kissed her desperately like a drowning man seeking air. "I love you."

Her legs wrapped themselves around his waist and Milenda whimpered as she felt him throbbing against her sensitive skin. She pulled him closer, her hands flattened across his bottom in silent supplication for more contact. Supporting himself on one arm, Jaali looked at her, his eyes misty with desire.

"Your beautiful face… I've ruined it." With his free hand, he traced the edges of her bruised skin, making her quiver with pleasure. "I'm so sorry."

Milenda brought her hand between them and caressed him, surprised by her own boldness. Jaali moaned.

"I told you already," she whispered in a voice made thick with yearning. "You didn't ruin anything. The bruises will fade and I will still be here for you."

Jaali arched against her hand before bringing his lips down on hers again. She felt him tremble against her and she came undone. Jaali moved his hips and in one single move became one with her. Their bodies joined in a frantic dance, their rhythm bringing them so high, Milenda thought she was flying, until Jaali climaxed and quaked in her arms, surrendering into his release.

They lay quiet for a few moments, enjoying their body contact, wrapped in each other's arms. Milenda kissed the corner of his mouth. "I told you, you wouldn't hurt me."

She smiled wide, relishing in his expression of awe and surprise. He returned the smile, relief washing all the worry away from his face. "I didn't hurt you," he whispered to himself, as if trying to make sense of it all. "I didn't hurt you at all."

"Much the opposite, *wimbo wa moyo*, you made me feel like I was able to fly and catch a star." She paused and kissed him again. He gave in to her demanding lips and kissed her back, confident this time, sure of the effect he had on her.

"Did we chase your demons away?" The look on his face was all the answer she needed. Jaali now knew he had none of Mnyama's cruelty in him. He was free.

Bliss

———————————————

Still in a dreamlike state, Jaali washed himself in the stream, grateful for the life-giving water that refreshed his aching body. Every inch of him was covered in sand, and he could still feel the gritty substance between his gums and his teeth. The stream was not deep enough for full immersion, but just sitting in the cool water, scooping it in his cupped hands and pouring it over his head, was heavenly.

After a while, he just sat there quietly, muttering a prayer of thanks to the orisas who had allowed him that small luxury. Grateful didn't even begin to express how he felt, not only for the plentiful water, but especially for Milenda and what had happened between them the night before. A great weight had been lifted from his shoulders, and Milenda had everything to do with that.

He had never known love, not since he had been forcibly taken from his parents' home as a child. Never having experienced kindness or care toward him of any sort while growing into adulthood, Jaali had always assumed—feared, really—there was none to be had. Or worse, that all those years of cruelty and abuse at the hands of Mnyama and his cronies had broken him to the point where he would never be able to love or be loved. The sexual abuse he had suffered since he was barely sixteen, and the brainwashing Mnyama had inflicted on him for five years, had broken him inside. Mnyama had effectively convinced him that there was evil inside of him, and that was why he had been so savagely punished for years. The cruel slaver had him convinced he would never be able to have a healthy, satisfying sexual life with anyone; he had him believing that, when the time came, he would be as barbaric and cruel to his partner as Mnyama and all the others, male and female, had been to him.

Milenda had proven the slaver wrong, and in spite of his situation and being stuck in an unyielding desert with an injured ankle, he felt like a new man. He was reborn, as if parts of him had mended the moment his gold-hearted princess had become one with him. His heart was overflowing with love and joy, and for a moment, he forgot where he was. He simply enjoyed the soothing effect of the water on his parched skin and the warm feelings inside of him.

The hated voice in his head brought him crashing down into reality. "Contender, we have decided on your last trial."

His stomach clenched. What were they going to have him do now?

"Your task is simple. You must keep going west until you find the first sign of the jungle. You will then be on the edge of civilization. We will further guide you then. May the orisas be merciful."

It sounded too simple, too easy. What were they up to? Jaali couldn't believe they were actually giving him a break, a respite from the troubles he had encountered so far. There was no point in musing about it though. He wouldn't know until he got there, so he might as well get ready for the journey.

It wouldn't be easy. His leg wouldn't allow him to walk very far, not even with the help of the makeshift crutch he and Milenda had concocted before she had left this morning. But he could at least move, and that in itself was a blessing. He could as easily be dead, or close to it, if Milenda and Mjusi hadn't stepped in to help him.

Dripping water, Jaali wobbled out of the stream and, not waiting to dry up, slipped into his freshly-washed clothes lying on a small patch of grass nearby. He briefly wondered how the other contenders were doing. Had any of them reached the end yet, and were their trials as difficult and cruel as his were? He doubted it. The Elders were truly trying to eliminate him from the race, so he guessed the other contenders were having a much easier time at it than himself. After all, the desert alone was a massive and difficult trial.

Supporting himself on the crutch, Jaali hopped his way to the shaded patch of sand where he had made love to Milenda the night before. A warm, fuzzy feeling coursed through his veins at the memory. Her golden brown skin had been like silk under his fingers, and her *matangazos'* glowing had told him she felt as happy as he did.

He smiled at the thought as he hid in the shade to take a nap. Milenda had made him promise he would wait for her before venturing into the desert again. Without too much sleep the night before, he was more than happy to oblige. It didn't take long for slumber to take him into its welcoming arms.

***

Peaceful and pure. Those were the two words she would have used to describe how Jaali looked as he slept in the shade of the wall. His almost-white hair was sticking out every which way, and his full lips were turned into a smile. Grateful he was having good dreams after all the nightmares he had experienced, Milenda sat next to him, reluctant to wake him.

However, it was early afternoon, and they had to get moving. This part of the desert was not as arid and there were plenty of green areas with abundant water sources, but if he was to ever get to the end of the journey, he couldn't stop for too long.

Leaning forward, she placed a light kiss on his lips, and then another. Jaali opened his lips and nibbled at hers, making her swoon in near ecstasy.

"Sweet Jewel," he whispered against her mouth. She smiled and pulled him up. "Was it a dream?"

Her *matangazos* burned a little as she lowered her eyes to hide her sudden embarrassment. "No, it was all real. Why?"

Reaching out, he held her hand and pulled her into his lap. He whimpered. "Gods. We shouldn't have, should we? You're the Jewel and I'm nothing."

Milenda caught his head between her hands and stared him straight in the eye. "Don't you start. Don't ruin the best thing that has ever happened to me, Jaali. We became one last night, and it was heaven. Wasn't it like that for you, too?"

She could feel him respond to her under her *kanga* skirt. "Yes, Milenda, it was heaven. Better than heaven. I was so scared, but… your love slew my demons last night. I can sleep in peace now, *msichana*. Thank you." Pulling her closer, he linked his lips to hers in a long kiss.

"As much as I would love to stay here and do this, we really must get moving, Jaali." Milenda got up on jellied legs, her heart beating frantically in her chest and her *matangazos* burning bright again.

Still sitting on the sand, Jaali looked up at her, a cocky smile on his face. It was the first time Milenda remembered him looking so relaxed, so young and confident. "Are you going to walk with me? Isn't that cheating?"

The princess laughed while picking up the makeshift crutch from the ground and handing it to him. "Cheating? Really? You know perfectly well that if we hadn't been cheating all along, you would be dead by now. The Elders don't play fair, so why should we?" There was a new bitterness in her voice, and she wondered if she would ever lose that now that she was privy to more than she had ever wanted to know about the Elders and her father.

With some difficulty, the Fjorden got on his feet, and leaning on the crutch, took a few steps toward her. His smile was no longer on his lips. "What's wrong? Something happened while you were gone?"

Milenda looped her arm around his, and they started their journey across the desert. "It was nothing. You shouldn't worry about it." Reluctant to give him any more to worry about, the princess focused on their labored walk on the sand. "Does it hurt?"

Jaali stopped and looked at her, his brows knitted in worry. "I'm not taking another step until you tell me what's going on. You are obviously upset about something. Tell me. We're one now. There should be no secrets between us."

"I found out that the Elders have been pretty easy on the other contenders so they could really cast their creative cruelty on you." Resuming their walk, Jaali let out a sigh and gave her arm a little squeeze. "I also found out that the first contender has arrived in the city."

Jaali started a little but didn't stop his limping progress. "Well, we knew it was going to happen sooner or later. More will come, I'm sure. You know who?"

Milenda silently cursed the sand that kept insinuating itself inside her shoes. "No, I don't. I will meet him sometime tomorrow for the ceremonial welcome." Silence fell on them for a few moments. "It should have been you." The wistful whisper hung between them. "Instead, here you are, hurt and still way off from the finish line. It's not fair."

Jaali laughed, making Milenda turn to him suddenly. "Nothing in my life has ever been fair, Milenda. Or in yours. I mean, is it fair that you had to grow up without a mother and barely a father? Is it fair that you must choose a life partner in spite of your youth? Is it fair that a group of men dictate everyone's lives in Natale?"

Milenda shook her head, her eyes on the sand.

"It's just the way of the world. But we can change it—we are changing it already, you and I."

"Mama Nyeusi says that once I'm a full-blown monarch, I'll be able to do a lot more. I just don't understand how my father can allow the Elders to do what they do and do nothing about it. You have to have a heart of stone to just… not care."

Tears danced in her eyes. Her heart was having such a hard time reconciling the fact that her father was not a good man, a caring man. When had he turned into this person? Had he always been like that, or had the whole thing with her mother turned him into this?

"You will be different." Jaali stopped and turned her toward him. "Look at me, *msichana*. You will be the best queen Natale has ever known."

"With you by my side." It was a question. The closer they got to each other, the more she feared something terrible would separate them. "You will be there with me, right?"

Jaali held her face with his hands and kissed her briefly. "Always. I will always be there." Their eyes locked for a moment, and Milenda felt a small fire sparking inside her again. She forced herself to look away and resume their walk.

The journey took a lot longer than it should have, but Jaali needed frequent stops to rest and to change the bandages on his ankle. The swelling had gone down quite a bit, but with the effort of the walk, it was starting to swell again. Milenda fussed over it while the young Fjorden made light of their situation. She smiled inwardly, knowing he was trying to ease her mind.

Not easily accomplished. Her heart felt as if someone had clenched it within an iron fist. She worried about everything; Jaali's future, her future, the future of her country. Not for the first time, she wished she had been born a regular girl without the weight of the responsibilities that fell upon a princess.

It was already dark by the time they arrived at a sheltered area that seemed safe enough to spend the night in. There was a running stream and plenty of shade. The trees were becoming bigger and more luxuriant as they headed west, approaching the borders of the city. They were on the very edge of the desert.

All this meant was that the earlier obstacles had been replaced by different ones, just as dangerous. Here there was not much of a risk of becoming dehydrated or suffering heat stroke, but there were more animals and even some wild tribes who prowled this area of the desert. Mjusi had joined them at the end of the day at her request. He would be a good guard against the dangers lurking in the dark and afford them some sense of relief.

While Jaali went to the stream to wash up, Milenda built a small fire to heat up their meager supply of food. Mjusi had followed the Fjorden to the water to keep an eye on him in spite of all the protesting.

"Mjusi has a surprise for you," Jaali said, limping toward her, hair dripping water.

Mjusi extended his massive head and dropped something furry at her feet. Much to her surprise and some horror, Milenda realized it was a small rodent. Jaali, trying to hide the amusement in his voice, dropped to the ground next to the fire.

"He thought he would go hunting for us."

Controlling a dry heave, the princess managed a small smile as she patted her scaly friend's head. "Thank you, my friend, but you should eat it. You'll need your strength to keep guard all night." She could see Jaali snickering from the corner of her eye. "Please, I insist. We have enough for tonight."

The winged creature let out a grateful groan, and in a smooth move, swooped his mouth over the dead rodent and swallowed it whole. Milenda averted her eyes, her stomach churning in a mixture of hunger and disgust. Finished with his feast, the lizard-like beast flew away to keep guard from the treetops.

"Stop laughing. It's not that funny." But she was also laughing now, chuckling under her breath while she heated up the leftover meat from an earlier kill, smaller but much more appetizing than the rodent Mjusi had generously offered them.

As tired as they both were, sleep wouldn't come easy tonight, with the events of the previous night still fresh in their minds. Suddenly shy of each other, they sat close together by the fire in silence. Their bodies alive and burning like the flames in the pit, both afraid to acknowledge it to each other.

Finally, tired of sitting still, Milenda stood. "I'm just going to wash up in the stream. Why don't you sleep? Mjusi will keep me company." As she walked away, she saw Jaali stretching in the grassy sand, ready to take a nap.

Mixed feelings of relief and frustration filled her chest as she undressed by the stream, the moonlight falling on her like a beam of light from the gods. She felt different somehow. Not better or worse, just different, as if a piece had been added to her. Maybe when they joined, Jaali's soul had fused with hers, and she carried them both within her now. With that pleasant thought, she waded into the water.

***

Jaali was not sleeping. Watching Milenda from underneath half-closed lids, he struggled to decide what to do. She seemed so ill at ease around him, or maybe shy. What was the right thing to do or say?

He hoped with all the passion of his young heart that she was not regretting last night. He didn't think he could handle the disappointment. Being with her had been the best thing that ever happened to him in his whole twenty-seven years of life. Sure, he must have had some very happy moments in the bosom of his own family as a child, but the darkness of what happened later had muddied the memories, jumbled them up to the point where he couldn't make out any details or even tell for certain they weren't just dreams rather than real recollections. The last thing he wanted was to mess up his relationship with the Jewel of Natale.

She was everything. He had lived all the years since he freed himself hiding in plain sight. His life had no frills. Jaali woke up, went to work, came home, worked on his wooden art, ate, and slept. Nothing as capricious as friends or any kind of relationships other than passing acquaintances had been part of his daily living for the past few years. Not being able to bring himself to trust anyone enough to share himself with at any level, the young Fjorden was more than happy living a solitary existence only broken by his daily lessons at the university—until Milenda had crashed into him that rainy day. Ever since then, his life had taken a surprising and unsettling turn. Suddenly, he found himself wanting more, so much more.

Jaali sat up and watched as Milenda reached the stream. With a hunger he had never thought he would have, he followed her with his eyes as she, oblivious of being watched, peeled her clothes off and walked stark naked into the water. The moon beamed down on her as if the gods themselves wanted him to see her in every detail. Her *matangazos* shone along her shoulder, giving her skin an otherworldly gleam. Her bare back plunged down to her small, round hips and her hair, freed of the *iqhiya* she wore earlier, stuck out wildly, as if having a will of its own.

Jaali's stomach clenched, and he felt himself respond to her. Savoring the feeling, Jaali uttered a small groan of pleasure. Until yesterday, that surge of desire had never been welcome, but now he allowed himself the chance to enjoy it, to encourage it even, because he knew it was wholesome and stemmed from a good place. He stretched, picked up the crutch, and stood, making his way quietly to the water's edge.

Milenda looked like an angel, splashing the cold water over her body, unaware of his presence. Jaali dropped the crutch and began stripping off his clothes. Once freed of all clothing, he wobbled slowly into the water, ignoring the pain in his ankle.

The princess turned around, startled by the noise, and he almost fell as her beauty hit him full force; her petite shape was pure perfection. His breath caught in his throat, and he lifted a hand to calm her. His own heart had started a crazed gallop inside his chest. To his surprise, Milenda, eyes misty with longing, took a few steps forward until she was standing right in front of him, so close he could feel the coolness of her wet skin.

"You shouldn't be walking around without the crutch," she said in a whisper, as her hand reached out and slid along his arm from his shoulders to his fingers in a maddening caress.

"I couldn't sleep." Mimicking her, he slid his fingers along her shoulder, down her silken arm until they met her hand. Their fingers interlaced, Jaali brought them to his lips and kissed hers slowly, his eyes never leaving her glittering emerald jewels.

She moved closer until their bodies were touching. She could surely feel his obvious desire for her. There was no way to hide it, as close as they were, and for a panicky moment he wondered if it would scare her,

Instead, she pulled him closer. "I love you."

Head tilted upward, Milenda offered him her lips. Gladly, he took them between his in a gentle nibble. His body was on fire as she pried her way into his mouth, her tongue caressing his. Forgetting his leg couldn't carry him, Jaali shifted his weight to it as he brought his arms around Milenda.

Together they fell into the cool water with a big splash. Their laughter broke the quiet of the night, and Mjusi came to check what had happened. Milenda waved him away.

"It's okay, Mjusi. We're just playing." The winged creature tilted his head as if doubting her words. But then, apparently satisfied, he flew up into the trees again.

Lying entwined in the shallow stream, they stopped laughing and locked eyes. Jaali could feel her heart thudding against his chest, joining his in a deafening chorus. Their intimate contact had sent her *matangazos* into a frenzy. He lowered his lips to her shoulder and felt the throbbing of her markings against his mouth. The knowledge that she was as aroused as he was set his whole being on fire.

Abandoning her shoulder, he kissed his way to one of her breasts. They were perfect; small and round, they fit completely in his hand. Drunk with desire, Jaali brought Milenda close to rapture with his tongue. Despite his haze, the young Fjorden remembered that she had not reached a climax their first time, and he so wanted her to. Milenda had taken him to heaven the night before, and he wanted to take her there, as well.

Milenda's shy hands came alive on his body, exploring every plane, every curve. Tracing Jaali's well-formed muscles proved to be a source of great pleasure for her, it seemed. It certainly was a source of great pleasure for him. Every touch of her fingers along his back, his chest, his hips, and his lower abdomen brought along waves of ecstasy.

"I didn't know." His voice in her ear startled her.

"You didn't know what, *wimbo wa moyo*?" she asked, her fingers stopping their exploration.

Jaali cupped her breast and gently brushed his lips over it. "I didn't know it could be like this."

Arching her body toward his mouth, Milenda promised to make him forget all of the horrible things done to him by making all-new, beautiful memories.

Her legs wrapped themselves around his waist and he thrust himself into her—gently at first, still scared of hurting her, but picking up momentum as Milenda whimpered in his arms, coaxing him to keep going. Faster and faster until they both reached their climax, their bodies tensing and then relaxing into each other's arms in blissful exhaustion.

Milenda fell asleep soon after, shivering a little from the effects of cool air on her still-wet skin, as Jaali watched her. There was a serenity about her that he had rarely encountered before. It made him feel calm even when life was not too promising.

He knew something bad was waiting for him at the end of this trial. No, he couldn't guess what it was, but the Elders had made it sound so simple—simple enough to trigger alarms in his brain. They were up to something. Not wanting to worry Milenda any more than necessary, Jaali kept his suspicions to himself.

In spite of it all, he couldn't stop smiling. His life as an *indent* had left him with deep scars and lots of terrible memories, but Milenda was erasing all of those, or at least replacing them with magical memories. On the outside, he had always come across as someone who was full of confidence and who had no fear. However, his insides held something far different.

Jaali was often scared of his own shadow. When you grow up thinking there is something evil lurking inside of you, you have no way of knowing that was an idea planted there by someone who wishes you ill. After years of keeping himself away from most human contact other than what was needed for everyday life, Jaali had no way of knowing he was wrong about himself. Milenda had uncovered that lie for him by loving him so much. She was not afraid of testing him, even when he was terrified. He had never felt so happy, so satisfied and confident.

Dipping his head a little, he kissed Milenda's forehead, which rested on the crook of his neck. Her wild hair still held droplets of water within its kinks, and her *matangazos,* now at rest, shone a little in the moonlight—a nice, reddish-brown, velvety smooth and glossy. With a deep sigh, Jaali rested his chin on her thick hair and closed his eyes. Whatever awaited him at the end of this journey, it had been worth it.

Pain

"What do you mean you don't know?" Losing all perspective of to whom she was talking, Milenda's voice rose to a feverish pitch. "You're the ones who make the rules. You have to know."

The Elder had risen from his chair and had crossed the few steps between them to place an appeasing hand on her shoulder. "Holy Jewel, even if we knew, we are obligated by our office and the gods not to disclose any of the details of the Trials."

Milenda bit her lip. She was hot under her *kanga* and feeling too angry for her own good. Of course, they would give her some cockamamie excuse not to tell her anything. They were afraid she would somehow rise against them or help Jaali. The end was very near, and she was finding it hard to believe that the Elders were just going to allow him to cross that finish line without trying something nasty. She knew they were plotting something, but there was no way of forcing their hand without revealing that she had been in constant contact with him.

She got herself under control and took a few deep breaths.

"I apologize, honored Elders, but I am worried for the few contenders that are still out there in the wild." The words came out with some difficulty, but she owed it to herself and to Jaali to be in the Elders' good graces. "After all, I am responsible for their welfare as it is. I just want to make sure that nothing bad happens to them."

The Elder, with his hand still on her shoulder, smiled—or was it a frown? "Exalted princess, you may rest in peace. All contenders are close to the end and are safe and sound. We would let you know if something terrible had happened."

Right, like you told me about Jaali's fall.

"You must not worry yourself about that, and instead start the preparation for your upcoming nuptials. It is tradition to follow the Trials with a royal wedding."

A quake ran through her body. Amidst all that happened, she had not even thought about the actual wedding.

Until the Elder uttered those words, everything seemed to be merely in the realm of possibility, the misty future. Now, the idea hit her like a ton of bricks; she was to be married soon. Whether with Jaali or someone else, all depended on his safe arrival at the finish line.

"Thank you, and I won't take any more of your precious time. I bid you my leave." With a slight bow, she turned her back on the power-hungry men and left their chambers.

Feeling helpless, Milenda walked the hallways with no particular destination in mind. She needed to think, but her thoughts were not being kind to her. Images of Jaali hurt or dead kept crawling back into her mind. There was not much she could do. So far, she had only been able to fix what the Elders had broken, not quite prevent it. What if what they had in mind for Jaali's last trial was so bad, he wouldn't escape with his life? She couldn't possibly fix things if he died. At first she thought she may be able to reach out to the place the Elders would send Jaali to, but unless he was there already, she couldn't pinpoint the exact location.

As the days had gone by, she had learned more about her gift. She knew now she was only able to reach out to where Jaali was. It was as if she had a direct line into his consciousness, some kind of lifeline attached to his brain waves and turned into a pathway of sorts. If he wasn't there, she couldn't reach out.

Thoughts of maybe appealing to Yemanjá had crossed her mind, but she already owed the Orisa so much. Everyone knew it was not wise to owe the orisas too much. They could ask for just about anything in return, and the faithful may not like what they asked for. The only thing she had left to do was to spend as much time as she could with Jaali, so she could hopefully be there when whatever it was the Elders had planned for him happened. Maybe then she could prevent it somehow.

Even that was proving to be difficult. The more contenders who crossed that finish line, the more ceremonies she had to preside over. Today she had the official welcome of the third contender to have finished. The past three days, as Jaali had painfully and slowly crossed what was left of the desert heading west, she'd had to excuse herself from his side every day. The contenders trickled in like a dripping faucet, and considering she was the one person they were doing this for, she absolutely had to be present during those long and boring events.

Not only did the ceremony itself take a long time, but the preparations were endless. Every time she had to be rubbed clean as if they were afraid the contenders would catch something from her. She was dressed to the nines, her face painted and her hair braided in elaborate hairdos that went totally unseen under the towering *gele* she was made to wear on her head.

When I'm queen, these ridiculous rituals will be gone forever. With that self-promise, Milenda kept walking around the hallways.

Mama Nyeusi almost crashed into her around a corner of the palace. The woman looked agitated, which was unusual for her. Beads of sweat hung on her forehead and her breathing was shallow and rapid.

"Mama, what's wrong? Are you sick?" Milenda reached out her hands to hold the woman who seemed on the verge of falling to the ground.

"Child! Just the one I was looking for." Her choked voice scared the princess. Something was terribly wrong. "Let's go to your chambers. We need privacy."

The short walk to her room seemed never-ending, as

Milenda's anxiety grew every time she took a peek at the old woman's blotchy face. *Please, let it not be Jaali. Please.*

Slamming the door behind her, Milenda took the woman to the relative comfort of a chair and crouched at her feet. "Tell me, Mama. What's going on? You're scaring me."

The *iyalorixá* held her hands in her trembling ones. "Child, I just heard. Jaali's gone."

Milenda blinked her eyes several times, trying to make sense of the woman's words. "What? Gone where?"

Tears flooded the old woman's eyes. Milenda had never seen her cry. A sense of panic rose to her throat, almost choking her.

"He's dead, child. Jaali's dead."

The young princess dropped to the floor, her breathing quickening and her eyes opening wide.

No! No, it was not possible. She had left him this morning, alive and well. His leg was healing nicely, albeit slower than it should because of the lack of repose. His strength had been recovered, and Jaali was as happy as anyone in his situation could ever be. They had been making plans for the future about things they were going to do once they were married and Milenda was officially a royal adult. *No, it's not true. It can't be.*

"Ibis, the chambermaid for the Elders, just overheard them talk. He has been killed by a bounty hunter not too far from the city walls." The *iyalorixá* was talking, but Milenda had stopped listening. Her ears rang loudly and her eyes could only see big bright spots of light. All her strength had left her, and her legs wouldn't carry her if she tried. Having trouble breathing and with her heart beating fiercely on her throat, Milenda began to slowly slip out of consciousness.

When she woke up later, there was a doctor tending to her. Asha was nearby, fussing as she normally did, and Mama Nyeusi stood beside her bed, holding her hand and cooing words of comfort.

"Jaali!" It was a primal scream of grief as the memory of the news came back to her. "No, no, it can't be. Not my *wimbo wa moyo*. No!"

"She is too agitated," the doctor said. "Maybe we should call her father."

Bitterness colored the old woman's words. "For all the good that would do. He hasn't been there for her ever."

Nevertheless, Asha was sent to look for the sovereign, to ask him to come to his daughter's side in her hour of need. Milenda's wails of pain could be heard through the hallways of the palace and stopped every servant and every visitor in their tracks.

Despite Mama Nyeusi's doubts, the king didn't take long to come to Milenda's side. For once, he seemed appropriately worried, and even more so once he set eyes on the flailing figure of his daughter in bed.

"What happened to her, Mama Nyeusi?"

"She just heard that the boy, Jaali, is dead." There was no point in hiding the truth now.

"Jaali? Who's he?" If at first she thought he was just being difficult, a quick look into his face told her he was serious. He truly had no idea who Jaali was.

"One of the contenders," Mama Nyeusi said, trying hard

not to cry herself. "And the one Milenda's heart had already chosen for a consort."

The king seemed confused. "But the Trials are not finished yet. How can she already have chosen a consort?"

Was he really that oblivious to the affairs of the heart? Had he never been in love before?

"They were in love even before the Trials started, your majesty." The old woman took a deep breath, trying to keep patience in her voice. "This was just a formality for Milenda. In her soul, she had already chosen."

A look of utter confusion clouded the king's face. "How do you know he's dead? I have not been informed of anything of the kind."

"I beg your forgiveness, your majesty, but servants sometimes overhear things. The Elders have just received the news."

Clenching his powerful jaw, Milenda's royal father was silent for a few moments, staring at his daughter still wailing in pain.

"Milenda, child of mine." He sat on the edge of the bed and, for the first time Mama Nyeusi could remember, held his daughter's hand. "You need to calm yourself."

His words had the power that nothing else seemed to have until then; her eyes snapped open, and she sprang up to a sitting position, tears running down her cheeks, hair in disarray.

"Calm myself?" Anger colored her voice. "How can I calm down when the love of my life, my soul, is dead? Have you never loved anyone, Father? I know you don't love me, but didn't you love my mother even a little bit? Did you even cry when she died?"

The staff threw evasive looks at each other and slowly started leaving the room, giving the king and his daughter some privacy. The only one who did not leave was Mama Nyeusi. She calmly sat on the other side of the bed, listening in, her eyes somber and her mouth set in a sad frown.

"I know you are upset, daughter, but you must not speak of things you know nothing about." The king's voice was low, almost a whisper.

"I know more than you think, Father." Milenda spat her words, anger and contempt dripping from them. "I know what really happened to Mother, and you did nothing about it. Have you ever loved us at all?" Tears resumed falling from her swollen eyes.

The king looked at the *iyalorixá* and then his daughter, lost for words. With a big gulp, he replied, "I do love you, child. More than you'll ever know, but I was hurt once, and it is sometimes easier to pretend I have no feelings. I did love your mother. More than life itself, and I was devastated when she died. I don't think I ever recovered."

Great sobs were coming from Milenda. "If that's true, why didn't you do something about the Elders, Father? They had Mom murdered, and you did nothing."

King Melchior's expression fell, and his breath caught in his throat. "What do you mean? Your mother died in an accident."

"How can you be so blind? Mother was murdered because she had the misfortune of picking a Nyota for her child's seed.

Don't tell me you didn't know." Spittle flew from her mouth, and her *matangazos* were burning fiery red.

Suddenly pale, the monarch let out a groan of grief. "No, she died in an accident. They told me she had fallen off a cliff while on one of her daily walks." He seemed to be trying to convince himself rather than arguing. "She fell."

His voice trailed as he realized the truth in his daughter's words.

The look in her father's eyes had managed to calm her. She had never seen him so emotionally broken. "You didn't know…."

For a few moments, they sat quietly while they both collected themselves.

"Tell me about this Jaali," her father suddenly said. "Did the Elders have anything to do with his death, as well?"

Milenda told him about the young Fjorden who had stolen her heart and how she was sure the Elders had tried to foil his progress and success at every turn of the Trials, all because Jaali was an Outlander and thus unfit to be a royal consort in the eyes of the Elders. Now she would be expected to take a husband from the rest of the contenders, and she couldn't even bring herself to live, much less love again.

Her father held her hand in his while she poured out her heart to him for the first time in her young life. "I will find out exactly what happened, Milenda, for all the good that will do." His voice had become softer and gentler. "I promise you though, if I find out the Elders had something to do with this, they'll have to deal with me."

Even though it was probably an empty promise, it brought

Milenda a measure of comfort. When her father left, Milenda held on to Mama Nyeusi's hand. "I have to find out if it's true, Mama."

"What do you mean?"

"I will reach out to him. If he's dead, I won't be able to do it, but in my heart, I just can't believe it. I can't believe it, Mama."

Milenda didn't waste any time. Closing her eyes, she reached out to Jaali and found only emptiness. A sob rose in her throat. She tried again and found nothing. His consciousness was nowhere to be found.

Her heart broke into a million pieces again. Where she thought there were no more tears, more sprang out, and when she thought she could hurt no more, she did. Jaali was dead.

***

For the first time since he had started the Trials, a gusty wind blew across the desert, lifting up sand and throwing it uncomfortably against his skin. There was very little desert left as it quickly turned into a much greener stretch of land. He was definitely getting close to the end. In spite of his fear about what the Elders were planning for him at the last stop in this torturous journey, he had a song in his heart. He might not be in the clear just yet, but he was closer to finishing and claiming Milenda as his wife. For that, he couldn't be happier.

They had spent the last three days in bliss in spite of the lack of food and comfort. When they were together, it was as if all the other needs vanished, and all that mattered was the two of them. Jaali was still shocked at how amazing he felt in her arms and how good he could make her feel, as well. It was all like a dream, and he hoped not to wake up from it for a long time.

Rounding a corner in a small forested area, he saw what looked like a stone wall. Was it possible that he had finally arrived at the city walls? His heart jumped for joy and his step quickened.

His injured leg was a lot stronger, even though he still limped. In fact, he had a suspicion the limp would never really go away completely. But for now, he could walk a lot better and faster than just a couple of days ago. His ankle was better able to hold his weight, and even though he was still using the crutch, he knew he could probably have made it without.

Rushing toward the wall, Jaali almost missed a glint of something coming from behind a tree. By the time he realized what it was, it was far too late to take cover.

Two men, guns aiming at him, came out from the shelter of the trees.

"Stop!"

The scream hit him with the force of a stone. What was this now? What were these two men doing here?

They were both big men, tall and heavily muscled. They wore white clothing and red scarves over their heads.

Bounty hunters.

Jaali froze. What would two bounty hunters want with him? There was no bounty on his head, and he was not someone anyone would want to catch. He raised his hands over his head in a gesture of surrender, even though he was not sure what he was surrendering for.

"What's going on? What do you want?"

The tallest man advanced a few steps, never letting the gun down. "Jaali Asker—is this your name?" he asked, in a low, booming voice.

Jaali nodded, still confused by it all. "Yes, that's my name." No one had called him by his full name in so many years, he almost hadn't recognized it. At the university, he was simply known as Jaali Outlander. "Why do you ask?"

"There's a bounty on your head."

Jaali started. A bounty? Who would have put a bounty on his head?

"We are here to collect you."

"There must be a mistake. I am nobody…" In his head, he could almost hear the sweet voice of Milenda chiding him for saying that. *You're everything,* wimbo ma moyo. *You're everything.*

"You killed Mnyama and now there is a price on your head."

Jaali's heart fell. Mnyama! Even after four years, the slaver was still haunting him.

Yes, he had killed the slaver those years ago, but nobody knew. They had been alone in the woods when it happened.

The cruel slaver had been doing what he did best, tormenting Jaali in that special way of his that broke his victims from the inside out. Jaali was twenty-one by then and had grown to be strong and tall. For the first time since he had been taken as an *indent*, Jaali was not going to take it anymore. He fought the slaver. They had rolled on the jungle floor like rabid animals, kicking and punching each other. Mnyama was huge, and his weight alone was a massive weapon against someone strong but slim like Jaali. The young *indent* knew he was about to lose the fight, and he knew just what that meant: a session of sexual and other physical abuse until the slaver tired of it and left him to bleed and cry among the trees.

With his last strength, Jaali had seized a big branch lying near his hand and swung it with all his might against the head of the big man. When Mnyama had collapsed on top of him, motionless and quiet, Jaali thought for a moment the man had fallen asleep. Then, a stream of hot, sweet-smelling liquid had started dripping on Jaali's face and he knew the slaver was either dead or severely wounded.

Jaali had rolled over and examined the man's head.

Mnyama had no pulse. He was dead.

Joy and a healthy amount of fear had filled Jaali's heart. Mnyama was dead. Finally, he was free!

He knew, though, he wouldn't be free for too long should anybody find out he had been the one who killed him. *Indent*s had no rights, and self-defense was not accepted as a good reason to kill your owners. Jaali had to pretend he didn't know anything about it and let someone find him.

He ran to the river, jumped in to wash himself and his clothes of the man's blood, and then took the long way home to allow the clothes to dry.

The body had not been found until the next morning. Someone had followed a predator to the jungle, only to find the half-eaten corpse of the cruel slaver. Nobody had ever known he had done it. So how did these bounty hunters know?

"I don't know what you are talking about," he replied, his hands still held up in the air, his heart beating too fast.

"We don't care if it's true or not." The man had taken another couple of steps toward him. "We are here to get you and collect the reward."

"Who's offering the reward on my head?" In spite of the fear in his heart, he was curious.

"The Elders. And a generous bounty it is."

Jaali almost choked on his breath. The Elders! So that's what they had been planning for his demise, another murder disguised as a legal act. He wondered what they would tell Milenda once they brought his body back.

"So, say your good-byes to this life. Your head is ours."

Jaali turned and ran as fast as his injured leg could carry him. But it wasn't fast enough. He felt the bullet hit him from behind, first in the back of his thigh, then his shoulder. Losing his balance, Jaali fell face first on the dry sand, hitting his head on a rock.

His last thought went to Milenda, her beautiful young face shining in the sunlight, green eyes glittering like emeralds.

I'll love you forever, Milenda.

The light became darkness, and he faded away.

Resilience

Being the heir to the crown of Natale, Milenda was not allowed time to mourn. That same day she was dolled up and almost carried away to the royal gardens where a welcoming ceremony was being held for the last of the contenders arriving at the finish line. Numb, she survived through the whole three hours of the ritual event, smiling only when the poor man who had survived the infamous Trials came to stand in front of her, his eyes full of hope she'd pick him for her consort. She allowed him to kiss her hand, and then she sat on the throne-like chair while her father and other members of the royal court made their speeches.

During the following banquet, she ate nothing, never once touching the food on her plate. Asha fussed over her, trying to coax her into eating something or at least drinking some water or juice, but Milenda had lost all her will to live. If Jaali was dead, she wanted to be dead as well. He was her life now, as intrinsically connected to her as her own soul. Living without him would be like living without the sun or the water that sustained all life. Her body was present, but her mind was not.

Shortly before the end of the ceremony, the contender came to bid his good-byes, and noticing the deep sadness in her eyes, he whispered, "Exalted Jewel, whatever brought those clouds to your eyes, may the orisas dispel it from your heart."

Milenda looked up into this man's eyes. He looked tired and thin, as if he had not eaten properly in a while. The Trials had not been easy for him either, by the looks of it.

"Was it hard?" she asked, low enough so only he could hear it.

"Yes, but for the sake of my family, I never gave up."

Milenda smiled at him then and wished him well. Maybe he would be her chosen consort. Now that Jaali was gone, it didn't really matter to her whom she picked. Her heart belonged to someone else.

The man's words lingered in her head. *Never give up.*

She excused herself as soon as she could and returned to her room, locking the doors behind her. Mjusi had come for a visit; he had felt her pain and wanted to be close to his mistress.

Milenda sat on the floor, close to her winged friend, and closed her eyes. She would try to reach Jaali one last time. She wouldn't give up yet.

With her mind, she extended a connecting line, looking for

signs of Jaali's consciousness, but she could find nothing. She extended her mind again, like long anxious fingers searching for the hand of a beloved one.

Just as she was about to give up, there was a little twitch on the other end.

"Jaali!" she exclaimed, her eyes popping wide open.

She was not dreaming. She had felt something on the other side. Closing her eyes again, she reached out one more time, her heart beating furiously in her chest, her mouth dry, and her hands trembling. There was no mistaking it now; Jaali's consciousness was on the other end, weak and faded, but definitely there. He was not dead. Something was very wrong, but he was alive.

Jumping to her feet and almost toppling over Mjusi, who gave her a disapproving look, Milenda ran out the door and straight down the hallway. At first she was going to go to Mama Nyeusi's room, but then she changed her mind and decided to go to her father's. If someone could help her and Jaali now, it was her father.

The royal room was on the other side of the palace, where it was quiet and only family or trusted staff members were allowed. She knocked on the door furiously, hoping he had already returned from the ceremonial welcome event, and heard a faint voice from the other side.

"Father, I need to talk to you!" she yelled through the thick wooden door.

The king himself came to open the door and invite her in. He was wearing his house robes and looked as disheveled as she had ever seen him.

It occurred to her that she had only been in this room a couple of times her whole life, and both times as a child. The room didn't look any different from the last time, years ago.

"Father, I need your help." Not wasting any time, Milenda closed the door behind her. "Jaali is alive."

"What do you mean? You told me he was dead." Once again, the king looked confused and bewildered.

"Don't ask me how I know, because I can't tell you yet, but I know he's still alive. I just don't know where for sure." Milenda was talking fast, and her eyes darted around from her father's face to his hands. "I need your help to go retrieve him before he does die."

Her father stared at her intently for a few seconds. "What can I do?"

"Send your most trusted men with me to the *Jangwa Pori* to get him." It was almost an order. "I can find him. He shouldn't be too far from the walls."

"Too dangerous for a princess," he protested immediately. He scratched his chin. "Besides, the Elders assured me the Outlander boy is indeed dead."

Milenda took a step forward and grabbed her father's hands. "Father, for once listen to me, and do the right thing. The Elders lie to serve their own grand purposes. They don't care about this nation. They don't care about us. Please, Father, save Jaali. He will be a good royal consort—strong, faithful, and fair. Please."

The monarch swallowed hard and looked down at their entwined hands. A few seconds later, his eyes came back to rest on Milenda's.

"All right, my child. I will let you go with a few guards. When?"

"Now. Before it's too late."

Her father nodded and called out his private guards from the guardroom down the hall from his.

In less than an hour, she was on her way to the edge of the city, with an escort of three strong, armed guards. Once in a while, she reached out for Jaali, and every time she felt signs of life, not enough for her to form a complete connection, but enough for her to know he was still alive.

They reached the walls before nighttime and began scouring the area. As the night fell, it became harder and harder to see even with the torches the guards had brought along with them. Milenda had just begun to lose hope when she spotted a lumpy mass a few yards away, half hidden by a tree. Taking off at a run, she almost tripped over Jaali's backpack, which lay discarded a short distance from his body.

Milenda fell to her knees next to her beloved. The sand was stained dark beneath him and he was not moving. Sobbing loudly, she turned him around. His face, even lifeless, was a balm for her soul.

She cleaned off the sand that covered his eyes, nose, and mouth. He had a head wound, still bleeding freely, and there was also a bleeding wound on his shoulder. As she cradled him in her arms, she felt for a pulse and was overjoyed to feel his heartbeat, faint but steady.

"*Wimbo wa moyo*, hold on. We'll get you out of here."

Two of the guards removed a collapsible stretcher from their bags, clicked it into place, and placed the young Fjorden on it.

"Careful, he's bleeding a lot. We need to get him out of here and stop the hemorrhage." She walked beside them, holding Jaali's hand while they carried the stretcher and the man upon it up to where they had left their transport. On the drive back to the palace, Milenda sat by him, caring for his wounds. She applied whatever was left of the *dawa* leaf in his bag to stop the pain and bandaged the wounds the best she could with the sparse materials she had available.

In the palace, a few more guards came to help carry Jaali inside. Milenda insisted he be placed in her room, and for once, nobody denied her.

While the palace physician was called, Milenda undressed and cleaned the young Fjorden, checking his wounds. She was no doctor, but she could tell both bullets had gone through and exited the other side. There was some sand in the wound, but other than that, they didn't look infected. On the other hand, the wound on his head—a great big egg-shaped bump on his forehead and a long gash—was red and angry. She cleaned it with a tenderness she didn't even know she had.

Only then did she allow herself to believe Jaali was really alive and finally out of the desert.

The doctor did his magic and gave Milenda instructions on how to take care of him for the rest of the night. At the princess's request, he also removed the tracker from Jaali's ailing body.

"Call me if he doesn't regain consciousness by the middle of the night. I'm hopeful that the ice and the rest in a cool place will bring him back. He lost a lot of blood, so he's weak, but he's young and strong. He will pull through."

The princess felt a strange urge to hug the doctor, but quenched it by twisting her hands compulsively while thanking him.

The room was finally quiet, with Jaali and her the only ones left within. Milenda hadn't had the time to think much about what had just happened.

Now, though, for the first time that night, a weight left her chest, and a bubbly feeling of relief and happiness came all the way to her mouth. The uncontrollable laughing came, quickly followed by weeping. She stretched herself alongside Jaali on the bed and cried on his good shoulder, stopping once in a while to bestow little kisses over his chest, on his chin, and all over his face. She couldn't stop the happiness—or the anger she was feeling. It was overwhelming, and she was afraid she would explode if she couldn't put an end to it soon.

Before she knew it, the sound of his heartbeat against her ear lulled her to sleep. For the first time since Jaali's death had been announced, she slept peacefully, his heart singing a song of hope against her face. A heavy, rejuvenating sleep came over her, and she didn't stir until she felt a movement under her head.

Jaali was waking up. He tossed on the bed, as if he were being stung by the bullet ants again. She sat up, supporting herself on an arm, and looked at his pale face, blotchy with scratches and bruises. Then her eyes traveled to his muscled upper arms, which were a mess of black and purple, and his bandaged shoulder with its strange hue of red.

"Jaali, can you hear me?" Afraid of startling him, her voice came out in a barely audible whisper. "Are you awake?"

His eyes suddenly flew open, the sky blue of his eyes startlingly bright in someone so sick. He seemed disoriented at first, but he quickly focused on her.

"Milenda." His voice was hoarse, but it sounded to Milenda like a choir of a thousand angels uttering her name.

"I thought I lost you." Tears danced in her eyes again, a mixture of sadness and joy. "I thought my life was over, *wimbo wa moyo*."

Jaali's lips turned up in a smile. "You will never lose me." His shaking hand searched for hers and held it against his chest. "Don't cry. I'm alive and we're finally together."

In spite of his words, Milenda burst out in tears. Relief and anger washed over her whole being.

Pulling her against his chest, Jaali held her tight and allowed her the time she needed to air out all of the frustration and anxiety of the past couple of weeks. When the tears ran out, she kept her head solidly attached to him, his rapid heartbeat soothing her nerves.

"What do we do now?" Jaali asked against her hair.

"Now, we rest. Tomorrow, we go to war." The determination and seriousness in her voice did not leave any room for doubt. She meant it.

***

In repose, Milenda looked almost angelic. Her hair, wild as usual, belied the peace reflected on her face as she slept stretched out alongside him, her head resting on his shoulder.

Jaali smiled in spite of the non-relenting pain that seemed

to have taken over his whole body. The wound on his shoulder burned as if someone had poked it with a flaming torch. The rest of his body was not doing much better. Aches and pains permeated every muscle, every joint. The Trials had finally taken their toll on him. The simple act of moving his eyes sent him into a spiral of dizziness, and for the first time in his life, he had no wish to go anywhere. The bed—was it Milenda's bed?—felt like heaven, and his exhausted brain wished he would never have to leave it.

Jaali thought about what had happened at the end of his Trial. Had those men really known about the Mnyama's incident, or had they been instructed by the Elders to say that? He couldn't imagine how anyone would have known since there was absolutely nothing to connect him to the man's demise. By the time they had found his body, the slaver had been ravaged by wild animals, and it was impossible to tell what exactly had killed him in the first place. The common notion was that he had been attacked by a predator in the jungle. Jaali was okay with that explanation. As hard as it was for him to deal with the fact he had taken another human being's life, it was also true that the slaver was hardly human, and the young Fjorden was more than happy to see himself freed from such a monster.

The attack was a surprise, but Jaali had been half expecting the Elders to try something to stop him from finishing the Trials in one piece. In spite of what they had told him when he had first volunteered, the only reason why they had allowed him to compete was so they could have him in a position where it would be easy to get rid of him. They had been unsuccessful, thanks to his stubborn, determined princess who, against all odds, loved him.

How fortunate was he to have her on his side! Once in a while, he wondered whether he had been dreaming all along. How had a lowly *indent* attracted and inspired such love and devotion from someone like her? Yet he had, and that knowledge filled his heart with a happiness he had never known before.

With a groan, Jaali moved his legs just enough to help blood circulate. Milenda stirred, and her head lifted from his shoulder to look at him. Her bleary eyes barely opened, and she brought a hand to his chest as if checking to see if he was still breathing. "Something wrong?" The panic in her voice made him cringe.

"No, *msichana*, I'm fine. Just a little sore." He tried to move his arm and managed only to send a shooting pain along his chest and back. He moaned softly. "My shoulder, on the other hand, is not happy." He chuckled.

Smiling now, Milenda kissed him on the lips, catching him by surprise. "This is for being alive." Her eyes had recovered that gemstone gleam he so loved. "You worried me sick, *wimbo wo moyo*. Don't you ever do that again."

Jaali laughed. "I will do my best."

His eyes locked on hers for a moment. "Thank you. You are truly an angel, my own *malaika*. I would be dead, being eaten by animals in the desert if it weren't for you not giving up on me."

"Another contender reminded me you should never give up on what you truly care about," she explained, her fingers playing with the bandage that crossed his chest. "I have much to thank that man for."

"How did you find out I was still alive?"

"I reached out to you until I could find signs of life." Her face grew somber. "It was a dark time, Jaali. To reach out and feel… nothing. I just didn't want to accept you were dead, so I kept reaching. Finally, I felt you." Tears welled in her eyes, and her voice trembled. "I just couldn't imagine a life without you."

In spite of the pain it caused, Jaali lifted his arm and caressed her face, wiping the tears away. "Don't cry. I'm alive and well—or will be, given time to heal. We're together."

She sat up straighter. "Tonight I will be announcing to the populace my official choice. After that, the Elders will have no choice but to accept you as my future consort."

"Unless they try to kill me again." The comment was out before he could stop himself.

In one swift move, she had jumped off the bed and was now leaning across the edge, disbelief in her eyes.

"What did you say? Are you telling me the Elders did this to you?"

"They paid bounty hunters to come and finish me off before I could enter the city walls." She deserved the truth. If she was going to be the future monarch of this land, she had better know exactly what she was up against.

Silence fell. Jaali could almost hear her heart beat, her eyes becoming distant as if she had gone deep inside herself. Then she walked to the door, opened it, and yelled out a name he didn't recognize. A young girl came running in, giving him a furtive look of curiosity before focusing on the princess.

"Asha, I need to get dressed. I am going to see my father."

Surprised and a little worried, Jaali watched as Milenda went on with the business of getting dressed. It was mesmerizing to watch her undress, her body—now as familiar to him as the air he breathed—was resplendent under the dim light in the room. The young servant girl's eyes flittered nervously toward him, obviously uncomfortable with the fact he was witnessing such a routine.

Asha slid a *kanga* shirt over her mistress's head and then wrapped a skirt tight around Milenda's narrow waist and hips. He watched as an *iqhiya* was placed over the princess's out-of-control hair, giving her a more decorous air.

When she deemed herself ready, Milenda came to the bed again and, not waiting for the young girl to leave the room, kissed Jaali's dry lips fully and deeply.

"I will be back soon. Asha, take care of my future husband." The young girl's eyes opened so wide, Jaali thought they would come out of their sockets.

Left alone with this stranger in the room, Asha bowed nervously.

"You don't have to stay here, Asha, if it makes you uncomfortable," Jaali told her. "You can wait outside if you prefer. I'll call if I need help with anything."

The young girl uttered a faint thank you and turned to leave, obviously relieved. But before opening the door, she turned around and asked, "Are you really going to marry the princess?"

The Fjorden laughed, amused by the girl's confusion and surprise. "Yes, gods willing. I love her very much."

Much to his surprise, the girl lifted her eyes to him and spoke again. "I'm glad. The Jewel deserves to be loved and cherished." Turning around, the girl left the room.

A smile slowly spread across Jaali's face. At least somebody besides him was happy about it!

***

When her father opened the door to his room, Milenda couldn't have been more surprised.

Just beyond it, inside the royal chamber, Mama Nyeusi sat in a chair, looking up at her with her wrinkle-bordered eyes. The princess took a few steps inside before she was able to articulate her shock. "What are you doing here, Mama?"

The old woman smiled sadly and waved her into the chair next to her. "Sit, child. Your father and I have been talking."

Her father, dressed in his everyday clothes, closed the door and joined them in the center of the room. He didn't look happy, but then again he rarely did. Milenda couldn't remember ever seeing him without the tightness on his lips or the distance in his eyes. This time though, his eyes were not distant, just… sad.

"I called the *iyalorixá* so we could talk," he explained in his low voice. "There is much, it seems, I don't know about my own nation and my own family."

Milenda looked to her father and back to Mama Nyeusi, confused and a little unsettled by the whole thing. "What's the matter, exactly?"

"After what happened to Jaali, your father was curious

about certain things you had said. It appears he knew a lot less about what happened than what we thought at first."

"And why are you here, daughter?" Her father, all six feet four of him, loomed over her as she sat. She was not sure whether to be excited her father was actually showing interest in her and her life or to be worried. After all, she couldn't be sure he was not in on the Elders' plans for the demise of her beloved Jaali.

"I came to talk to you about Jaali. I want to make the official announcement that I'm choosing him for my consort. And I want to do it tonight, before the Elders come up with some other plot to maim him or kill him." In spite of her doubts, the truth came spilling out of her mouth, desperate as she was to believe in her father again.

The king raised an eyebrow and studied her. "Are you sure this is what you want? Are you certain this is the man you want to marry?" When she nodded emphatically, he added, "It won't be easy at first. He's from a different culture, a different race. He was an *indent* and has no fortune."

"Neither do the other men who ran the Trials, and yet no one is asking me the same questions about them." Milenda realized her voice had raised an octave and had taken on a defensive tone.

"I'm not doubting you, child. I'm just telling you the facts. You're a future queen and people are going to find all kinds of things to criticize. Bringing in an Outlander as a spouse will start evil tongues wagging."

She took a deep breath. "I know that, Father, but I love him, and between the two of us, we will strive to be good rulers and change a lot of the things that are wrong in our country."

Surprising even herself, Milenda reached out and held her father's hand in hers. "I can't imagine living my life without him. If I were to marry somebody else, I wouldn't have the motivation and the joy to even try to be a good monarch. You understand that, don't you?"

The sad look he gave her spoke volumes of how well he understood. For the first time, she felt sorry for her father, who had been caught in a no-win situation where his choices were either bad or worse. Being a king, he had to have offspring, but to do so he had to hand-deliver the woman he loved into someone else's arms. And then he'd lost both her love and her life. It was no wonder he had been such an apathetic king; he lacked the joy, the drive, and the will to live because he had lost the one person who had previously given him all of that: her mother.

"Did you ever love me, Father?" Milenda was almost afraid to ask, but she had to know. "I wouldn't blame you if you didn't, considering the circumstances of my birth."

He gave his daughter's hand a squeeze. "In spite of everything, I do love you and always did. You look so much like your mother. I couldn't help but love you."

He dropped to a crouching position in front of her. "I haven't been a good father or a good king, I know that. I'm just hoping that it's not too late to fix things." Timidly, he brought her hand to his lips and kissed it. It was the first time Milenda had ever seen her father doing that, and her heart fluttered with an unfamiliar feeling. She had waited her whole life for this moment, and now that it was here, she couldn't help but wonder whether it was sincere. She hoped with her whole heart that it was.

"Will you help us announce our engagement tonight?" she asked, her voice trembling with emotion.

"I will go now and arrange everything. I'm guessing Jaali is in no condition to be in public yet." Her father's eyes looked softer now, their usual harshness and ice gone.

"He needs to be present for this. We will have him carried on a stretcher to the… royal gardens?" She didn't want to do this announcement in the more formal venue. It was important that the people saw this as a change in the winds of power and society. Making the announcement in a friendlier, more down-to-earth place seemed to be the way to go.

"I will make it happen." Milenda couldn't believe how much more confident her father seemed to be. She smiled at him as a way of thanking him, and he left the room.

She turned to Mama Nyeusi. "Is it for real?" Her anxiety made her breathe harder than usual.

The old woman rose from her chair and took a couple steps toward Milenda. "I can't swear, but I think it is. I believe he is finally realizing what's been going on all these years. After all, in some ways, he was also a victim of circumstances."

Milenda sighed deeply. "I better go back to Jaali. I'm scared of leaving him alone for very long. Who knows what the Elders have up their sleeves now?"

***

The heavy curtains had been pulled over the windows, drowning the room in darkness. In bed, Jaali slept soundly, his face relaxed into a peaceful expression. She couldn't begin to imagine his relief at being out of the desert, especially considering all of the terrible things he had been made to experience while there. A new wave of red-hot anger filled her heart and made her *matangazos* burn like fire. No one was going to hurt her heart-song again. Ever!

With the door locked behind her, she stripped off her clothes before climbing quietly into the bed and molding her slim body against his. He had lost so much weight. She could feel his bones where his flesh should have cushioned her. She brushed her hand across his chest, feeling his ribs right below his skin. Her face, leaning against his shoulder, could feel his clavicle poking her as she held him tighter against her.

"Milenda?" His voice, a little slurred by sleep, was like music to her ears.

"Wimbo wa moyo, did I wake you?"

"I cannot think of a better way to wake up than having my beautiful princess curled against me." He looked at her upturned face. In the dark, she could see his warm lips curled into a generous smile. She squeezed him tighter.

"You have lost so much weight," she whispered. "Do you want something to eat? I will call Asha."

"I'm not hungry… not for food, anyway." His hand had traveled to her hips and discovered the lack of any clothing. "You're not dressed."

She giggled. "Obviously. Why? Do I make you uncomfortable with my skinny body wrapped around you?"

In a swift move, he turned so he was supporting himself on his arm and looking directly into her eyes. "I love your skinny body against mine. So much so I don't want you to go away from me ever."

"You shouldn't do that. You are not well yet." Her smile belied her admonishments.

"When I am with you, I forget pain. I forget injury. You fill up my thoughts and take over my senses." His liquid blue eyes seemed to shine in the dark. "I love you, princess."

His dry lips fused with hers. She could taste and feel the desert sand in his mouth.

Would those specks of rock ever leave his body for good? Would the memories of those days ever fade? If on the one hand she wanted them to vanish into the mists of the past, never to be revived again, on the other hand, there had been moments of true happiness she would sooner not forget. Why did the good always seem to come attached to something bad?

Jaali's mouth became more demanding, and her heart started the usual crazy race his touch always provoked.

"My father agreed." Breathless, she found it hard to focus on what she needed to tell him. "We will announce our engagement tonight."

The young Fjorden stopped, lips hovering over her neck. "He agreed?" He sounded so surprised, Milenda almost laughed.

"Yes. My father wants to atone for his mistakes." Yes, she still found it hard to believe, but her heart sang in joy in spite of her doubts. "We will have to get you ready to come out in public with me tonight. You think you'll be able to manage?"

Jaali chuckled and dropped a butterfly kiss on her nose. "Are you joking? To announce our engagement, I would drag myself through fire. I will be there if they have to carry me."

Milenda smiled widely and then kissed him. That was just what she was hoping to hear.

The Plea

———————————————

The whole city's populace gathered in the royal gardens. People squeezed among trees and flower beds. Some had climbed onto branches and found a high spot to sit and watch, and the dignitary dais was equally full with members of Natale's elite class and some foreign representatives. Milenda watched this from a window of the palace, biting her lip so hard, Jaali was afraid she would draw blood.

"Stop biting your lip. You do not want to go out in public with blood dripping from your mouth. Bad enough that you still have those bruises on your face." He rolled the wheelchair back a little to make space for her to move away from the window.

Truth be told, he was so nervous himself, his stomach was somersaulting inside of him. His life as an *indent* and then as a professor of languages had not prepared him to face a crowd as big as the one awaiting them outside. He would sooner stay within the relative protection of Milenda's room than face the crowd. However, he needed to be beside the princess when she made the announcement. What would hiding say about him as a future royal consort?

Milenda exhaled loudly. "I'm a nervous wreck," she admitted, taking her eyes from the window and looking at him. "There are an awful lot of people out there."

"You are going to do fine. Your people love you, the beautiful Jewel of Natale. You have nothing to worry about." Yet nobody knew him, and being an Outlander who stuck out like a sore thumb among the Natalian people did not give him a fuzzy feeling about how Milenda's subjects would react to him.

"Still, I'm afraid of their reaction when I make the announcement. What if they resent me marrying an outsider? Our nation has been buried under tradition for so long, I'm not sure people are ready to accept a change this big." She came up behind Jaali, wrapped her arms around his neck and shoulders, and rested her chin on the top of his head. "What do we do then?"

Jaali placed his hand over hers. "We'll cross that bridge when we get there. No point in fretting about something we don't know will happen."

They remained silent for a while and then resumed their position by the window. Together, they watched some of the palace staff erecting a giant screen, where they would project her image so people in the back could see as well. Technology like that was rarely used for fear of draining national stores of electricity, but this was a momentous occasion, and her father had seen fit to break tradition for once and bring out the old technology.

Soon enough, it was time to go. Jaali had been meticulously dressed in ceremonial white clothes—long, wide pants and a silk tunic, richly embroidered in metal thread and small diamonds. After a great argument with the stylists, Milenda had convinced them to forego a head covering. "I want people to see his beautiful, pale hair shining under the lights as a symbol of a great change to come." On his feet, he wore only simple sandals, since his ankle was still too swollen to allow any other strappings. The humble wheelchair disappeared underneath all the whiteness and sparkle of Jaali's clothing and his own coloring.

"I look like a ghost," he complained with a chuckle. "People may not even see me, blending into my clothes."

"People will see you, trust me." She looked at him with such pride and love, his heart melted. "You look beautiful, my enchanting consort from the northern lands."

He pulled her into his lap.

"You are going to wrinkle all that silk." Her protest was halfhearted, and she didn't fight him when he brought his lips to hers. "We really have to go," she whispered with a little sigh, as he reluctantly let go of her.

Melinda wheeled him along the hallways and up to the back doors that opened into the gardens. They had discussed it earlier and agreed people should see him, not her, rolling himself onto the makeshift stage built just outside the gates.

Even though his injured shoulder prevented him from moving without pain, he was determined to grin and bear it.

Milenda straightened, smoothing the golden *kanga* skirt and shirt with her hands. With an almost defiant stance, she opened the doors and walked out onto the stage. Jaali hesitated for a moment, watching her marching toward the crowd with a confidence he knew she did not feel.

A warm sense of pride invaded his heart. He was in love with the most incredible young woman, and he still found it hard to understand how he actually deserved to be loved by her.

Knowing that he couldn't delay the inevitable, Jaali wheeled himself behind her, a sharp pain making each movement torturous. The crowd hushed at their entrance, only to explode in applause once Milenda reached the edge of the stage where she was fully visible to everyone. They did love their Jewel.

But would they love him, too?

Cautiously, he approached the front of the stage and rolled into his place beside Milenda. The crowd hushed again at the sight of him. He could only imagine what he looked like, the snow-haired Fjorden who so obviously did not belong among them. The ghost from the north who dared steal the crown Jewel. Jaali could see it in their eyes, the set of their lips, and the stillness of their bodies. He was nothing but an *indent*, a slave in their minds. Jaali stubbornly stared at the crowd, fighting the urge to lower his gaze. He put a hopeful smile on his lips, but his heart clenched inside his chest.

"Beloved people of Natale, your Jewel greets you."

As the ceremonial words were uttered, the crowd forgot about Jaali for the moment and cheered in response. Milenda smiled and scanned the throng of people cheering her on. "I come before you today to announce my choice of consort."

Silence descended, and every eye nervously darted toward Jaali.

"All of the contenders fought bravely during the Trials, and I couldn't be more proud of each and every one of them. I am also happy that all of the contenders reached the end with their lives."

Jaali noticed a murmur riding through the masses like a wave. He recognized a few of the other contenders among them. They were surely asking themselves why he was on stage and they were not. His throat felt dry and scratchy, and he swallowed a few times, his chest tightening as the weight of their whispering hit him full force.

"I have made my choice." Milenda's words echoed throughout the gardens aided by an old system of speakers that amplified her voice. "After careful consideration and listening to my heart, I have chosen Jaali Asker to be my royal husband."

A crescendo of voices speaking in whispers reached his ears and he flinched. They were not happy with her decision. Did he really expect them to be?

"I know it looks like a strange choice, a man from another land, another race, someone brought to us as an *indent*. I understand your confusion, maybe even a little anger, but Jaali is my *wimbo wa moyo*, my twin soul, my life. He fought valiantly during the Trials and was very seriously wounded.

His strength of body and character is exactly what is required for a good ruler. He understands the common man because he is one of them. His life has been a series of struggles to survive, and the fact that he is here now, badly injured but determined to introduce himself to you speaks volumes of his will to be a fair and strong monarch. I beg you to welcome him and love him as I do."

The quietude of the crowd was unsettling, but Milenda seemed unconcerned by it. Jaali realized the king was not present at the ceremony. Was this part of the ritual? That the princess must stand alone to face the consequences of her choice? Or was he too cowardly to endorse such a choice?

Much to his surprise, Milenda bent down, slipped her hand under his arm, and pulled him up from the chair. The sudden weight on his ankle made him stumble, but her steady hands supported him.

"Trust me," she whispered in his ear.

Limping beside her, Jaali moved forward so he was right on the edge of the stage. Without warning, Milenda proceeded to unbutton his tunic, and much to his dismay, she carefully removed it.

Suddenly he found himself standing in front of a mass of thousands, bare chested and vulnerable. Cheeks burning in shame, with harrowing memories of his time in the slave market, Jaali looked at Milenda with barely disguised pain.

"Trust me," she whispered again.

The Jewel turned to her people again, and still supporting him, she addressed the crowd again.

"Behold! This brave man displays the scars and wounds

inflicted upon him by unscrupulous men who sought to prevent him from surviving the Trials. He sustained great injury of both body and heart because he loves me. When all looked dire and others would have just given up, he fought like a warrior to stay alive because he loves me. I may be a princess, but I am a woman first, and this man loves me and I love him."

Understanding why she had undressed him in public, Jaali straightened his back, for once feeling proud of the scars and bruises he carried. He could feel every eye upon him, scanning his chest and his arms, studying every inch of his mottled, pale skin. Those were badges of honor, physical proof he was willing to go the distance for Natale's royal heiress no matter the cost.

The air filled with gasps of shock at the sight of Jaali's badly bruised chest and bandaged shoulder. The fact that he limped and could barely stand without support just added to the level of shock from the onlookers. None of the other contenders had suffered the same fate. They were standing on their own among the people, looking refreshed after having rested and been well-fed for a few days. There was no denying that something was not right.

"So I ask you, people of Natale, will you accept Jaali Asker as my beloved consort? Or will you deny me my happiness?"

Milenda helped Jaali into his chair and helped him put the shirt back on again while the populace mumbled to each other. "Sorry, *wimbo wa moyo*," she whispered in his ear. "I had to get their attention. Are you mad?"

Jaali grasped one of her hands and brought it to his lips.

"You could never make me mad." He smiled.

"Just give me time." With a wink, Milenda turned to the crowd again.

"Have you come to a decision? Are you going to deny me my happiness, or are you going to join me in welcoming Jaali into the royal family?" The voice that he loved so much, usually sweet and melodic, was authoritarian and mature.

First, there were only a couple, but these were soon followed by dozens, then hundreds. People lifted their arms in the air, signaling their acceptance of the Fjorden into their midst. On the faces of the common people of Natale, a smile slowly emerged, and Jaali's own lips curled into a heartfelt grin of gratitude.

Milenda, a regal smile plastered on her face, raised her arms up in the air and waved at the crowd. "Thank you, wonderful people of Natale. I knew I could count on your love to help me through this."

She turned suddenly toward the palace, and putting a hand over her heart, she called, "Father, may I also have your blessing?" As she had explained to Jaali, her father's permission was a mere ceremonial gesture. Being over eighteen, Milenda required no permission from her father to pick a consort.

The king, impressive in his ceremonial gold garb, appeared from behind the doors. Slowly, and with a rare smile on his lips, the monarch stepped forward. He took hold of his daughter's hands and turned to the people.

"It makes me very happy to bless this historic union between my daughter, the Jewel of Natale, and Jaali Asker of the northern kingdoms. May they be blessed with many joys and many children." He raised Milenda's arm in the air, and reaching out for Jaali's, the king raised it up on his other side. It was followed immediately by a fierce roar from the crowd.

It was both exhilarating and unnerving to hear the people react with such enthusiasm. Jaali had never been in the eye of the public in a favorable position, and he couldn't help being nervous about this situation. He so much preferred going unnoticed. Being noticed was not something he would normally perceive as a good thing. His whole being cringed and shook.

It's a good thing this time. Forcing himself to ignore the instinct to flee, Jaali smiled and waved at the crowd. *For Milenda. I'll do whatever it takes for her.*

The ceremony was over quickly after that. All of the dignitary formal congratulations would be postponed until the state banquet, which would take place a few days later.

Mama Nyeusi was waiting for them inside. They gathered in a small sitting room with the king to talk about what needed to be done from then on. Milenda sat next to Jaali, her hand firmly within his trembling one. Mama Nyeusi rubbed a hand gently over his shoulders and smiled at him before sitting down across from them.

"Jaali will be moved to the consort chambers tonight," the king announced, his eyes darting to the Fjorden in concern. Jaali flinched, still not used to being in the presence of the nation's ruler. "It is required by tradition, and it wouldn't be wise to break tradition any more than we must."

Milenda bristled beside him. "Father, I don't like the idea

of Jaali being separated from me. You know the Elders are waiting for the chance to take another stab at getting rid of him."

"He will be well protected. I will personally pick the guards to keep an eye on things." The king sounded sincere, but Jaali still couldn't totally trust him. "It behooves us to follow tradition when and however we can. The people are behind you now, but we must also have the noble houses and foreign dignitaries with us. Your engagement in and of itself breaks so many traditions already."

"We want our nation to embrace change. Won't the following of silly conventions like the consort chambers solidify the opposite vision?" Milenda's hand squeezed Jaali's, and her whole body tensed as she talked.

"Change cannot be sudden. It has to be fed in small spoonfuls." The king looked toward the *iyalorixá* for support.

"The king is right, Milenda." Her poufy white skirts fell in big folds to the floor around her chair. "We have to pick our fights carefully, and this one is not one worth fighting right now. Jaali will have the protection of the king's guards. He'll be safe enough within the palace. And you are just a short walk away."

The princess turned to Jaali and there was a silent question in her eyes. He gave her a little nod. As much as he didn't want to be away from her, he understood the wisdom behind the king's advice. "All right, we will move him to the consort chambers tonight after the doctors check him."

"And after that, we have a wedding to plan," her father said, a rare smile on his lips.

The wedding would take place as soon as everything could be planned and with the least amount of fanfare as tradition allowed. Invitations would go out to neighboring nations and even to Jaali's native country up north. No one really expected a reply from Jaali's old world, though. With luck, they may be able to be married within the month, but there was a lot of work to be done.

That evening, Jaali was taken to the consort's quarters. Even though not happy about being separated from Milenda, he couldn't help but be amazed by the size of this room.

The whole space was about four times the size of his *hema* and richly furnished in masculine colors and pieces. The bed could welcome five or six people and was covered in satiny, brown sheets and throws. The headboard was a massive piece carved of what looked like ebony. Two enormous windows stretched from the floor to the high, vaulted ceiling, allowing the light of a sleepy sun to shine through in all its glory. A door, equally massive in size, which he assumed led to the bathroom, gaped at him from behind heavy panels.

I like my hema better.

Impressive as it was, this room was empty of character, empty of personal touch. He hoped he didn't have to stay here long as he wheeled the chair around the room. So used to the warmth and artistry of his own home, the coldness of this room chafed at him as sandpaper on bare skin. The two servants turning his bed and laying out his nightclothes seemed oddly out of place in this lifeless room.

"Yikes! This is awful."

Milenda's voice soothed his ears and worked as a salve for

his aching head. He turned around to look at her standing by the door. Hands solidly set on her hips, the princess seemed aghast at what her beautiful emerald eyes were seeing. "Who decorated this horror?"

Jaali laughed. "It's not that bad. It just needs a little personal touch, that's all." He rolled the chair closer to her and held her hand. "Didn't hear you come in. Miss you already, *msichana*."

Milenda bent and kissed him lightly on the lips. "Don't be cheesy. We just saw each other ten minutes ago."

He smiled, licking his lips and tasting her lingering sweetness.

She frowned. "I still hate this idea. It makes me nervous."

"Do you really think the Elders will try something?"

"You don't?" She sat on the edge of the bed, Jaali's chair right in front of her. "I really think they have something up their sleeves."

As if on cue, Milenda's father walked in. He dismissed the servants and closed the door behind him.

"There is something you need to know," he said, pulling a chair close to them. "The Elders have arranged a new marriage for me."

Milenda's jaw fell. "What? Why? It's not like you can have children." Jaali cringed at the comment.

"I know. They are arranging a surrogate again." The king looked tired, his eyes a little swollen and droopy. "It makes me nervous for you Milenda."

It was Jaali's turn to be surprised. "Why? What would Milenda have anything to do with having another child?"

"Normally nothing. Milenda is the firstborn and the heir to

the throne no matter how many other children I may have." The king paused and his eyes darted between the two young people.

A terrifying thought emerged in Jaali's mind. "But if something was to happen to her...."

"Exactly." The monarch combed his wiry hair with his long fingers. "If she were to die, then the next child would inherit the right to the throne."

"You think they are trying to get you to father another hild, so they can get rid of me?" Milenda almost shouted, jumping to her feet. "How can they?"

"I didn't put much meaning to it until you told me what had happened to your mother. Now, I'm worried they are indeed planning your demise." He bit his lip. "They are not happy with you and your talk of change. Change means less power for them, and they won't have that."

"So what do we do?" Jaali asked, his hand shaking in outrage.

"I have a plan," the king said, his voice lowered to a whisper. "But you are not going to like it."

The Wedding

———————————

In the month leading to the wedding, Jaali and Milenda barely had time to rest, caught in a whirlwind of preparations and social obligations.

Now, shadowed by royal guards constantly, an annoyed but resigned Jaali limped his way around the palace, his wounds healed but his leg was permanently damaged. There were few moments of privacy, and Milenda found herself almost missing their time in the desert. Their physical contact had dwindled to a touch of the lips and hands here and there, for fear of being caught in the act by overzealous staff. The wedding date had been settled, and the princess counted down the days to when they would finally be together. It was pure torture to be next to the one she loved, feel his body heat and see the smoldering flames of desire in his pale blue eyes, and yet not be able to freely pull him into her arms and be one with him, again. The wedding day could not arrive soon enough.

"I just saw the dress, child." Mama Nyeusi was fussing over her unruly hair, her bulky skirts brushing the side of Milenda's sitting figure. "It's the most beautiful thing I have ever seen."

The princess sighed and smirked. "I'm sure you're exaggerating, Mama. I told them not to go crazy with it."

The old woman laughed. "Well, they sure didn't go crazy. They just went… very creative. You are the crown Jewel. Did you really expect them to make you a plain wedding dress?"

Milenda shook her head, and the *iyalorixá* dropped the brush. "Do I really have to braid my hair for the ceremony? I hate it!"

"You must give the populace at least a little bit of tradition." Mama Nyeusi bent to retrieve the brush. "Tradition makes people feel comfortable and safe. You marrying an ex-*indent* is a huge detour from tradition, so just give them the ease of a traditional wedding ceremony. It's a feast for the eyes and a psychological muscle relaxant."

Milenda laughed at the old woman's choice of words. Muscle relaxant indeed. She did not feel relaxed, knowing the Elders could try to ruin it all at any time. Maybe the people were relaxed, but Milenda and Jaali were anything but. "That's exactly what the Elders want—a nation of sleepwalkers. Easier to manipulate."

Mama Nyeusi resumed her patient braiding of the princess's stubborn hair. "Your hair is just like you. No sense at all and hardheaded. These walls have ears, child. It behooves you to be careful with what you say out loud."

As Milenda snorted, the older woman smacked her not so gently over the head. "I'm serious. You need to watch what you say. You and Jaali have worked so hard to get where you are, why would you risk jeopardizing all of it? Be smart."

Milenda rubbed her head where the *iyalorixá* had hit her. She saw the wisdom in the woman's advice, but it was getting harder and harder to keep all her feelings and ideas locked inside for fear of what the Elders might do. As she was quickly finding out, it was not easy living in fear. Jaali had endured fear for so many years. She couldn't imagine how someone could live like that and still open their eyes every morning and go on existing. The young Fjorden had admitted to having thought of and even attempting suicide, and even though the orisas regarded killing yourself a shameful way to solve problems, she could not blame him for his desire to vanish from the world of the living. How painful it must have been to subsist in constant fear of being raped and hurt in so many different ways; her mind was still unable to wrap itself around it. To be at the mercy of someone as evil as Mnyama was too horrifying to even contemplate, and yet that had been the life of the sweet Outlander she loved above all else.

"Well, in another week, I will be officially married, and there's nothing the Elders can do about it." Even as she said it, she knew there were indeed so many things they could do to stop her and Jaali from being the heirs to the throne. However, there was not much point in dwelling on it. She must be positive about their future together, or she would drive herself crazy.

After Jaali moved to the consort's quarters, Milenda had felt lonely. Her room was suddenly too big and too empty, and even Mjusi seemed to miss him every time he came to visit. The flying reptilian creature took to sniffing the whole room, as if looking for something, before settling in his usual spot on the rug, whimpering sadly. Milenda sympathized. She felt the same way.

There had been a few times when she felt so empty without Jaali that she had defied all sense of traditional bridal decorum and had reached out for him during the night. The visits had not lasted long. Wiser than she was, the young Outlander had quickly made her realize that nothing was worth risking their future together, not even a night in each other's arms. Begrudgingly, she'd had to agree with him and leave.

Now, she was alone again in that big room, Mjusi sleeping and gently snoring on the rug while she pouted on her enormous bed. Tossing and turning, Milenda fought to find the peace needed to fall asleep and was foiled at every attempt. She needed Jaali. Not just in the physical sense, but her soul needed his to feel complete, to feel satisfied and restful. A week just seemed like an eternity to wait.

I'm being childish. Punching her pile of pillows, she bounced on the springy mattress as she tossed to the other side again.

"Stop doing that, child. You are making me dizzy."

The deep, rich voice made her sit up, startled.

Yemanjá sat in an armchair to the right of her bed, her beautiful face obscured by the darkness of the room. Milenda switched the nightstand light on.

"Do you ever get any sleep, girl?"

"Yemanjá, when did you get here?" Silly question, of course. The Orisa could come and go as she pleased.

"I've been watching you for the past half hour." The Orisa stood and crossed the few feet between the chair and the bed. "You are in grave danger. And so is your consort-to-be."

Milenda swallowed. "I know. My father is taking care of it."

Yemanjá sat on the edge of the bed and reached for Milenda's hand. "You are dear to the orisas, Milenda. We want you safe and sound because you have a lot to do for this nation in the future. We want you to know that no matter what, we will keep an eye on you and Jaali, the blue-eyed Outlander who will change our way of life."

The Orisa's hand was warm and soft, and Milenda fought the urge to hug her. "My father has a plan. He hasn't shared it with us because he thinks it's better if no one knows, but for once I trust him."

"Good. It's about time he did the right thing and stopped being a puppet to the Elders." She huffed, obviously frustrated.

"This new wife of his has been carefully selected for her fertility and lack of morals. She won't put up a fight when ordered to be fertilized by whatever male the Elders decide will produce a nice, malleable heir. Then all they have to do is get rid of you and Jaali and they have it under control again."

The Orisa lost a little of her usual coldness as she spoke to Milenda, her eyes softening and gathering moisture. "You must be kept safe until such time as you are to assume the throne of the kingdom."

The princess nodded, her voice silenced by a knot of emotion in her throat. She sincerely hoped her faith in her father was not misplaced and he did indeed have a plan to keep them safe from harm. Hope and an undying faith in the power of love kept her optimistic and secure.

She squeezed Yemanjá's hand. The Orisa smiled and stood again, smoothing the imaginary wrinkles of her diaphanous white dress.

"I will bid you farewell for now, but be sure I will always be close, watching over you."

In a sudden soft "poof," the Orisa vanished. Milenda was alone in the room again. Mjusi lifted his head, finally aware of movement, only to lower it again with a whimper.

Milenda knew she should feel safer knowing the Orisa was looking over her, but just the idea that she needed to be looked after was distressing. Why couldn't she just be a commoner, able to love whomever she wished and not present a threat to anyone?

Her own mind corrected her; Jaali was a commoner, and look at what had happened to him. There was no safe place in Natale for anyone until things changed dramatically. That was her job, her mission. She needed to stop feeling sorry for herself, grow up, and face her problems head-on

It was time.

***

The mirror reflected someone he barely recognized. The blue scarf tied around the high collar of his white linen shirt made his pale skin stand out and his blue eyes even bluer.

Milenda had somehow convinced the stylists to make him a traditional Fjorden wedding suit. Not that it looked in any way familiar to him. Having been transplanted to Afrika at such an early age, Jaali had few memories of his own traditions. He couldn't remember a single wedding he had been to, and this strange, slightly restrictive costume he was now wearing felt as foreign to him as to any Natalian. The shirt had black embroidery on each wide sleeve, and a skirted black vest was laced tightly over it. The pants, made of soft, creamy cotton and tucked into black knee-high boots, were by far the most comfortable item of clothing he was wearing. The soft leather boots were a far cry from the sandals he was so used to and rubbed uncomfortably against the sides of his feet and legs.

When he protested, favoring the loose tunics of a local wedding, Milenda had given him a stern glare. "The people must get used to the fact that they are going to be ruled not only by a native Natalian but also by an Outlander. People see what they want to see. So, if you show up dressed in local clothing, the crowd will soon forget who you are and how you got here. They must remember in order for us to change the way things are."

She could be very royal when she chose to.

Mama Nyeusi came storming through the doors. "Are you ready, child? The guests will only wait so long before they get restless."

Jaali turned to look at the old woman, her white skirts sashaying across the tiled floors like a giant broom, hands on her hips, and a frown on her face.

He smiled. "I'm ready, Mama. Uncomfortable, but ready."

She scanned him with her eyes and clicked her tongue in disapproval. "That bride of yours has the strangest ideas sometimes. What kind of getup is that?"

"Traditional wedding clothes from the northern lands," he explained, opening his arms in defeat. "I hate to admit it, but she has a point. I guess I can be uncomfortable for a little while if it achieves something good in return."

Flanked by royal guards on all sides, Jaali limped his way along the hallways of the palace, his ears trained on the growing rumble of voices and cheers. His stomach somersaulted, and his heart skipped a beat.

It was still painful for him to be the center of attention. A small, private wedding would have been his choice, if he'd had a choice, which, of course, he hadn't. Neither had Milenda, who was expected to put on a show for her people on the most important day of her life, the day she joined her life with him, a stranger from another land. He took a deep breath and licked his lips. He could do this.

Mama Nyeusi had vanished around the corner, probably to sneak to Milenda's side in her chambers where they would wait for the sign to make her appearance.

The guards stopped by one of the main garden doors, the one he would use to enter the wedding stage. By now, Milenda was doing the same on the opposite side of the stage. The idea was for them to make a simultaneous entrance and awe the public.

Trying to control his galloping heart to no avail, Jaali waited for the signal to move forward onto the stage. The weight of his clothing was beginning to make him sweat. The stylists had chosen the lightest possible fabrics for it, but it was still a costume from the cold lands, not for the heat of the jungle. He swept a finger between the high collar and his neck and swallowed.

Once the door opened, he could hear the clamor of the crowd, yelling in expectation of what was about to happen. He remembered being one of them, excitedly waiting for some special event or ceremony. Amidst the doldrums of everyday life, these occasions were more than welcome. He understood, but he did not like it because this time he was in the center of it all. The crowd stretched as far as the eye could see, and he blinked against the harsh sunlight as he stepped outside.

His gaze shot immediately to his right, where Milenda was making her way to the middle of the stage. She looked beautiful in her blue bridal dress, and for a moment, he forgot he was being watched by thousands of people. He smiled, and Milenda looked at him and smiled back.

"You look exquisite," he mouthed, hoping she would understand. Her petite figure was clad in a skintight, two-piece dress that enhanced her soft curves. The bottom, a simple mermaid skirt, was made of ocean-blue satin. It hugged her hips only to flare out at the bottom. The sleeveless bodice was the color of a twilight sky and decorated with silver satin and diamonds. Her *matangazos*, purposely left bare to allow no doubt as to her ancestry, shone almost as bright as the jewels in her top. Her wild hair, which had been tamed into a million braids, was covered in a warm orange-yellow *gele* almost a foot high. It fanned from the center to both sides of her head in a sunny cascade. Her neck was cuffed in a two-inch wide, golden ring and an *isigolwani*, a beaded neck hoop traditional in Natalian weddings. As a princess, she should have been wearing many more golden rings around her neck, but because he was poor and not able to buy her the traditional rings, she had decided to wear only one. However, it was thicker than the habitual, to symbolize his humble background.

A few more steps and they were standing before Mama Nyeusi who would be performing the handfasting ceremony. The old woman, her back to the crowd, smiled at them and reached out for their hands. Carefully, she placed Milenda's hand over Jaali's and tied them with a golden rope to symbolize their imminent union.

Milenda's eyes fixed themselves to his, and Jaali fell in love all over again. His heart melted, and he forgot where he was, his focus solely on her. This amazing girl would be his wife in a matter of minutes. She had been there for him through thick and thin, and he could only hope he would be able to return the favor. Could it be that his love was enough to keep her happy for years to come?

"Jaali Asker, this is your wife Milenda Nwosu, Crown Jewel of Natale," Mama Nyeusi said, raising their hands in the air. "Will you love, honor, and protect her for the rest of your life?"

Jaali looked briefly at the old woman and then returned his gaze to his bride. "I will." He squeezed Milenda's hand and added in a whisper, "I will love you forever."

"Milenda Nwosu, this is your husband Jaali Asker, Outlander. Will you love, honor, and protect him for the rest of your life?"

Milenda's eyes were suspiciously moist. "I will." The crowd whispered in excitement as Milenda mouthed an *I love you* to her groom.

The *iyalorixá* released their hands and motioned to Asha, waiting on the side of the stage, to approach. The young girl, dressed in red, stumbled across the stage with Jaali's family blanket draped across her arms.

"Take the *nguba* and wrap your wife with it as a symbol of your love and protection for years to come."

The bridegroom took the blanket from Asha and placed it over Milenda's shoulders, thus symbolically sealing their union.

"I knew we were meant to be together the moment I put this blanket over your shoulders the first time we met," Jaali whispered for her ears only. "It's only fitting this old blanket be our *nguba*."

Green eyes twinkling like stars, she grasped the edges of the soft wrap against her chest and smiled.

"Kiss the bride! Kiss the bride!" the crowd shouted in unison. Jaali obliged. Sweeping her into his arms, he brought his thirsty lips down on hers and kissed her, much to the delight of the populace.

Loose Ends

The reception that followed seemed to last an eternity. Dignitaries from all over Afrika—but none from the Outerlands—lined up to congratulate the young, royal couple. Delicious, rich dishes came out from the kitchen in the hands of a never-ending, red wave of servants. The wine poured freely into the crystal chalices of the guests, and the musicians played an array of popular tunes for everyone's entertainment.

Milenda and Jaali had eyes only for each other, both desperately yearning for the privacy of their wedding chambers and the comfort of each other's arms. Together they sat, hands entwined below the table, hearts fluttering in excitement. The princess's *matangazos* would have been hard to hide if it weren't for the *nguba,* which Milenda refused to remove from her shoulders. How she felt about her new husband was not anyone's business, and she had no wish to have the crowd witness her markings shine and throb as her body responded to his proximity.

Hours passed before they were finally ushered by the guards to their quarters and left alone. Guards would be just outside the door, they knew, but Natalian doors were thick and impervious to sound.

The wedding chambers were strangely smaller than their usual ones, but much cozier. There was an enormous bed against one wall, a couple of dressers, and many soft, furry rugs covering the tiled floor. Milenda recalled some of her tutors referring to it as the "baby-making room," and she giggled nervously.

It was all becoming real: the wedding, her future as a queen, her future as a mother and a wife. But it was all overshadowed by the dangers still lurking in the dark minds of her nation's powerful Elders.

She folded the *nguba* carefully over an armchair, then took a few steps forward to stand before her new husband.

Jaali seemed as overwhelmed as she did about all of what was happening. She could feel him trembling as she unbuttoned his vest.

"You must be so uncomfortable under all these heavy clothes." Her voice was soft and wistful. She was still not totally used to the intimacy she shared only with him.

Jaali tilted her chin up with his finger and looked into her eyes. "I would put up with a lot worse to be with you."

She knew it to be true. Her beloved had endured more than any human should have to, just to have the right to ask for her in marriage. She had no doubt as to his love for her.

"I can't believe you're my wife, *mke wangu*." He paused, as if tasting the words. His lips curled upward. "*Mke wangu*. I like the sound of that."

"*Mme wangu*, my husband. That sounds good, too."

Their lips met in a kiss, Milenda's hands trapped between their bodies.

"Let's get you out of these clothes." Realizing too late how that sounded, her *matangazos* shone bright red.

Jaali laughed and hugged her tight against him. "I can't wait," he said, once the laughing subsided. "I'll help."

His tone made her frown. "Stop teasing me. That's not very kind." Needing a distraction, she resumed the unbuttoning of the offensive piece of clothing as he joined her efforts. "Kidding aside, you have to be hot. Aren't you?"

With a soft chuckle, the Fjorden nodded. "I feel like a pig roasting over a fire."

Buttons undone, Milenda helped him remove the vest. Then she turned her attention to the laces of his shirt.

"This collar feels just slightly less uncomfortable than the slave collars I had to wear on my way to Afrika." The princess froze, her eyes shooting up to his. He bit his lower lip. "Sorry. I can't believe I just compared my wedding shirt with *indent* paraphernalia."

"You don't think marrying me is a form of slavery, do you?" Milenda felt suddenly insecure. She knew he loved her, but marrying a royal heir and every restraining thing that went along with it, could not be easy for someone who had finally earned his freedom. She reached out to caress his face.

"Gods no, Milenda. Of course not. I was just making a joke." He covered her hand with his and held it against his cheek. "Marrying you is all I want. It's freedom from a life of bad memories and loneliness. I love you, *msichana*."

Slowly, hesitantly at first, he brought his lips down on hers again. Milenda melted against him. It all still felt like a dream.

Working together, they removed each other's clothes, one layer at a time. At first they giggled as if playing a children's game, but soon the blood ran too fast and too hot through their bodies. Urgency and yearning took the place of playfulness, as they got rid of the last items of clothing and stood naked and vulnerable in the center of the room.

Jaali's eyes devoured her with such intensity, she shivered in anticipation. "You're beautiful. Did you know that, Jaali?"

"Not as beautiful as you, my *malaika*." His hands slid over her shoulders, one hand sweeping along her bright *matangazos* up to her neck. Instinctively, she leaned her face into his hand, closing her eyes as the warmth of his skin radiated into hers. "You're an angel. You've saved me from myself, from my night terrors, from my fears—"

She didn't let him finish. Interlacing her hands behind his neck, Milenda pulled his head toward hers and muttered, "I love you," over his lips.

As if their legs had stopped supporting them, the couple dropped to their knees on the soft rug and lost themselves in a long, deep kiss. When they parted, the princess could feel her markings burning hotly, matching the feelings inside of her. Trembling with desire, Milenda brushed her hand down along her husband's chest to his hard and well-defined abdominal muscles and then lower in a teasing caress that made Jaali moan. Not shy anymore, she wanted to feel it all. No secrets, no unknowns, just twin souls melded together for eternity, two bodies joined into one.

***

Milenda woke suddenly with a hand tightly pressed against her mouth. Several dark figures had entered the room and stood silently around them, as if trying to decide what to do next. As Milenda made a move to warn Jaali, one of the black-clad figures reached down and pressed a hand over his mouth to discourage any screaming. Milenda, disoriented and suddenly scared, struggled against the strangers, while another man threw a blanket over her and Jaali's naked bodies. They were unceremoniously pushed toward the door.

"Do not speak. Do not yell," an unfamiliar voice told them. When Milenda protested, another hand covered her mouth, rough skin scratching her lips. "If you scream again, I'll have to gag you."

They traveled quickly and silently through the deserted hallways of the palace. No guards in sight, no servants.

What's going on? A terrible suspicion rose in her heart. Were these the Elders' men coming to kidnap and kill them?

Once outside, they were both hoisted up onto the bed of a land vehicle, a rare sight in the city these days. They barely had time to sit before the speedster moved forward with a lurch. In spite of their name, none of the existing motor vehicles were very fast, but this one was going at top speed throughout town, on roads that were no longer fit to be driven on. Tree roots and other vegetation provided constant obstacles that the driver tried to avoid by steering left and right in sudden shifts, not always successfully. Milenda, sitting next to Jaali, was thrown against him several times.

Her husband lifted a bare arm and encircled her shoulders, pulling her protectively against him. "Elders?" he asked in a whisper, his eyes studying the men around them. Their faces were covered with black scarves, and they did not speak at all.

Milenda scooted closer to him. "I'm afraid so. We need to come up with a plan. They are going to kill us at the end of this trip."

Jaali looked strangely calm. "Why didn't they kill us in the palace? There was no one around to hear it."

The princess brushed a tear from her cheek, hating herself for the show of weakness. She was scared; however, anger was really what was eating her inside out.

How dare they ruin her wedding night? The one happy day in her life, and they had to pick this one to kill them both? Couldn't they have chosen a later date? She realized how irrational her thoughts were running and snorted.

"They made sure my mom and my biological father were killed far away from the city, so there would be no questions about the accident."

In a comforting gesture, Jaali tucked the blanket tighter around her. It was warm, as it always was in Natale, but the breeze on their naked skin added to the discomfort. "We'll be okay. We're together. That's all that matters."

He seemed so sure of himself, Milenda relaxed a little in his arms. She watched the other men with curiosity. They didn't seem too interested in what the couple was doing. In fact, their focus was solely on the road around them, as if they were just as ignorant of where the speeding vehicle was taking them.

The night suddenly turned into day, unannounced as it usually was, and the speedster stopped. Milenda realized they were on the coast, not far from where the nation's seaports were located. The two men in the back with them jumped off the car, and one went around to talk to the driver and his companion.

Jaali exchanged worried glances with her, but neither dared say anything. If they were going to do anything, her instincts were telling her it had to be now.

In silent agreement, they both jumped from their spots and made a run for it over the side of the vehicle, knocking the remaining man to the ground. Blankets flying behind them, they held each other's hands and fled toward the ocean from where she was hoping they could have a better view of the land around them.

With a silent prayer to Yemanjá, Milenda hurtled herself as fast as her short legs could carry her toward the friendly immense sea of blue, the Orisa's home turf. Maybe once there, she would help them somehow.

But before they reached the edge of the water, hands grabbed them from behind and threw them to the sand beneath them.

"Stop running!" a voice yelled behind them, while they struggled against the two burly men pinning them to the ground.

"What do we do with them, boss?" asked one of the men. "They're going to try and run again before we do what we have to do."

Kill us. Panic rose in Milenda's throat.

"Kill me, but leave Jaali alone." The desperation in her voice surprised even her. She didn't want him to die. With or without her, it was of utter importance that he lived. "Please, I'm the Jewel. I'm the one who will inherit the crown, not him. Leave him be, please."

Much to her surprise and dismay, the men burst out laughing. "She's a funny little thing, isn't she?" one of them said with a loud chuckle.

She glanced at Jaali, whose blue eyes darted quickly around, searching for a way to save them. Only there was none. A deep sadness grew in her heart, and tears rolled down her cheeks and into the sand. It was the end.

"Take them to the meeting place and get rid of them." The command was given in a low, but authoritative voice by the man who had driven the vehicle. "I tire of this game. Do it!"

Hands reached out to pull them onto their feet and pushed them forward not so gently. Milenda sought Jaali's hand and held it tight.

Yemanjá was not going to help them now.

***

Inside the cabin, the air was a little stale, as if it had been closed for a long time. Jaali didn't care. The important thing was they were still alive. Confused for sure, but still breathing.

The men in black had taken them into the bowels of a ship anchored not too far away in a hidden cove and had locked them inside that cabin. As soon as their eyes had gotten used to the dimness, they found their own clothes lying over the back of a chair. They dressed quickly, happy not to be so exposed anymore, and sat holding each other on the edge of the berth, silent for a moment, ears focusing on the outside noises. There were voices shouting out orders and the thumping of many feet running over wooden floors above their heads.

The common noises heard on a ship, Jaali remembered.

Milenda was the first to break the stupor they were in.

"Why did they bring us to a ship? And why did they have our clothes here?" There were too many questions, and no one to answer them. "Why haven't they killed us yet?"

The Fjorden brushed a hand along her cheek in a soft caress. "I don't understand any of it, but I am happy we're still alive." His attempt at a comforting smile failed miserably. The truth was, he was still pretty sure they were going to end up dead.

Milenda pointed at a covered dish on the little table by one of the walls. "Is that food?"

They both stood to go check it. Sure enough, under the metal dome there was warm food. Lots of it. Beside it there were two goblets and a bottle of water.

"Do you think it's okay to eat it?" she asked.

Jaali was starving. He had barely touched the food during the reception, his stomach upset because of nerves. Not stopping to think twice, he nodded emphatically and reached out for the food. Milenda followed suit.

The food was tasty and satisfying, and the water was cool. They poured themselves some more and took the platter with them to the bed.

"Don't understand any of this..." The princess looked up at him, her mouth full of food.

Jaali couldn't help it. He laughed. "You look like a squirrel, with your cheeks all puffed up with food."

Forgetting their situation for a moment, she slapped him playfully. "How dare you compare me to a squirrel! Now that we are married, you don't think I'm pretty anymore?"

Jaali put his food down, flattened his hands on her cheeks, and kissed her on the mouth. "Squirrel or not, you are the most beautiful creature in the world."

Food forgotten, the young couple slid down onto the bed, lips sealed in a kiss, bodies glued together in an embrace.

"I love you, little *ekorre*." His native word for squirrel sounded like a compliment coming from his honeyed voice. She giggled against his mouth and gently bit his lower lip. "Ouch. Didn't know *ekorrar* could bite. Now, I will have to bite back." Instead, he suckled on her lower lip, making her moan softly.

The door to the cabin opened suddenly, and the room became inundated by the bright light of sunshine. They sprang up as if their bodies were made of metal coils.

The light edged the figure standing there in an eerie halo, and for a moment, they were both dumbfounded by it. The silhouette seemed familiar somehow, but they could not see it well thanks to the glare of the sun.

"Oh, for gods' sake, you young people are like rabbits." The familiar voice of Mama Nyeusi brought a relieved smile to Milenda's face.

"Mama!" Milenda ran to hug the woman, who stood with her arms wide open in invitation.

Jaali didn't move, paralyzed by the surprise. Mama Nyeusi

looked at him over the princess's shoulder. "Come on, there is room for one more in these old arms."

The Fjorden walked into the hug with a wide smile on his face. Maybe they weren't going to die after all.

"Aah, my two favorite royal heirs."

"Mama, what are you doing here? Are you a prisoner as well?" Milenda had finally detached herself from the old woman's arms.

She frowned when Mama Nyeusi started laughing.

"What's so funny?" Jaali looked at the woman in disbelief.

"You are. You really think you're a prisoner here?" Tears were rolling down her cheeks as she held her stomach. "That's too funny. Child, of course you're not a prisoner. Why would your father keep you imprisoned?"

"Her father?" Jaali blurted out, his hands on Milenda's shoulders. "What does the king have to do with this?"

"Let me sit down, child. I'm not a young woman anymore." Her laughter finally stopped, and the old woman sat herself on one of the two chairs in the cabin.

She sighed deeply. "You father promised he would come up with a plan to protect you. Well, this is it."

Milenda and Jaali sat down side by side on the edge of the berth and were staring at the *iyalorixá,* bewildered.

"What is?" Milenda's voice came louder than even she seemed to expect. "Mama, what plan?"

"As long as you were in Natale, you were at risk. The king realized this, and came up with a plan to protect both of you as long as need be." Mama Nyeusi smoothed the wrinkles in her vast skirts with one hand. "The only way to protect you is to make the Elders believe you disappeared."

The couple exchanged a questioning look before staring at the woman again. "Disappeared? What do you mean?"

The *iyalorixá* sighed again, exasperated with them. "As in dead, gone for good. Child, the only way the Elders will not be looking for you and trying to kill you is if you are already dead."

Jaali practically jumped off his perch on the bed. Just when they had finally relaxed, the word *kill* came up to haunt them again. "What do you mean by that? The king is going to have us both killed, so the Elders can't get to us? That makes no sense at all."

Mama Nyeusi wiped her eyes with a hand and blew out a heavy breath. "Young people can be very thick," she mumbled. "Of course he's not going to kill you. Why would he do that? He's going to make the Elders believe you died."

The princess, who had been unusually quiet, squeezed her hand around Jaali's arm to calm him. "How will he do that? We are a little too well-known to be able to hide anywhere in Natale."

When she said that, something clicked in Jaali's brain. He suddenly knew what the plan was.

"Your father is sending us north."

Both Milenda and the old woman looked at him, one in surprise, the other with a smile and a nod. "Where up north?"

The *iyalorixá* looked him in the eye and said, "Isvärld, the land from which you were taken."

A tremor went through his body. He hadn't heard that word in so long. Everyone always called him an Outlander or Fjorden. To most Natalians, it didn't matter exactly which nation had birthed him. They were content with the knowledge he was from somewhere in the Outerlands, where the fjords abounded and the weather was ice cold. After all these years, he himself had almost forgotten the name of his native land.

Isvärld—a nation of snow, ice, and beautiful blue oceans and skies. For the first time since he was a boy, he felt his heart contract with yearning, a tinge of nostalgia for a land he could barely remember anymore.

Unaware of his inner turmoil, Milenda gasped. "You're kidding! We're being sent to Jaali's home?"

The old woman nodded and reached out to hold Jaali's hands. The young man was almost paralyzed by shock, not sure whether to be happy or scared of going back to his own roots. He had lived in Natale for so long that, in spite of his obvious coloring, he thought of himself as a Natalian. To go back was like starting all over again in a foreign land.

He was suddenly aware that Milenda had pulled him against her and was holding him in a tight embrace. "You're going home, *wimbo wa moyo*. You're going home."

The ship was anchored in a small cove, protected on all sides by massive rocks. Looking over the railing on the deck, Jaali, still reeling from the news, thought it would not be a good place for a ship during rough seas. In his head, he could see sea crafts being thrown against the rocks by the restless waves and broken into tiny pieces, not unlike what he was feeling at that moment. Milenda, by his side, kept stealing worried glances at him.

"Are you okay, Jaali? You look a little green."

Jaali pulled her closer to him and lowered his lips to her ear so only she could hear his words. "I'm all right. Just trying to get used to the idea of going back to Isvärld. I don't want to sound ungrateful, but I really don't remember much of it. I barely remember my family, and I have no idea whether they are still alive or not. Everything I know is here in Natale. In a way, it's almost as if, once again, I'm being taken by force to a place where I know nobody. I am not sure how to feel."

Rising to her tiptoes, the princess placed a brief kiss on his lips. "There's a big difference, Jaali. This time you're not going alone, and you're not a slave."

He sought her lips again and feasted on her sweet flavor and warmth.

She was right. With her by his side, what was there to be scared of? Whatever awaited them in the land of ice would be nothing compared to what he had gone through in Natale. He was a free man, and he had his soul mate by his side.

"We'll make it home, and we'll be safe. When Father calls us back, we'll make sure things change in Natale," Milenda said.

They soon had to say their good-byes to Mama Nyeusi.

"Snow and ice would kill me for sure," she had said when they asked her to join them. "The king needs someone he can trust by his side. The wife they have picked for him is young and stupid. She will drive him crazy, for sure." She laughed at the thought. "I'm needed to keep him sane."

Milenda had a hard time letting the old woman leave the ship. After all, she was the closest thing she'd had to a mother. As the ship began to move against the break of the waves,

Mama Nyeusi waved from the beach, her voluminous skirts flying around her like the wings of an angel. Jaali squeezed Milenda's shoulder and wiped the tears rolling down her cheeks.

All of a sudden, a great commotion rose on deck. The sailors all screamed in agitation and pointed at the skies, fear obvious in their expression. The young couple followed the direction in which they were pointing and saw a great big shadow flying toward the ship.

"Mjusi!" Milenda ran to the edge of the deck, where the lizard creature had ungracefully landed with a thump.

"Gods, what are you doing here, my friend?" Crouching down to pet his scaly head, Milenda looked back at her husband with a question in her eyes. "He can't come with us. The cold will kill him."

Jaali approached and kneeled by them. "No, it won't. He's a *msitu*. They are creatures that easily adapt to their environment. That's one of the reasons they are so rare. Some say they actually originated in the north, and that, at one time, they breathed fire to protect themselves from the cold. Of course, there is no way of knowing if that's true."

Mjusi looked up at them with his big green eyes and growled playfully. "You really want to come with us?" Milenda asked him.

The creature nodded.

"Are you sure he'll be okay, Jaali?"

Jaali smiled and petted the flying lizard. "He's family, and family should stick together."

The sun had gone to sleep in the ocean, and the three of

them looked over the side of the ship into the bright, full moon above. The future was not clear, and they were heading into the unknown, but they had each other and their love.

"Look, Milenda," he pointed at the moon. "It's smiling at us."

Milenda hooked her arm around Jaali's waist and leaned her head on his shoulder, Mjusi curled up at her feet. Happiness filled Jaali's heart.

"See, Jaali?" Milenda said, pointing up at the smiling moon. "It's Yemanjá giving us her blessing. Everything will be all right."

Glossary

The Afrikan language used in this book is very loosely based on Swahili and other African dialects while Jaali's native language is based on several northern European languages such as Dutch and Swedish. Here's a list of the terms used in the story and their translations.

älskling – darling, sweetheart

asante – Thank you

barafu – frozen treat

batucadas – drumming competitions

buugeng – weapon in the shape of an S used in Northern martial arts

bwana – boss

duivel – devil

ekorre – squirrel

for søren – damn! Holy Crap!

Fjorden – someone from the northern lands

gele – very elaborate head-wrap that often reaches great heights

hema – primitive home

homa – a drug that elicits hallucinations
indent – Natalian term for slave
iqhiya – headband, turban
isigolwani – decorative neck hoop
iyalorixá – priestess serving as a go-between mortals and the orisas
kanga – printed fabric, typical wrap dress (skirt or shirt)
kidogo moja – little one
magie slangen – magic snakes
magiska fen – magic fairy
malaika – angel
matangazos – (noticeable) markings
mheshimiwa – sir, honorable sir
mjusi msitu – Forest Lizard
mke wangu – my wife
mme wangu – my husband
msichana – respectful term for girl
muwa pombe – alcoholic drink made of sugarcane
nasikitika – I'm sorry
nguba – wedding ceremonial blanket/wrap
orisas – minor gods
santulo – scarf that goes over the iqhiya to add volume and height
shetani – the devil
tukufu – dear, precious
tulia – calm down, all is well
wimbo wa moyo – heart's song

Acknowledgements

It may sound a little weird to thank a whole continent, but that's what I'm about to do. I'm so grateful to Africa for all the inspiration and insight it provided me not only for this romantic fantasy but also for so many other things throughout the years. I spent quite a big chunk of my childhood and teen years in several countries in Africa. Its wild beauty and stark social and cultural contrasts never ceased to fascinate me. Even though *Desert Jewel's* Afrika is very much a construct of my imagination, bits and pieces of the real Africa have "sneaked in."

I would be remiss if I didn't thank my awesome editors and beta readers for all their help and insights and my publisher, Hot Tree Publishing, for believing in *Desert Jewel.*

A special thank you to Sydney Everson who was my first

beta reader (way before the manuscript was ever sent to a publisher) and has been there supporting me every step of the way. To my wonderful Sippy Cups and Semantics, AKA my cheerleaders, you guys are the best.

To my husband and sons who have to put up with my frantic schedule, thank you for your patience and support. I love you always.

Finally, I am so thankful for my family across the Atlantic Ocean who have always believed in me. And of course, my dad. Without him I would have never lived in Africa and experienced places and things who made me the writer I am today. Thank you, Dad. The angels are fortunate to have you beside them.

About the Author

Natalina wrote her first romance in collaboration with her best friend at the age of thirteen. Since then she has ventured into other genres, but romance is first and foremost in almost everything she writes. Her novel, *We Will Always Have the Closet*, is her first published romance.

After earning a degree in tourism and foreign languages, she worked as a tourist guide in her native country, Portugal, for a short time before moving to the United States. She's lived in three continents and a few islands, and her knack for languages and linguistics led her to a master's degree in education. She lives in Virginia where she has taught English as a second language to elementary school children for more years than she cares to admit.

Natalina doesn't believe you can have too many books or too much coffee. Art and dance make her happy and she is pretty sure she could survive on lobster and bananas alone. When she is not writing or stressing over lesson plans, she shares her life with her husband and two adult sons.

Facebook: WWW.FACEBOOK.COM/AUTHORNATALINAREIS

About the Publisher

Hot Tree Publishing opened its doors in 2015 with an aspiration to bring quality fiction to the world of readers. With the initial focus on romance and a wide spread of romance sub-genres, we envision opening up to alternative genres in the near future.

Firmly seated in the industry as a leading editing provider to independent authors and small publishing houses, Hot Tree Publishing is the sister company to Hot Tree Editing, founded in 2012. Having established in-house editing and promotions, plus having a well-respected market presence, Hot Tree Publishing endeavors to be a leader in bringing quality stories to the world of readers.

Interested in discovering more amazing reads brought to you by Hot Tree Publishing or perhaps you're interested in submitting a manuscript and joining the HTPubs family? Either way, head over to the website for information:

WWW.HOTTREEPUBLISHING.COM